The
Sweetest
One

Melanie
Mah

The
Sweetest
One

Cormorant Books

**Canada Council
for the Arts** **Conseil des Arts
du Canada**    ONTARIO ARTS COUNCIL
CONSEIL DES ARTS DE L'ONTARIO
an Ontario government agency
un organisme du gouvernement de l'Ontario

Canadian Patrimoine
Heritage canadien   Canadä

The publisher gratefully acknowledges the support of the Canada Council for the
Arts and the Ontario Arts Council for its publishing program. We acknowledge
the financial support of the Government of Canada through the Canada Book
Fund (CBF) for our publishing activities, and the Government of Ontario through
the Ontario Media Development Corporation, an agency of the Ontario Ministry
of Culture, and the Ontario Book Publishing Tax Credit Program.

LIBRARY AND ARCHIVES CANADA CATALOGUING IN PUBLICATION

Mah, Melanie, 1980–, author
The sweetest one / Melanie Mah.

Issued in print and electronic formats.
ISBN 978-1-77086-432-0 (pbk.). — ISBN 978-1-77086-433-7
(html)

I. Title.

PS8626.A3758S94 2016   C813'.6   C2014-907699-1
                                       C2014-907700-9

Cover photo and design: angeljohnguerra.com
Interior text design: Tannice Goddard
Printer: Friesens

Printed and bound in Canada.

 MIX
Paper from
responsible sources
FSC
www.fsc.org   FSC® C016245

The interior of this book is printed on 100% post-consumer waste recycled paper.

CORMORANT BOOKS INC.
10 ST. MARY STREET, SUITE 615, TORONTO, ONTARIO, M4Y 1P9
www.cormorantbooks.com

The
Sweetest
One

1

THE LAST TIME I saw Trina was the best night of my life and I didn't know it at the time. It was my birthday, and I'd just had this massive blow-up with my dad. He said something I disagreed with — I can't remember what — and he thought I was talking back. My dad can't stand not being right, so he started yelling, and because I have my pride, I started yelling too. And when it got to the point where his face was turning red and he was spitting when he talked and he could barely look at me because he hated me so much, I left. Hadn't even had my birthday dinner yet. I pushed the front door so hard it slammed into the side of the building, bounced back into my face, and smashed my nose. It started bleeding, but I just kept going. I was hungry, I didn't have any money, and it was getting cold — it can be cold here in June if you don't have a jacket — but I wanted him to feel guilty, realize he was wrong. I thought I'd show him — what, I don't know. I pinched my nose with one hand, wiped it with the other, and went down the hill towards Anders Park. Halfway there, a set of lights came up behind me, and I turned around. Trina's car, a powder blue Civic, and she was whistling the happy birthday song out the open window.

"What do *you* want?" I said. It didn't matter. I didn't want to go back.

"Get in the car, Chris. Please?"

"Why should I?"

"We'll go for a drive," she said, "wherever you want," which she almost never did.

I kept walking.

She drove beside me, jolted her car from time to time to keep up. The stereo was on. Depeche Mode. "Come on," she said. "We could get some pizza, go to the lake? I saw meadowlarks there on Thursday." Trina likes birds. It's something we have in common. It's fucking nerdy knowing birds by sight, but somehow she pulled it off. People liked her. She made life look easy.

I got in the car, didn't talk at first.

"That's better, right?" she said, soothingly. "I've got the heat on."

The song changed to old-school jazz, Ella's voice thick like smoke. Dream a little dream of me. Trina cracked the window and lit a cigarette. Sang and blew smoke at the windshield. I asked if I could have one, waited for a reply, but Trina kept singing.

"Well?" I said. I was being bold. Then I saw the town limit sign. No.

"Put it out of your mind," she said when she saw me. "It's gonna happen or it's not. No sense being afraid."

It'd be the first time I'd leave town in two years, but I trusted her. We sped past and rocked the car into the drive-through of Perry's Pizza. Ali Meer's voice in the little foghorn speaker. Trina asked me what I wanted and I shrugged. "Mushroom, onion, tomato?" she said.

"Just mushrooms," I said.

She sneered but that's what she ordered — that and a bag of fries, the best ones in town. We pulled out to the side. They bring you the pizza when it's done. She opened the FRY bag and took a whiff, put her hand in and looked me in the eye. "So you're gonna take up smoking now?"

The trees hanging from the rearview twisted on their strings, pink red pink.

"No, I just wanted one."

She dropped the fries between us. Grease spots on the paper bag. "Don't smoke," she said. "It doesn't suit you."

"You smoke 'cause it suits you?"

"Well, I can't live without it now, can I? I'm addicted."

No, she's lazy. People never blame themselves, they always blame the drug.

"Chrysler," she said, levelling with me, "you're into books."

"Yeah?" I said. Probably rolled my eyes.

"You like books and weird shit. You think of patterns on bathroom tiles, which vegetables are actually fruits. You're smart. You're gonna do something good someday."

"If I live," I said.

"Just don't smoke, okay?"

Cars went by on Highway 11, streaks of white and red under yellow streetlamps in the dark. Highway 11 goes west to the mountains, east into Red Deer. No one ever stops here unless they have to. I was gonna say something about that, insult Spring Hills to make myself seem cool, but just then, Trina turned the stereo up, some loud punk love song. When the pizza came she started the car and it roared to life, cantankerous. Her little piece of shit, a boxy metal hatchback from the eighties. We drove with the windows cranked down and the music up. We ate straight from the box, no napkins, and a slice went cold in half a minute because of all the wind. We sang along. I made a joke about the Wanderer, this local guy in a black turtleneck who spends his time walking through town, no job or anything, and then suddenly, we saw him on the shoulder. We stopped at the Red Mart for slushes, then turned around, went to the Dairy Burger for ice cream, where Mr. Berkson, our old science teacher, lurked in the bushes installing irrigation, and we waved and beeped our horn at him and he scowled at us because he hates our entire family. We went west down the highway, past another town limit sign, to the lake, where we chased rabbits on the bike path with the car, whipped shitties in open fields, sped down Half Mile Hill like freefall, and even though the car slipped on our second pass of the hill, and I got scared, it was the most fun I'd had in years. I felt happy, lucky, proud to be with her. Cool Trina Wong and her weird little sister. We were fine.

Eventually we parked by the water where she convinced me to get out of the car. I fucking loved it. It was totally black, the peaceful lap of lakewater on shore. There was a ghostly noise. We gripped each other and laughed so hard, louder than the loon. I told her about the time our sister Stef and I caught fish with safety pins, that other time we saw an owl. I wasn't used to doing all the talking, I'm still not, but I liked it. Her eyes on me, she huddled in like I was a fire. Her smell. Perfume, shampoo, makeup, cigarettes. Sweet.

Still, the fight was in my head. I started talking about when Gene, for fun, yelled down from our apartment window at some Christian parade, and without meaning to, went on to rant about our dad.

"You have to understand where he's coming from," Trina said, putting on her big sister hat, though I didn't want advice then — not from her or anyone. "Dude's got a Grade Three education, but Mom lets him walk all over her. He wants us to do the same. You know you're smarter than him. We all know. And it's a shame. He has the money, and he has a bad temper. He can make your life hell. But someday you'll graduate and then you'll be gone, and he won't be there, cutting into you."

The lights were out when we got home and snuck in together. Our room a grubby apricot, stinky beetles in the crevices, walls streaked grey where our hands and feet had rubbed while sleeping. Dreams of fighting or running away. We talked some more, about her boyfriend Kirk and whatever guy I was crushing on at the time, about the clothes she wanted from the store and the things we wanted in general. Good boyfriends, long lives. She described the house she was going to live in, a purple bungalow — orchid purple, like the number five crayon — with white trim and a concrete step. I told her I thought it would be cool someday to go to university.

"You should," she said and flicked out the lamp. "Happy birthday, Chris. Have a good year, okay? Be crazy if you want to."

I collapsed in my dirty bed smiling. *Everything'll be good*, I thought. *Happy birthday. Seventeen. Your sister loves you.*

At 3:06 a.m., I woke up. Sometimes you just know. I felt for her in her covers, lightly, in case she was there. It's something I did a lot back then to see if she'd gotten home from wherever she was. No one to check if not me. Sometimes I did that and felt an arm or a leg, then went back to sleep. A few times, she woke up and yelled at me. This time there was no one there. I turned on the light. Her bed was made — she'd never made her bed in her whole life — and on top of her blanket was a folded sheet of paper, a note that said she'd gone to see the world, that she would write, that she was sorry, that she might come back someday, maybe to visit, maybe to live, she didn't know, and that she hoped I'd have a good life, whatever I chose. I had already chosen to stay.

I went through all the rooms and closets in the house. I kept expecting her to jump out. *Boo! Fucking scared you, didn't I?* she would say. I went downstairs and turned on all the lights and went aisle by aisle through the store like a snake. Only when I came up empty did I go out back, outside. Her car wasn't there. I woke my parents to tell them that thing no parent wants to hear. "We have to go," I said.

My dad and I had been fighting nine hours before, but he cared about me again and didn't want me to leave. "You know why," he said, and didn't need to.

I said, "If you don't come, I'm going on my own."

It hurt him, I saw it and was sorry, but he got out of bed and into some outside clothes while I called the cops, who said call back in two days.

My mom insisted on staying home. She said she didn't think she could help, even though she's always talking about how fast her eyes are. I didn't push because there wasn't time to hear all her excuses. *Saturdays are busy during rodeo. No one else can open the store.* Truth is, she's scared. She thinks her body will evaporate the second she leaves town. Part of me, a big part, understands, but she still should have come with us.

My dad and I went to Kirk's house first. I thumped on the door, rang their bell for a whole minute. Kirk's mom was probably awake and just didn't want to get it. I stumbled around in the dark to the back of the house, where her bedroom was, yelling "Hello! Is anybody there? Hello!" I would've woken the neighbours if I had to. I came back to the front of the house and thumped on the door some more, till I heard shifting and rustling inside, someone mumbling. The door opened.

"She's not here," Kirk's mom said, all squinty in her housecoat. *Don't mess with me,* I thought. *I'll knock your fucking teeth out.* "Please," I said, and explained the situation. My dad stood around awkward in his orange hunting cap maybe ten feet behind me.

She made us wait in the hall. Kirk came out in a grey sweat-suit, hair smushed in the back, face scrunched against the light. He knew it was bad news. We went into the kitchen and he sat down right away, head in his hands as I told him what had happened.

"Do you know where she might have gone?" I asked. "Did she borrow any money from you?"

He spoke quietly, didn't have any useful answers. He said he'd last seen her the day before, asked about the note, said she wouldn't have left without telling him. That he couldn't believe it.

I looked for signs of her anyway. The house was messy, socks and gossip magazines on the floor, junk piled high on every surface. "Call us if you find anything," I said as we left.

TRINA HAD AT LEAST an hour on us. She could've been anywhere by then. My dad drove slow so we could see down side roads, then sped up so we could look into cars as we passed them. Around Alhambra, he said something about bad luck and then went quiet. I wanted him to say more, about how it felt, how it was happening again — another kid gone, the fourth one — but I knew it wasn't something he could give me. Instead I thought about the people and animals who leave their clans and go wandering into the woods when they know their times are coming. *Why would they do that,* I asked myself, and thought of reasons: They don't want to spread sickness. It's their last chance to see that pond, or the aurora by themselves. Solitude before death is just a thing some want. But there is no want, just instinct. I decided then that when it came time for me, I'd choose to stay with the people I love.

Dawn came a couple of hours in. I peered into ditches, forests, and fields, down other roads, wishing that my dad was a better driver or that I was fast enough to take it all in. The sun, rising ahead of us behind a hill, seemed brighter than normal. I was staring into fields. Everything I saw was yellow and blue. But then I looked out the windshield and saw we were on the centre line. "Ba," I said, but he didn't respond. A sad look in his eyes, or maybe not. His hands were steady on the wheel.

As we reached the top of the hill, we saw another car, so sudden it was like it wasn't there. It blocked out that sun, so bright if I were a believer, I'd say it was God. Does God even exist? You'd think with all we've gone through I might have faith in something, that I'd be like my dad and fear the power of ancestors and dead people, or I'd go to church, but where's the proof?

I wrapped my hand around the wheel and yanked hard. We lurched into the ditch — the pull and speed — and things flew around in the car, coins, bits of dirt. I was so fucking scared. I tried looking at him, my favourite person left alive besides Trina, I would've been okay if he were the last thing I saw, but I couldn't, I tried harder, inertia, PLEASE, then something big hit me in the face and chest, and everything went white.

I didn't see him. I missed my chance. The afterlife is white. We come from nothing, then go back into nothing. But then the white started to shrink, and there was pressure on my shoulder and lap. I was upside down, held in by my seatbelt, and the airbag was deflating. My dad was rubbing his head, slow and confused. He was hurt. I reached out for him, but he shoved my hand away, yelling, "Why you grub the wheel?"

"What do you mean? You almost killed us!"

He started swearing at me in Chinese, things I mostly don't know the translations for, though one of them means *I hate you.* I almost told him off, but stopped myself. Part of why we fight so much is that one of us can't be the bigger person. That's what Stef used to say, and I saw it was true when Trina or my brother Gene fought with my dad. I remember thinking, *If only you could just shut up and walk away, we wouldn't have to hear all this, we could go back to laughing about the chicken head on Trina's plate and her acting mad about it.*

I'm not an athletic person, but I somehow got out of the car without hurting myself. My dad had his window down by the time I got to him, still obviously pissed, his arm resting on the frame. "Are you okay?" I said. He didn't answer. It was like he was pretending I wasn't there. *Who's the adult now, fuckhead*, I wanted to say, but instead I told him I was gonna get help. I asked if he wanted to come.

"Why I come with you?" he said, sputtering.

It was beautiful where we were — sunshine, rolling hills, a couple of old barns a few miles away. A car passed, loud.

"Are you hungry?" I asked. He has diabetes.

"No."

"Lei ho noi mo sic yeh," I said. *You haven't eaten in a while.* There was nothing to dispute. "We'll get you something to eat."

Eventually he said "Aww, hell!" and got out. We started thumbing for a ride, beseeching RVs and big trucks towing boats and trailers to stop. Turns out a Saturday morning in June is a very bad time to hitch a ride — one of those things you won't know until you try. Everyone is in a rush to set up at a rodeo or to get the last good spot at the campground. They assume someone else will help. I imagined Trina going by in her car. What would that be like, her leaving home then seeing us all pathetic on the side of the road? She would stop. *Oh my god*, she would say. *I put you through hell. I'm so sorry.* We'd drive home, leave my dad's broken-down car where it was, and she'd promise not to leave again.

After a while, we started walking — slow because of his low blood sugar, his foot problems, a bad hip, a bit of arthritis. My dad's not a runner. A truck with jet skis in the back honked its

horn at us, roared by. I saw some bushes at the edge of a field
and went to take a better look. Stef told me that white berries
are usually poison, blue berries are often edible, and with red
berries, you have a fifty-fifty chance. The berries were blue. I was
scared — there's always an outside chance, right? — but I tried
one. Seemed okay. Saskatoon? I called my dad. He limped over
to where I was, arms pumping, perked up, not mad anymore.
My photogenic dad, eager and roguish like a little kid who loves
adventure and who for some sad and awful reason got stuck in
a decrepit old body. I had him wait a couple of minutes, in case
the berries were poison, but when nothing happened, I picked
a few for him.

He stopped me in the middle of picking and said, "Do you
think we steal?" There was a house two hundred feet away —
it was green and white, well kept, with bushes and windows like
knocked-out eyes.

I said, "You need the energy."

He chewed on his guilt for a while, then reached out, dainty,
and took a berry, then another and another and another. I ate
some, too, put more in an bag I had in my pocket. Always carry
a bag. It was something else Stef used to say.

We crossed the highway and started thumbing for a ride
again. Didn't have to do it long before this old steel truck pulled
up, rolled down its window. Sometimes luck rains down on
you and a bunch of good things happen all at once.

"You goin' to Carstairs?" I asked.

"Yep," the guy inside replied.

We got there in under fifteen minutes, bought insulin, had
breakfast, called my mom and a tow truck, which dropped us
off at the hospital in Spring Hills. The clinic was closed, so we
waited at Emerg six hours to be told we only had deep tissue
bruises. My dad and his cute black eye.

We walked home from the hospital, down Main. My mom was upstairs watching Chinavision, a slice of hot yam on the TV tray beside her. She shuffle-ran towards us when she heard the door, all jazz hands and incredulous eyes, this weird, sprightly smile on her face. A smile. Hadn't we almost died? I guess it was a smile of relief. She told us to never leave town again.

STEF ONCE SAID THAT when someone is missing, you're more likely to find them the sooner you start looking. So even though the world almost succeeded in killing us that day, I had to give it a chance to finish the job.

I went out to the living room, where my dad was telling my mom the story of what happened for, like, the fifteenth time. She was still in her chair. He was taking bone plates out of the microwave. One had a sausage bun, the other a piece of yam. Speaking in a mix of English and hillbilly Cantonese, he told my mom I caused the accident. "But she know how to help if trouble."

"Of course, she does," my mom replied. "She knows how to do things."

He perked up when he saw me.

"Wanna go back out?" I said.

"What," he said, both a question and not.

"We could go back out with the truck."

"No," he said. He hasn't driven in the five months since. It's not a thing I'm supposed to ask him about, so I don't.

I called Kirk. He said he came up empty, too, but fired off explanations left and right, said she needed time alone, that she was just in Edmonton, that she'd be back, I'd see, note or no note, he knew her. He was scrambling, like someone bailing water from a sinking boat.

I tried keeping my anger in check. Kirk was cool, but a part of me knew he took her away from us — not because he encouraged her to leave, I don't know if he did — but because a family like ours has its own rich life and that's not something you should fuck with. They used to go out every night, and she loved him, maybe more than she loved us. Before she left, she was already gone. Kirk and I were united by our shared misery, by this shared goal of finding her, and I needed him for his car and licence. But we weren't close, and I suspected we never would be.

He picked me up and we took another road out of town. We drove around, made random left and right turns. Though he seemed really sad, like he wanted my condolences, Kirk was chatty. He asked me how things were at school, how the store was, how my parents were, had I applied to universities for early acceptance yet?

I looked across the empty fields. Maybe they weren't empty. Maybe I just couldn't see what was there. It was getting dark again. I put my telepathic feelers out and wondered what she could possibly be thinking. Could she be happier somewhere else? Maybe she couldn't be happy unless she knew what else there was. What else did there need to be?

When Kirk dropped me off at home, I went to my room and saw that Trina had taken things: clothes from the closet, makeup and perfume, a box of tapes and CDs, and her little player that skipped on bumps. Everything else was where she left it. The rest of her clothes. This red leather jacket I always loved. Her hat, a turquoise blue kids' cowboy hat she wore almost every day for two years, even to Grad. Why wouldn't you take your one iconic piece of clothing with you when you left? Maybe she wanted to start fresh. Maybe it was insurance, a promise she'd be coming back. Or it was something for me to remember her by. As if I'd forget. The room smelled like her.

I took a moment, just stood there looking around till I

couldn't. Then I left, closed the door behind me, and went to the boys' room. I plopped down on Gene's bed and snuggled into the wall. Sometimes you can hear mice on the other side, but I didn't that night. I pulled the blanket over my head and lay there wondering if and when she'd be back and how it would've been if my dad and I had died instead of only getting hurt.

We filed a missing persons report two days later, but what was the use? She was long gone, maybe already settled somewhere by then, maybe — I wish she'd call. One call, one letter, just to let us know that she's okay. Would that really be so much to ask?

2

THAT WAS FIVE MONTHS ago. Since then, summer played out. I started sleeping in the boys' room for good, moved my stuff in there. A few times I thought I saw Trina's car and walked around all night looking. The store was quiet, a trickle of customers and some German tourists. It was a lean-your-chin-against-the-heel-of-your-hand-with-your-elbow-on-the-counter kind of summer. We didn't go anywhere or do anything. We worked all day, and at night I watched my parents shrink, watched them do nothing but watch TV. I guess I could have been better. I could have joked, helped form a sense of family cohesion. But I wasn't in a joking mood and my parents aren't the kind to talk about feelings.

It's November now and I'm in Grade Twelve. Over summer, word got out about Trina. She was cool, as I said. Though she was outside the social order at school, and though she couldn't give a fuck about that, she was liked.

Summer gives your identity a chance to shift. If you're lucky and try real hard, you can come back as someone else, someone better in their eyes. I came back a weirdo who likes to read, who likes music no one else likes. Doesn't help that all the kids in my family but me are gone. First day back at school, Curt Mayhew called me Dead Girl and it stuck. Pretty soon, that was my name to everyone. I don't mind. I have my friends. I have my cold, black heart and thoughts of Ty Rodriguez.

The first week of school brought him here. I don't know where he came from, but he's six foot two and has a low-rider bike, Buddy Holly glasses, clothes from the seventies, and dyed orange hair. All week I float home from school, still looking for Trina's car, but in a daze, dreaming about Ty Rodriguez. I pretend to do homework at the front counter of the store while imagining what it would be like to kiss him — he smokes, the smell and taste of that. Sometimes my mom will come and talk about university — *will you be going? What will you take? More calendars came in the mail for you* — and I'll shrug off the stool, slink away, go find someone who needs help. Carly Anderson needs a size for her husband. Boyd Nielsen needs a claim ticket made for the pair of boots he's bringing in for a half sole and heel.

University is university. I always said I'd go, but I'm in Grade Twelve, and I'm gonna die this year, so what's the point? Rather than read Aristotle or Marx or learn the finer points of botany or abnormal psychology for a couple of months, I'm gonna spend the time with my parents. Who would fault me for making a choice like that?

MONDAY MORNING, MRS. BLACKBURN opens the door to her office, wearing a red and black polyester skirt suit and sheer black pantyhose. "Chrysler! Come in," she says.

We sit across from each other. Her office is small with no windows and metal shelves you can buy at the hardware store. She has posters on her wall. *YOU CAN DO IT!* one of them says in blue handwritten font, multicultural kids doing jumping jacks below. But all the kids in this school are white except for me, Aabidah Meer, and some Natives. Files and papers everywhere.

There's this thing on her desk, a clear glass globe the size of a softball with seashells trapped inside. I think of the factory it was made in, millions of live sea creatures shipped in one end and crates of glass balls coming out the other. Where would they have found all those shells?

I look up, and she's smiling at me. "You wanted to see me?" I ask.

A baby starfish in the glass ball, tiny bubbles caught in its skin.

"Is it true you're not going to university?" Her face is earnest.

I look down. "I don't know," I say.

"You could do big things, you know."

It makes me smile, and I don't want it to. "You're supposed to say stuff like that."

"What happened with all those calendars we sent out for?"

"My mom got kind of crazy when she saw the one from Harvard."

A teacher smile, then she waits for me to say something else. When I don't, she says, "Well, you got a bunch, didn't you?"

"Yeah." It was nice, getting mail.

"But you haven't applied anywhere."

I don't say anything.

"And you didn't look at the calendars?"

"No, I looked at them." I thought it'd be a way to see places without leaving town, but all universities look the same. Stone buildings, weird buildings, big green lawns and trees, multicultural students. Even the University of Hawaii was nothing special to look at — just a bunch of people wearing leis over their normal clothes.

"And?"

I shrug.

"Chris, I think I know why you're not applying, and it's sad. But you can't just let go of your future because of what might happen. You owe it to yourself, and the world, I think."

The world? It's not like I'm gonna discover the cure for cancer or something.

"Isn't there something you want to do, as a career?" she asks.

"Yeah," I say under my breath, but she doesn't hear.

"I look at your grades, and I guess you could do more work in English and Math, but let's see: Bio, 87, Chem, 92 —"

"Mrs. B., I know I get okay marks in some things, but that's not the issue." I'm trying hard not to tell her I'm probably gonna die within the next nineteen months. There's a lot of ways to die — probably more than there are ways to live. You could get hit by a car, get a bad case of food poisoning, be the victim of armed robbery. Maybe you crash your bike or come down with something: tuberculosis, pneumonia, bronchitis, lupus, Ebola, diabetes, complications from diabetes.

"Would it hurt for you to try?"

Yes, it would. I see myself in a dorm room, lying awake at night, worrying about a pain in my chest that could be the start of a heart attack or heartburn — worrying about whether or not Trina came into the store that day looking for me, about whether or not she left when she couldn't find me. Or say the pollution in whatever city I live in is bad and I get cancer, say someone jumps me on my way home from the library one day.

"Can we just try something? You don't have to answer me, but it's probably better if you do. Are there any jobs that interest you?"

"Yeah, dental hygienist," I say.

"What?"

"A dental hygienist. You know, the people you see before the dentist? They clean your teeth."

"Anything else?"

Entomologist. Ornithologist. Urban planner. "I wanna write." You don't have to leave town to write.

"Like journalism?"

"No, like stories." I'm reading *The Illustrated Man* by Ray Bradbury. If I knew an Illustrated Man, he'd tell me stories with his skin. He'd fill me up with words, pictures, ideas, everything exotic, so I wouldn't have to leave.

"So you want an English degree."

"No, I just want to write. What's so bad about staying in Spring Hills? Work at my parents' store all day, come home and write stories at night."

"It sounds like you've put some thought into this."

"I mean, I may go to university, but I don't think now's the time."

Of course it's the time, I expect her to say, but she doesn't. A phone rings in another room. Mrs. B. is looking at her hands on the top of her desk. She picks at a cuticle. Then she looks at me.

"Chris, I have to tell you: you don't belong here."

I look down.

"There are lots of kids in this school I can't imagine anywhere else. Their parents grew up here, their grandparents grew up here. But, Chris, your family —"

No.

"— has always been special. Reggie, I thought he was going to do something big, go off and be a doctor or scientist. Trina, I thought she'd move to the city, be an artist."

Fat lot she knows.

"I just want you to think — if you could live somewhere right now, anywhere — I want you to close your eyes and think of where."

"I'd live here."

"Because you love it so much."

"No," I say. "No one seems to understand. I have constraints."

"I know about your constraints," she says. She pushes buttons on her plastic watch. Mrs. B. needs a timer because she also teaches gym. "But for three minutes, I want you to pretend you don't have them. I'm going to time you, and at the end of that you're gonna tell me where you want to be."

I don't need three minutes to know. I've been thinking about it for years. New York. The most mythologized place you can name besides heaven. All the movies in the world probably play there. It's got hundreds of clubs, all kinds of music. Fresh vegetables at all-night corner stores. Pigeons, bookstores, the Lower East Side. Ten million people, all strangers, at rush hour, a hundred thousand out in the middle of the night. Hundreds of nationalities. Good pizza. But it's hard to move to the States, and school is expensive there. Honestly, I'd be okay with Edmonton. Anywhere with lots of people and a university. Or Toronto. That's somewhere new. I don't know anything about it, except it's big.

I tell Mrs. B. New York, Toronto, and Edmonton, so she'll let me go. Nice ideas but they're not gonna happen.

AFTER SCHOOL MY DAD and I go shopping at the Co-op. That's where we go for groceries — and insulin at the in-store pharmacy. They have a senior's discount. Everyone says hi to my dad, and he waves and replies in kind, using their names when he remembers — "Frank!" "Jim!" "Rick!" — and a loud, vague shout when he doesn't. Spring Hills is a town of six thousand, the kind of place where everyone knows each other and their cars, where more often than not people in affairs get found out when someone sees the wrong truck parked outside a house.

A flash down Aisle 3 — canned soup — catches my eye. Halfway down, a small, thin woman with long black hair. I go, telling my dad I'll be back. "I don't need anything," he says.

But I do. It isn't her, though. Why would it be her? It shouldn't be her. This lady looks at me like *what the*.

"Sorry," I say. "I thought you were someone else."

And then for some reason, from out of thin air, by a pyramid of cans, Ty Rodriguez is there in a brown Co-op uniform, writing in a notebook, this look of concentration on his face. He's smart. Writing with his left hand. I'm left-handed, too! I pull a can off the pyramid and read: *corn, water, sugar, salt*. Niblets. I take a deep breath. Smoke and musky cologne. He smells so good. His shoes are nice. You can't get ones like that here, maybe they're from Europe. I cough and his head moves. Dyed orange hair. *Say something*. I reach for another can, a few inches from his elbow. I imagine our skin grazing, the back of my hand, his arm, electricity. How many more ingredients are there in creamed corn? One, two, three, four — *say something* — five. A glimpse of his cool glasses, his nose has so much character. *Say something!* I don't. I put the can down and walk away.

When I find my dad he's in the meat section, in the midst of another good smell. He hands me a toothpick poked through a hunk of something brown and greasy. His thick fingers, bleached white at the tips. I look at him, he nods at me, his jaw working. "Go ahead," he says. English slang sounds weird coming from him, like marbles in his mouth, but it's still a comfort. I put it in my mouth and chew. Spicy, meaty, salty. Sausage. We try all the different flavours. The samples lady and her electric frying pan can't keep up. People jostle around me, someone shoves me. Hands coming at the plate from all angles. Nothing in the garbage beside her but toothpicks. She tells us how much they are and my dad looks at me, eyebrows raised, mouth open in surprise over the price, before limping away and coming back with five packs.

"So many?" I say.

"What, you think we can't eat them all?"

"No," I say like he's a little boy. "You have a prime rib *and* a chicken in the fridge, and five packs of sausage — *fifty sausages* — are enough for two years. Do you know how much fat is in one of those? Look," I say, turning over a pack to show him. "Thirty grams in one, and more salt than you're allowed in a day."

"Well," he says, scrunching his face and shooing the facts away like flies.

"No. Not 'well.' You're gonna buy five packs, you're gonna put them in the freezer, and you're going to try to feed me one a year from now, and I won't want it."

"Two forty-nine good price!"

"It's only good if we eat them," I say. "They'll be on sale again. Just buy two."

"I like smoky dog," he says. I like them, too, but I shrug my shoulders and smile like *what can you do.* He stands his ground — he's old and lives for food, I should let him — but eventually his face opens up, this guilty smile. He pinches me hard on the cheek, and though I'm more than old enough to hate it, I love it. Every time he smiles I want to take a picture. He puts some away, and we walk down the meat aisle, at peace with each other for now, a small, rare battle won by me in this lifelong war. I'm pretty sure that my departure from the world, as long as my dad is alive, will be marked by the purchase of a number of smokies, steaks, and roasts limited only by what the Co-op can carry. He will need to buy another three freezers for all the extra meat he will buy.

We walk back with our groceries in the handcart. As soon as we get home, my dad starts on supper. He's an awesome cook, works wonders with a wok. The first thing he did when he moved here twenty-five years ago was install a gas wok in the wall. It's still there — massive, three feet wide, the kind you'd find in the back of a Chinese restaurant, which makes sense, because he spent his first ten or twenty years in Canada working restaurants. His food is so good you could sell it.

He pulls a giant chicken out of the fridge on a Styrofoam tray and makes it halfway to the cutting board before the tray cracks and the chicken tumbles onto the floor. Flecks of dirt on it like pepper. My dad plunks it into the sink, sees my face. "It's just a little dirt," he says, rinsing it off, annoyed, probably thinking *what is it with this family and its health standards* as he pulls the chicken out, his hands under its wings like it's a baby.

With about an hour left in the workday, it's time for me to go back down to the store, but before I do, I watch him tie up the chicken. If you grew up poor in the old country — any old country will do — it means you know how to tie a knot — out of grass, reeds, string, rope, animal hair, whatever. Nothing more useful than tying a knot to keep your cow, to keep your door shut, to keep your stuff together on a very long trip, to keep your memories. The chicken's way too big for the pan, but in twenty seconds he makes it fit. My dad, the shoemaker, tells the chicken who's boss.

Downstairs, I sit around bored for most of an hour then run for the four customers who come in ten minutes before close. I come back upstairs just in time to catch my dad at the table with his shoebox of pills and his shirt pulled up. His age spots, his gallbladder scar — purple, eight inches long — and the bottom two inches of his triple bypass scar. He applies the alcohol, fills a syringe with insulin, and stabs himself in the gut. One time, I asked if I could help. *Why not?* he said, and showed me how. It felt weird, like poking a pin through canvas, resistance then give. He winced. I pushed the plunger down and he put his hand on my head and shoved it around, a loving gesture. *Do it faster next time,* he said.

When my mom's done the books, she comes up for dinner. The chicken, in pieces on a metal plate, smells really good but is a little too pink. Trina would have eaten it. I can't.

Two minutes into the meal, I drop a chopstick then duck under the table to find it and see my mom's already taken her shoes and socks off, her calloused, flaking feet hovering over the filthy floor. She's kicking them together like a little girl. Up top, a pained expression, her eating face. My mom doesn't eat for taste, she does it to stay alive. Probably wouldn't eat if she didn't have to. I grab a new chopstick and when I get back there's a chicken drum on my plate. "Thanks, Ba," I say.

His toothy, greasy-lipped smile, a piece of chicken in his hands. He sucks the meat off, happy as a clam. Then he gives my mom the giblets.

"Mo bei gnoa!" she yells. *Don't give it to me.* The giblets stay on her bone plate, I watch them get cold. He tries giving her other food, too, and she keeps yelling "Ngoa ji gei loa!" — *I'll get it myself* — but she doesn't.

At the end of the meal, my dad complains about all the leftover meat. Best chicken in the world and most of it will be thrown out in three days. Indignantly, he picks the congealed giblets off my mom's plate and eats them. Watching him chew it all up, I think of rocks and grit and coronary blockages. He looks back, astonished by my interest, like it's the most natural thing in the world to be eating that stuff, then his face melts into a smile, a guilty grin — but what's he guilty of? We smile at each other, hold it for a while. I get up for more rice and he swats me on the ass. Some dads hug you, support your decisions, tell you that they love you. Mine hits me, bites me, swears at me, shows his love with aggression. *Love hurt*, he calls this.

I'm hiding the chicken drum in the kitchen when the phone rings. It almost never does outside store hours. Trina. No, it's a telemarketer. We wash the dishes then hang out in the living room, my mom in her armchair, my dad flat out on the couch. They're watching Chinese TV on satellite. Me, I'm walking on my dad's back and legs, soft and firm like Jell-O that's been sitting in the back of the fridge for a month. When I'm done, I pull up a chair from the dining room table and watch the lawyer show with them till it's time to sleep.

When they're in bed, I go to my room and write in my notebook, *jobs that require the tying of knots: cook, cowboy, sailor, justice of the peace.* Creaking. My bedroom door opens. It's my dad, wondering why I'm not asleep yet. I'm a straight-A student, almost an adult, I can tell him what to buy at the Co-op, he trusts me with money at the store, but he still thinks he can tell me when to sleep. I guess he can. We take care of each other.

Soon after he turns out the light, I sneak down the hall past their room, then down the front stairs and out. I've got posters and a tape gun with me. I started making the posters in June — a description of Trina and her car, when she was last seen, all that. I need to know, does she live nearby? Has someone seen her? Maybe she's in danger or hooked on drugs.

One step out the door, cold wind slams me in the face. Mike Brown's dad Gary drives by in his cop car. I go walking down Main, down Fiftieth, putting posters on brick walls, lampposts, and windows downtown, and end up on the highway. Walk in this town long enough, and that's where you'll end up. That or a dead end. There are businesses along Main — my parents' store, for one — but the highway is where the action is. School, grocery stores, some fast food places. I tape posters by the bars, by the all-night truck stop diner, on gas pumps, even though I know they'll be torn down tomorrow. Gary Brown told me that business owners and town maintenance people have complained, that the posters constitute vandalism, but frankly,

I doubt he'd do any different if his precious little Mikey went missing.

I've halfway decided to tape a poster to the cop shop window when I see a single headlight on the highway, moving slow. A bike. Someone in an old man parka. Nice. And when I see who it is, my heart jumps. Ty Rodriguez. I wanna call out. He's smiling big, toothy, thinks he's alone, but I'm here, too. One a.m. We're the only ones in town still out. Say something. Thirty feet away but he'd hear you. Where's he going? Maybe just out for a ride. It's a great night for it. Freezing cold and fucking windy, but it's gorgeous and so dark out and the snow is blue. I've always loved an empty street. Even better when it's a highway. I guess he thinks they're special, too.

Should I call out or shouldn't I? I think as he sails by, past the town limit sign. A gust of wind goes through me.

I watch till I can't see him anymore, then walk up to the sign to see if I'll exist past it. Just one step, just a couple. What's the harm? One time I stood there for more than twenty minutes weighing the options, taking baby steps forward and big steps back. The streetlights are on but there's a lot you can't see. Maybe someone in a field with a knife. I could get hit by a car. It's stupid to walk on the highway at night.

Trina is right: I'm a chickenshit. There could be millions of dollars on the other side of this sign, or all the knowledge in the world, the perfect boy, the most beautiful thing I could imagine, all for the taking — but there's only one thing, one person, I'd leave town for, and she's already long gone.

I finish the posters and go home.

3

IN THE BEGINNING THERE was Sean. Or maybe it wasn't Sean. Maybe there were others. You can only go so far back. I don't remember what I liked about him, for years I only remembered him as a name. Something happened to him. Maybe he moved away or transferred to another school because he hadn't been around in so long, more than ten years, maybe. Then in March, this guy came into the store, this total rig pig with permanently dirty overalls and hands. I only knew it was Sean 'cause he was cashing a cheque. He smelled like alcohol. I wanted him. Can I say that? Something about him, about all those rigger guys. But he didn't remember me. I didn't ask if he did, but I knew. I cashed him out and didn't say shit. I guess it's fine. He's probably stupid now. He was probably stupid then, too.

Sometime after Sean was Craig Jamieson, with the machine-gun laugh. His dad owned the fruit stand. My dad and I would go on Saturdays or after schools, we would pull up in the grey Olds, and fear would creep up unannounced like a lion in a nature show, then pounce. My dad would get out of the car. Me, I wouldn't even unlatch my seatbelt. "Lui la," he would say. *Come on.* Then we'd stand out there on the gravel in the heat, my dad pointing at the baskets of cherries and peaches he wanted, changing his mind sometimes, while Craig and I would have an awkward moment, talk a bit about a light subject like school or the weather, I don't remember. Craig would joke. I wouldn't, not with my dad standing there. What's the worst that would've happened if I'd talked to him more? I don't know, didn't think that far, I was that scared. What I did know was I'd catch shit from my dad if he so much as suspected. He'd beat the shit out of me with a shoe, a hanger, whatever he could find when we got home. He would.

Between Sean and Craig was Derek Mason, who I remember one time on the steps of Spring Hills El drawing a big fucking tank shooting puny little soldiers. Pinpricks of spattered blood. That was our moment, me watching him draw. Five years later, in Grade Seven, some of us were at this glacial erratic on the bike path, a big rock people in town call Big Rock. I'm not sure why I was there. Derek was about to make out with Amanda Rice, and it made me feel weird, the way he was touching her, the way he was getting in. A nursery rhyme song about the eensy weensy spider, only it was going up her leg and she liked it.

I even liked Mike Brown at one time, until he came into the store with his dad, saying something about Stef or Trina's ass, something about a "nice Chinese butt." Fuck that guy.

There was Travis Ingmire, who I don't remember much of, and Steve McInnes, brother of Peggy McInnes, who used to date my brother Reggie. There was John Nelson, whose house I called. I found his number in the phonebook. I was so nervous, the moment after you dial the last number and it starts to call and you can't turn back, the ringing, one, two, three, four, the woman who picked up who must have been his mom, but I forged ahead and asked for him. When he got on the phone, I asked him how he was and what he thought of the weather. His answers were brief, so I asked him more questions, about basketball — he was on the team — and about some funny thing that happened in math class that week. Eventually he asked me why I was calling, and I couldn't handle it. He probably told his friends all about it. It scared me off calling guys I liked for years. I still don't do it.

There was Mark Petersen, this friend of Gene's who I ended up being friends with, too, whose first words to me were "You look ravishing." That ravishing thing was a joke, a thing he did to be weird, but I had daydreams of putting my face on his crotch on the benches in the hall at school. Things were not anatomically correct in my imaginings, warps in the space-time continuum were required. He didn't know how I felt — I didn't tell him — and before he moved away for university, he dated my friend Kay Berringer.

There was Jake Kowalchuk, handsome and friendly, who everybody liked. We had mutual friends, and when Jake's dad ended up dying in a fourteen-car pileup out on Highway 11, I thought our having something in common would make us closer. It didn't. He was out of my league. There was Jason Parsons in Grade Six, who I chased and kicked in the shins, John Niedermeyer last year, who was ugly and sweet, but still too scary to approach, Andrew Grabowski, this guy from Interior BC who wore skater clothes but wasn't a skater. There's a lot I'm leaving out. Other than John Nelson, none of them knew, or maybe some did but didn't show it, or they showed it and I was just too fucking scared to notice or do anything back.

Do you ever feel like there's maybe no one for you? Or that there's someone and you have to find them, and if you've found them, you have to win them, and only when you do will your life be forever changed for the better and in ways you could barely imagine? That's exactly how I feel, like there's no one for me. Or maybe it's Ty, and there's no goddamn way whatsoever he'd be interested in me.

I used to say stuff like that to Stef and Trina. Stef would encourage me, tell me in her no-bullshit way that I was smart and beautiful and that someday I'd know it was true, and guys would flock. One time, Trina started crying. "It's sad, all right," I said, laughing at myself, but she said she was crying because she didn't understand how I'd grown up in such a way that I could never once believe a single good thing about myself. It made me feel even worse — like not only am I totally not attractive to anyone but also I'm fucked up in a way that is even weirder than I thought, and can't be changed.

One time when I was maybe fourteen, I was talking to Trina about this guy, Dirk Klassen, who was a snowboarder, canoer, mountain-climber kind of guy. I was saying there wasn't any way, I barely even walked on the bike trail, and plus I was ugly.

"Fuckin' rights you are," she said.

"What?" I said, wounded.

"See, even you don't believe that shit," she said.

I guess she had a point. But being scared and worrying about whether or not someone good would want you is one thing. Letting someone else shit all over your self-esteem is another.

I KNOW THAT, AS a teenager, I'm supposed to hate teachers, but they're okay. Nothing special about me, just I like learning, and they've got my fix. Plus, they're all nice to me, even though I'm a bit of a dick at times. Biology is my favourite, and I do okay in French, but Mr. MacAvoy — Mac — my English teacher, is exceptional. There's something about him, he has this passion you can see when he reads something he likes. He's like that Dead Poets Society guy but less cheesy. He started the writing club, theatre club, music appreciation club, book club, and the school's literary magazine. Spring Hills is a town of rednecks and skids and Mac singlehandedly brought culture to it.

Today he spends class reading chapters eight and nine of *Lord of the Flies*. They're the ones where Simon, my favourite character, goes crazy in the jungle. The boys mistake him for the beast and kill him, and it's hard to read, devastating. Afterwards, Mac asks us questions, and I try to come up with answers, but after each of my attempts, he calls on someone else and builds their answer, not mine, into the teachable moment. It makes me ashamed of myself but I still try. There's so much to say about a book like that.

I'm surprised when he pulls me aside at the end of class to tell me about a student writing contest. He acts like it's some big news. I tell him that most of the things I've written are sad, cheesy, angsty, or plagiarized, but he gives me an entry form anyway.

At lunch, I find Nancy in the library, finger at her drooly mouth, reading *Mists of Avalon*. In the movie of my life, she would play my best friend, but "best" means "most good," not necessarily "very good." She's not the bottle I pour my life into — she doesn't always know what to say, and I don't run to her when things get tough.

Nancy wants to keep at it, so I get up, find *The Illustrated Man*. I love the idea of an illustrated man. If you were in love with one, you'd be allowed to stare. When you were together, he wouldn't have to tell you how he felt about things — all those moving pictures on his skin. For a while, he might stare back, but you're plain as a blank page. Eventually he'd get bored and leave. Or maybe he would see something. Maybe he's tired of all those tattoos and would be glad to look at you.

After school, some of us go to KFC. Nancy says she got a letter yesterday from the University of Alberta that said they'd keep her in mind for a full scholarship, and that they'd let her know early next year. I don't want to talk about this but we start going around the table anyway. Kay says, "Yeah, I don't know," and Luke says he got conditional acceptance to U of C.

"Seriously?" I say. Luke's marks are in the Cs.

"Serious as a pig's teats," he says, and I'm so happy for him that I get up and give him a noogie. "Yeah," he says. "Figured it's the only way to get out of this shithole. How about you?"

"Haven't really thought about it. I mean, I've looked into it, but I haven't made up my mind," I say, then ask — though it's only Tuesday — "What's everyone doing on the weekend?" Luke says Kat Mitchum might be having a party. Kay says she'll go if it happens.

When we're done at KFC, Luke and I go downtown. His dad owns Johnson Hardware on Main. We walk down Fifty-Second, turn down at the hospital. Fewer streets in this town than wrinkles, than blood vessels in my hand.

It's minus ten, but he's wearing shorts, no coat, and his arms are crossed. We're breathing clouds. "God, put on a fucking coat, will you?" I say.

"Fuck you," he says, overemphatic, and it hurts though I know he's kidding.

We pass posters I put up last night. Luke sees them but doesn't mention them. Not much of a talker, Luke. We pass the old IGA, the old Zellers, the Nutters.

"Fuck, I can't wait to be in Calgary," he says. "My mom's such a fucking dick." I agree, but don't say anything. Ruth Carcadian thinks she's hot shit, and likes nothing better than to gossip at the IGA.

After leaving Luke at his dad's store, I go to the library, the public one this time, to read the encyclopedia. Yeah, it's geeky. My brother Reggie read the dictionary because he thought it'd help him get into a better school. It didn't help his communication skills, though maybe all those words gave him a rich internal life. I hardly knew him, but I liked to think of him composing secret poems in his head about the conundrum of existence, or about butterflies, while he was pumping gas or folding jeans at the store. Me, I read the encyclopedia for fun. Learning for learning's sake. I'm a model citizen. Who needs university when you've got the encyclopedia? S for sloths and snails and squid.

I start reading about saints, enjoy it even though I'm not religious. Agnes in the brothel against her will, God striking men blind as they raped her. Anthony in the desert fighting the devil. These stories make me want to write my own, so I find the contest entry form Mac gave me earlier today. It's in Comic Sans, the font most commonly used by adults in their communiqués to kids they don't really understand. Thanks, adults. I wasn't going to read this before, but now I see it's in Comic Sans.

1997 Central Western Alberta
High School Non-Fiction Writing Contest

Theme: Travel. Where have you been? Where do you want to go and why? What does travel mean to you? (Is it the blending of cultures? A way to experience new things?) Keeping in mind that travel is an everyday part of life (eg., travelling to the grocery store or to a friend's house), what are some of your favourite places to travel?

The essay can be narrative, telling the story of someone else's travels. Does someone you know have a particularly touching, funny, or interesting travel story? (Newspaper articles count.)

Contest Deadline: November 30, 1997

Winners will be selected in the summer and published in a special travel insert in the July 3rd edition of the *Edmonton Journal.*

First Prize: $250 scholarship, and a $500 travel voucher, courtesy Destiny Vacations
Second Prize: $100 scholarship, and a $250 travel voucher, courtesy Destiny Vacations

Where have I been? Vancouver. Edmonton. Calgary. The mountains. Nowhere else. Where's Trina been? Where is she now?

4

✺

EIGHT YEARS AGO, MY mom got a package in the mail with Chinese writing on the front. Packages didn't come from China every day or even every week, but they came often enough that I didn't ask questions. Usually they were packing tubes with Chinese celebrity magazines inside, or letters from my mom's old school. This one wasn't anything special, I thought. But a couple of days after it came, I heard my parents talking, not angry and not about the store. Their tones of voice were weird, not ones I'd heard them use with each other before. They were solemn. I didn't understand some of what they said, but I got that he was telling her to go, he was insistent. Go where?

It turned out they were talking about my mom's high school reunion. The day after the letter came, while rummaging in a drawer, I found a black and white photo of her lounging off the front of this old car. It was a convertible, dark coloured with chrome details, a grill, a hood ornament that said MG. She had on a skirt, something I'd almost never seen her wear. I showed the picture to Stef, Trina, Gene, Reg, and finally to my mom, and when I did it turned up her face's dimmer switch.

"Whose car is this?" I said.

"I don't remember," she said, sly and playful.

"An old boyfriend's?"

"Yah, maybe. Do you know how big my waist was?"

"No."

"Eighteen inches," she said.

"How old were you?"

"Maybe eighteen?"

It's hard to believe anyone ever had a good time in high school, but my mom did. She loved those days. I've seen other pictures of her since: Pretty and excited with friends at a sock hop. Playing croquet with some guy in a suit, a toothy, formal smile on her face like she's winning the game and doesn't want to rub it in. It's only through these pictures that I can imagine her being my age. She loves dancing the Twist — when no one else is in the store, we do it while I sing Buddy Holly love songs to her. She was a good kid who loved to read. She likes talking to me about how she read Dickens and Shakespeare back then, how she learned to speak Mandarin fluently with only one lesson a week. She had so many friends and so much fun back then and no friends and seemingly so little fun now.

I asked her that night if she was planning to go to the reunion. She said she wasn't sure. I asked her again a couple of days later and got the same answer.

Eventually, Stef confronted her. "You're going, right?" she said. My mom had not been back in twenty years.

"Who will take care of the store?"

"I will," Stef said.

My mom wasn't sure about that.

"So Dad will," Stef said. "You have to go. You haven't seen those people in decades. You know you'll regret it if you don't, right?"

"I don't want to go alone."

"I'll go with you." Stef said it off the cuff, but it made sense. It was summertime, no school, and she spoke the best

Cantonese of all of us. She was fifteen, not too young for something like that. It was settled.

In the weeks before they left, my mom was happier than I've ever seen her, and the trip did not disappoint. Stef said she had a good time, too, though the weather was way hotter than she expected and she would have preferred less time on the bus and more time at destinations. Days were spent driving by rivers, mountains, pagodas, and fields, the tour guide speaking of the local vegetation and economy while my mom and her old classmates drowned him out singing their school songs.

They did stop at some places. One of them was this monastery in the desert: Sand Temple, it was called. It used to have old, intricate engravings on the outside but they'd been worn away by sand over the course of centuries. Inside it had no real floor, just drifting piles of sand and dust, and there were monks walking around in square hats and dark robes. Stef, who'd never been inside a church, said the temple was serious and silent, but the desperation of people begging things of gods was jarring. You could write a wish on a card then put it on a wall. There were hundreds of them there, overlapping out of lack of space. Imagine all those wishes, all those needs, all those impossible odds. Stef couldn't read Chinese, but she imagined people pleading for luck they'd never have, for terminal illnesses to be cured, for indifference to change to undying devotion. She thought it was a weird juxtaposition, the visitors — many of whom were probably poor — in this temple full of expensive sacred objects. There were silk scrolls, embroidered tapestries, glass mosaics, thrones, and pictures inlaid with gold. Stef checked all the rooms and saw gold statues in every one, but some rooms had curtains and she couldn't see in. She and I are alike. We need to know things. There were long lineups outside the rooms. Stef asked my mom what was going on and my mom asked the tour guide and translated his reponse. "This temple famous for fortune-telling," she said.

"How much time do we have?" Stef said.

My mom checked her watch. "Half hour."

"Can I have my fortune told?"

My mom hesitated — she's different from my dad in that she's generous with us in terms of money and things we want from the store — but eventually said yes. Stef joined a line and ended up spending most of her time in the temple waiting while my mom looked around some more. She got in less than five minutes before they had to leave. Inside the small room, a smiling monk sat on the floor behind a table. He asked her to shake a stick out of a jar and throw pieces of wood onto the ground, then told her fortune.

Stef and my mom went on to see the Great Wall and the Yangtze River, giant pandas and Tiananmen Square. They also stopped in on my uncle, grandma, and cousins. Before they knew it, two weeks had gone by, and they were coming home. It couldn't have been soon enough.

We fell apart without Stef. If a family is like ingredients in a recipe, she was our salt. Salt is vital. It brings flavours out of the other parts and makes everything work better together. Without it a dish falls flat. If you run out of salt, you might still get by with soy sauce, salted fish, or preserved sausage. In our case, though, there was no one to take Stef's place. My dad kept getting mad for dumb reasons, and there was no one to talk him down. When I tried we'd end up fighting. Gene had girl trouble, he always did. Too good-looking. Trina was caught cheating on a test at summer school. Reggie was depressed. Stef would have been the one to console us, but with her gone, we had to console ourselves.

"He's so stupid," I said to Trina about our dad. "I wish he was dead."

"I didn't cheat," Trina said to me. "I was just getting paper from my notebook."

"What do you do," Gene said, "when two girls like you and you like both of them back?"

Stef and my mom's return flight arrived in Edmonton on a Sunday morning. My dad came in to wake us so we could pick them up, and one by one, Reggie, Trina, and I stretched, yawned, and got out of bed. We knew how my dad can be. He'd come by once, twice, and if you weren't awake by the third time he came, depending on how he was feeling, there could be trouble.

When my dad started yelling, I was on the other side of the house, brushing my teeth. I came out of the bathroom — I was always missing out on stuff — and saw my dad and Trina standing in the doorway of the boys' room. The light was on. Something felt off so I ran there.

Gene was lying in bed, looking scared, which surprised me. "Wuck's wong?" I said, my toothbrush in my mouth. *What's wrong?*

"I told you I can't move," he said to Trina, who was by the bed now. She put her hand on his chin, maybe to force his mouth open and closed while she said something funny, but he made a terrified dog noise and screamed, "Stop it," without trying to knock her hand away.

That was when she started to believe him. She squeezed by me, started running to the phone, and I followed her. When we came back, Reggie was standing there, dumbstruck. He was never much help in crunch times, but he helped my dad bring Gene to the car. Gene was having trouble moving on his own. I pictured him playing basketball earlier that week and it distressed me even more.

We drove to Emerg, where they did X-Rays, took a blood sample, asked Gene about his medical history. We did what we could, told him when the elastic cuff was going to go around his arm and when the needle was about to go in, but Gene was panicking and there wasn't much we could say to help. Trina was thirteen and I was twelve and nothing bad had happened to our family yet.

My dad was leaning forward in his chair with his hands on his thighs. He looked like how I felt, worried, dazed, and like we needed some propping up. Reggie seemed to be thinking about something else entirely. Maybe it was school. He looked a little annoyed.

Eventually Dr. Bosch called us in. He said he'd looked at the X-Ray and blood results and didn't know what was wrong. "His muscles are fine, and his vitals are intact." he said. "No sign of stroke, not that we'd expect one at his age."

"Something wrong," my dad said, drawing out the words for emphasis. "He can't move."

"I'm suggesting he see a neurologist," Dr. Bosch said. He didn't know which of us to talk to now, so he was talking at all of us.

"Special doctor?" my dad said. The doctor looked at him.

"Yes. For the brain." He spoke louder, slower than before. "I'll get him an appointment. It'll take a couple of weeks."

"Brain," my dad said, astonished and worried. "He don't need to see special doctor now?"

"It takes a long time to see one," Dr. Bosch said. "There's a waiting list. But it might not be as bad as you think. His heart and everything else is fine. He'll live. What we need to work on is … the connection between his muscles and brain."

"How do you know he be okay?" my dad said.

"Well, you can leave him here for another day or two if you want, and we'll keep watch."

"Yah. Please," my dad said. It was past noon. Stef and my

mom would have been at the airport for hours by then, and we had no way to get ahold of them.

My dad left us at the hospital and drove to the airport alone. Reggie, Trina, and I took turns staying at home to wait for a phone call from Stef and my mom, and staying in the hospital with Gene. He was scared. Of course he was. I brought books so we could read to him. It was hard to choose which ones, since most of the best books are sad or weird. I read some of *The Hobbit* to him because it's fun and long and has a happy ending, but reading never was Gene's thing. He said, "Keep talking to me," so Trina told him fun stories about people who came into the store, like the guy looking for horse deodorant and the drunk guy our mom chased out with a boot. It was all stuff he already knew about, but he didn't complain.

THERE WAS LOTS TO do when Stef came back. It was back-to-school, one of our busy times. Gene was going to the city for tests around once a week or every other. No one knew what was wrong with him, but we heard different theories: Multiple sclerosis — which was weird for someone his age — young-onset Parkinson's disease, Lyme disease, lupus. When he was home, we fed him and helped him go to the bathroom — I turned away when I took off his pants for him, saw it anyway but pretended I hadn't so he'd feel okay — and we helped him with homework when school started.

We also shot the shit. Stef told Gene about her trip to keep him amused and calm. She talked about the temple, its dust and monks. She said she saw a fortune-teller, but she didn't tell us what he said.

"Come on," Trina said. "That's the best part."

"Naw," Stef said. "It's private."

"Private?" Trina said. "Even to your own family? I bet he

said you'll end up a millionaire, a professor with ten kids and a good-looking husband."

Stef was grim. "No," she said.

"I bet he said you'll be famous for your survival skills," Trina said.

Stef said, "No. Stop asking about it."

"I bet he said you'll get the store."

"No," Stef said for the last time, ferrying a spoonful of rice with beef and greens towards Gene's mouth.

Gene said, "I bet it's about me. It's why she doesn't want to say." He closed his mouth around the spoon.

He was right. Later that night, with Gene in the next room, Stef told me and Trina about the fortune. *Sickness in your family and premature death.* I'm not religious — I don't think Jesus died for our sins or that ancestors pull for you to win the lottery after you visit them at their graves — but what happened to Gene sounded an awful lot like sickness to me. You don't have to believe in it, but fortune-telling is a very old art. Stef, though, said fortunes were like horoscopes: you could read a lot into them and find what you were looking for. She was too rational, too scientific, to believe that stuff, said that she only got her fortune out of curiosity, because it looked fun. *When in Rome, right?* Still, I wondered if she was pretending not to believe so we wouldn't be worried about the future.

5

※

THE LIGHTS IN THE library start going out. Closing time, five-thirty. I walk out, past a brown metal cart full of university calendars, flimsy and useless as phonebooks for a town you know you'll never visit. Nancy showed me one of hers the other day. I had to pretend I wasn't interested. But Abnormal Psychology, Classics of Dystopic Literature, Invertebrate Zoology — fucking hell. My mouth was watering.

There's a bite in the air. Two minutes out the door, the feeling of pins pricking at my face. I'm cold even with my coat on. It's from the 1970s, I got it from the White Elephant.

I come home through the back just in time to hear my dad yelling at my mom about why I'm never there, as if it's her fault. They're in the main part of the store, in front of customers, which is bullshit. *Get some self-control, you fucking ape*, I want to yell at him, but you don't want to be around my dad when he's in a bad mood. My bedroom door locks, so I head upstairs, climb into bed.

What do I want? I want to be in this family and I don't want to be in this family. Like Trina. She could be anywhere, even in Caroline. Maybe in love with some guy, maybe pregnant. Too busy to call. Maybe she doesn't want to. Maybe she's still travelling. She always wanted that. You can drive all the way to Peru from here, through mountains to the tip of Chile where South America, at the very last minute, points away from Antarctica. I'd like to go to there, to experience twenty-four-hour darkness or sun. There's not a lot I don't want to see, especially if it's weird like that.

A few minutes later, my dad clomps down the outside hall and opens the apartment door. Sometimes you can tell a person is angry by the sound of their walk, but this time I can't. He pauses outside my room. He'll start banging on the door any second now. I want a nicer dad. I love my parents, just wish my dad wasn't always so mad. Please. He keeps walking.

Half an hour later, my mom comes up. I unlock the door. "Can I come out? Do you think he's still mad?"

"I don't know," she says. She crossed the biggest ocean in the world for this, for a husband who takes everything out on her and a kid who can't stop getting into trouble. "Why can't you be home?"

"Why do I have to be home? What is there to do?"

At dinner, my dad is quiet, acts like he hadn't just embarrassed himself and us in public. Steamed chicken leftovers, they look fully cooked but I only take one piece. You never know. When we're done eating, my mom and I do the dishes while my dad lies on the couch, falling asleep to some show. There's one of us at each sink.

I turn to her. "Did anybody call?"

"What?" she says. She's watching TV, too, keeps putting dirty dishes in the rinse water. A film of oil on top.

I repeat: "Did anybody call."

A shock in her water. She looks at me. "When? Today? No. You expecting a call?"

"No," I say.

A period piece on the giant Magnavox. Guys with long hair,

royal headpieces, and Fu Manchu moustaches. TV in the morning, TV in the afternoon, TV in the evenings. Dishes crash together under the water. It sounds like hollow thumping to me. I throw dishes against the inside of the sink, just so I can hear more thumping.

THURSDAY AFTER SCHOOL, NANCY invites me to her house to make soup, but I tell her I have to work. You never know how it's going to be. The store ends up being dead, so my mom pays bills at the front while I put up Christmas decorations. Pure busywork. I guess it's fine. But it'd be better if Trina were here. We'd do it together, she'd think of fun and creative ways to arrange the tinsel and Santa cut-outs, then we'd go on a treat run, she'd go look for dead stock, maybe try some of it on, or get me to. Slacking was her specialty. But work she was good at, too. She might have been our best employee. She definitely was our best salesperson.

I liked to watch her work, serving three customers at the same time, which we have to do when it's busy — running a pair of boots to cash then whirling around, trailing scent and personality behind her on her way to get someone into the fitting room with jeans so she could help someone else with a jacket. I'd see her work and think, *how are we related?* and sometimes if she saw me looking she'd smile. Some smiles have energy, don't you think, or power? When she smiled at me I felt a connection. Was it something I did?

Trina has a better understanding of people than anyone I know. My mom asked her one time how she sold so much and Trina said, "Most people have too many clothes already. You have to think of what else they might want from you." I thought about that and started to see things differently. She was fond of suggesting people try things, not just things they came in to try, but a pair of red or yellow pants, or a weird skirt, or a shirt in a different cut from the one the person was wearing. When she did she'd usually make a sale. She sold an oilskin to Mr. Andrechuk, this suit and tie accountant guy, guessing he'd want to feel rugged on weekends. She sold the same red silky dress to two different conservative dressers. The lessons here? Some want to be seen as rebels, most want to wear something soft every now and then.

Some of my favourite clothes are the dead stock items she helped me find — these houndstooth pants, these old sneakers from the eighties — and stuff she stole from my parents' closets just to see how they'd look with accessories. I guess she made me look a little weird, I'm the butt of school jokes sometimes, but I'm proud to look the way I do.

Anyway, we need more tinsel. I'm about to go downstairs to grab another box of decorations when my dad comes up and asks my mom what a certain word in English means. In the middle of their conversation, he lets out a fart, one of those that really drag out, and he just keeps talking, acts like nothing happened, even though the fart is as loud as his voice and Mrs. Lawrence is five feet away looking at belts. I bust a gut, he does too, and my mom just sighs, probably thinking, *What is it with this family and fart jokes?*

This is what our life is now.

MY DAD HAS ALL kinds of good qualities. He knows about animals, he's a really good cook, he's got good business sense, strong emotions, and he works really hard. Plus, you should be there sometime when he busts out a poem, a bit of philosophy, or when he's cooking and thinks he's by himself and lets loose a song that's sadder, more beautiful, than anything I've ever heard. The other thing about my dad, he knows who he is. Where my mom talks and talks about reading Shakespeare or Dickens or Arthur Conan Doyle when she was a kid, my dad willingly admits to never having read a book in his life. He thinks he's dumb. It's far from the truth. You can't build a store like this from nothing if you're dumb, and reading books doesn't always make you a smart or worthwhile person.

Probably the thing I like best about my dad is his stories. First thing I'm gonna do if I become a writer is publish them.

The last time I asked him for one, I said: "Tell me about that time you got lost." He looked at me. "You know, that time with the guy in the chicken suit?" It's one of my favourite stories.

"Wah, I follow him," he said.

"How old were you?"

"Long about six, seven year old. I went to next town."

"Like, you walked there?"

"Yah."

I pictured a caravan of children, or just my little boy dad, following an oversized chicken across a field and down a dirt road. The moment curiosity and glee turned to fear and dread, or the way those feelings mixed, then faded in and out.

"How did you get home?"

"Wah, I cry and somebody bring me home."

Another time I said, "You caught a fish with your bare hands."

"Yah," he said and laughed at the audacity of it, the memory like a light bulb, his face a lampshade. "Eider me or Gnee Ba." His favourite brother.

"Were you standing in a river?" I pictured them without shoes, feet gripping a shallow rock bottom, hands poised for a stealth move.

"No. You know, my village yau goa pond." He made a circle with his hands.

"What, your family owned it?"

"No. Everybody, that whole village owned that pond. Everybody have share. You know, that big," he touched his thumb almost to the tip of his finger, "the fish put in the pond. Later on, you know how big? That big!" He held his hands more than a foot apart.

"Wow! That's huge!"

"It was so good," he said slowly, emphatically. "We so hungry, we eat the head, eat the eye, eat the bone. You know, lo mai ne jip heng ga faan."

I knew. He taught us that. Whatever meat you're eating, put the juice on your rice. It tastes good.

"How'd you cook it?" I said. "Muy choy? Geung chong?"

"Muy choy, geung chong, haa deng." He told me more — I wanted to picture the kitchen, the pots, the stove, what kind of floor, maybe it was made of dirt — and then he said, "You know, before, no meat. Just some fish, just some rice, wegetable." The rhythm of his voice. I tried to capture it. Everyone's voice has a rhythm.

I said, "No chicken?"

"Couple time."

I knew. They tried raising them from chicks but they wouldn't take. "Tell me about the pig."

"The pick?"

"Yeah, you know, umm … every year there was a pig?"

"Not every year."

"Okay, but when there was one, every family took a turn to raise it, right? Like, every week the pig would go to a different family?" I imagined the pig bumping around inside their house against the furniture. "And then, you know, the Japanese came?" I was careful with how I put it. Maybe not careful enough. He didn't say anything for a while, just looked down to the centre of the table. Then I saw his face change. I wanted to know and thought I had a chance.

"Well?" I said.

"Gegai mun kut oo yeh?" he said. He was angry, quietly angry, and maybe he looked older. Both were rare.

The first and only time he told the story, he said there was a scout. I picture him running down a hill as fast as he could to tell everyone the Japanese were coming. The villagers left, maybe to hide in forests or ditches, and they came back hours later to find the place ransacked, everything on fire or already burned. There was garbage everywhere, and the pig lay dead in a field with a hole in its side. My dad said that one time he told the story that he thought the Japanese were about to eat the pig when they got called away by their general. The villagers had nothing left, not even dignity. Or, well, they did have one thing: that dead pig. They ate it, probably thinking of how much more food there would have been in a few more months, how angry they were, and what they'd do if they happened on the Japanese again.

Another time I asked, "How old were you when your dad died?"

"Long about ten, eleven year old." I wrote it down in my notebook. "You know," he said, "he never have energy. Always have to —" and then he said something in Cantonese.

"What does that mean?" I say.

He said, "Wah, you know," and raked the fingers of his left hand over his right arm. "To get blood mooing."

"What, all over his body?"

"Yah."

"How did he die?"

"Wah, he diabetic people."

"I thought he died because he drank too much."

"Wah, coulda be that, too. You know, before, no test tape, no needle, no nothing. You know how people find diabetic? They look at the *nil*—"

I had learned a few months before in Biology. "Your pee has flies if you have diabetes," I said.

"Yah," he said, glad to be understood.

"So he probably had it. How about your mom? How old were you when she died?"

"Three, four year before my fadder die."

"How did she die?" I said.

He used a Cantonese word I didn't understand.

"You always said she had cholera."

"Coulda be," he said, nodding. Then he got sheepish. "You know, coulda be you think I'm crazy, but," then he said more things in Cantonese. It took a while to figure out what he meant. My mom helped a bit, but it was mostly my dad talking and me guessing what he was trying to say. Turns out he and his mom had just gotten home from planting rice in their village plot when she sat down on the curb, exhausted — it was sunny and hot — and said, *Look at all those dogs.*

"What's wrong with that?" I said. He told me, again in Cantonese, and I figured it out soon enough. "Oh, there weren't actually any dogs there," I said.

"That's right."

"Okay. No, I don't think you're crazy."

"She so tired. She lie down in sleep. Nex few day, she sweating and sleep, dilehla, gnau."

"Sounds like cholera," I said. I went to the reading room and came back with my encyclopedia. It's not great, just a single volume, but it confirmed hallucinations are a symptom. I told him that. I also told him how it's transmitted.

"Oh," he said. "Yah. Three, four day later, she die."

"So fast," I said. "That's really sad."

"Oh, yeah," he said in the dismissive way he does when a fact is self-evident. He didn't make a big deal of it, which I guess made sense, since it happened so long ago.

I've known a lot of my dad's stories for years, but it's hard for me to wrap my head around the things he's lost. He tells me things and I don't know what to say, don't know what he'd want me to say. We don't talk about feelings. I ask him about his life, he tells me stories, but what can you say in response to that pain? *I'm sorry? I can't imagine what it was like for you? What was it besides sad? How exactly did you feel that loss?* These aren't questions I know how to ask him and not questions he'd be able to answer, I'm sure.

The last time I asked my dad for a village story, my mom sulked. "Gnoa m jongee gum sad," she said glumly.

"But all good literature is sad stories," I said. "Dickens, lots of Shakespeare."

"Goagoa hai story," she said. "Neegoa hai real."

"Yeah, but that's life. You can't just pretend it didn't happen."

"What's passed is past."

"Yeah, but it shapes who you are now, don't you think?"

"Still," she said.

One time we were watching TV. The show was a romantic comedy set in modern day Mongkok. When commercials came on, I asked my mom, "So, uhh, before in Hong Kong, did you have a lot of boyfriends?"

She looked up and to the side, as if she was trying to figure out how much she should tell me. That sweet smile of reminiscence. Look at her. Of course she had boyfriends. "Yah. Kind of," she said.

"How did you meet Dad?"

She shrugged.

"Come on," I said. "You had to have met somewhere." I used to joke with Stef and Trina that it was in a Chinese tearoom. They met eyes from across the room, shyly started talking, and soon realized they couldn't live without each other.

This secret smile on her face. She liked having information someone else wanted and the knowledge that she didn't have to share it.

"Well?" I said.

She shrugged.

"It's not a big deal. Why won't you tell me?"

"I don't have to tell you," she said. Her accent — a lot of China and a little bit of England there — and the way she over-emphasized her words, the defiance, made it funny.

"But like, when you die, no one will know the story."

"Baa la," she said. *Too bad.* "I don't need anyone to know."

My mom lords it over my dad sometimes, how she thinks she's so much more rational. She thinks she's smarter because she knows more words and went to university and doesn't believe in ancestor worship. She can't go a single week without bringing up Shakespeare or Dickens or Arthur Conan Doyle. She'll correct his poems, his bits of philosophy. *It's three grains of rice, not three bushels,* she'll say in Chinese.

I've asked her why she married him if she thinks she's so much better. I wanted to see what she'd say, wondered how my mom, with her priorities and love of book smarts, ever looked at my dad — this semi-literate rube from rural Canada and a Chinese peasant village before that — and thought *yes, him,* when there had to have been more educated local candidates.

She told me it was because she saw he worked hard.

"What else?" I said.

She shrugged.

"Well, did you love him? Did you think he was handsome? Was he nice to you?"

"Work hard is important," she said. But imagine leaving your parents, your friends, your favourite place in the world, your whole charmed life of sock hops and warmth and Great Works of Literature and little glass bottles of Coke and Chinese desserts for cold and snow and racism and some uneducated guy you barely know. Just because he works hard. Seriously, is she some kind of martyr?

6

✳

THE NEXT DAY, FRIDAY, I have Band. I sit in the back of the music room with Luke Carcadian. When we started Band, we took a test to see what we would play, and Luke got a bad mark so he plays tuba. I play baritone because Gene and Trina did, though I've often thought I'd like the trumpet better — high and sad the way Chet Baker played it or *bwah bwah* goofy cheerful like Armstrong and Beiderbecke. Luke and I barely know how to read music, so we spend class goofing around. He gropes his tuba like it's a girl, then tries to empty his spit valve on me. He thinks he's badass, but who are we kidding? We're in Band. Ty Rodriguez would never take Band — not Band or Calculus or Chemistry or Biology or anything else I'm in this semester. He's nineteen, probably in the slow stream. Guys like him don't belong in towns like this.

After school I call the cops to see if there's any news on Trina. As usual, Mike Brown's dad is the one who picks up.

"What file is this for?" he says, even though he knows my voice.

It's for my sister, you creepy fuck. The one you and your son used to circle jerk about, remember? "Trina Wong," I say and give him the file number. I try to sound nice. I hate faking it, but they won't help you if you're rude.

"Nope. Nothing new." He says it right away because he hasn't looked it up.

"Okay, well, you have our phone number? Eight four five —"

"It's the store?" he says.

"Yeah."

"Got it," he says, then hangs up on me. The prick. Gary Brown is as much of an asshole as Mike. He stopped me one night on my way home — swooped up parallel across the angle parking spots in front of our side door, cherries on — even though he's seen me, like, five hundred times. He also blew the whistle on the Meers, said he got food poisoning from their restaurant. People stopped eating at Perry's even after the Meers checked out. Aabidah Meer goes to my school. You should see her wash her hands. It takes a whole five minutes. Been that way since grade school. I bet her parents are clean, too.

As soon as I get off the phone, it rings again. It's Kay, asking me if I wanna go to Kat Mitchum's party. I say sure, even though parties are not my thing, and after dinner, I tell my mom I'm going out to a friend's, even though I'm not friends with Kat Mitchum. My mom doesn't have the balls to ask more than that, and my dad won't check to see if I'm around as long as he doesn't need me. I kind of wish he did. Stef and Trina were his favourites. Me, I'm just what's left.

Kay comes by in her car around eight-thirty, her hair like coiled-up pasta. Took her hours to do. We drive to the Voyageur Motel on the south service road and ask people going in if they'll buy us alcohol, and we hang around freezing our asses off until someone does, this guy with a mesh cap, brown nylon coat, and tobacco-stained moustache. He gives us a bag, heavy with wine coolers, then shorts us ten bucks on our change and asks us where the party is and can he come. I wanna punch him in the face, kick him in the balls, kick him while he's down till I break something.

We drive off east down the highway, to the Red Mart. My body clenches as we pull in. Josh McMurtry is there behind the counter. His eyes follow me as I walk in. He was friends with my sister Stef, and if there's anyone in my family I look like, it's her. I wait behind a woman with four bags of chips and a thing of dip. She pays with quarters and pennies, and he's looking at me — smiling — like *what can you do*. Beige coat with the Red Mart logo.

"Hey," I say when she leaves, and his eyes shift to the pile of change in front of him. It's cold even in here, despite the fried chicken and wedge fry heat lamp. I see cigarettes I know on the wall behind him — Camels, Marlboros, Gauloises, Lucky Strikes — while he puts the change away. He says they're all American.

"Except for Gauloises," I say, thinking of Picasso and Camus, George Orwell in *Down and Out in Paris and London, Asterix the Gaul*. I've never smoked before, but now I'm going to a party, why not have some fun? I ask him to close his eyes and run his hand along the cigarettes, and though he's in his twenties, close to getting his degree, he does it with a smile and a little kid nod. I close my eyes, too, then count to five and tell him to stop — Belmont Mills — then I hand him ten and change for the pack, some matches, a medium slush, and a one-piece meal. He gives me an extra piece, extra fries, doesn't ID me.

"Thanks," I say.

He nods. The box is hot, heavy, moist.

"So ..."

He looks at the counter.

"I'll see you around," I say, and leave.

Six big steps outside and I'm in Kay's car, the heat and Eazy-E on high. It's a song I know from Trina. "Open wide, now don't you waste it. Ah, shit! All over your face, kid," Kay raps along.

"You're dirty," I say, and mean it. We laugh. I like that she doesn't give me time to be sad. "Do you mind if I eat?"

"No, go ahead." She reverses hard — sliding a bit on ice — then turns, starts going east down Highway 11. Are we getting Luke? I'm trying to figure out her plan. Eventually, we run out of turnoffs, and the only way left to go is straight out of town.

"Where are we going?"

"Oh, I didn't tell you," she says. "Kat's parents cancelled their trip. Party's moved to the bush."

She must be joking. It's too cold for an outdoor party.

"What the fuck?" I say, but the music's loud and she can't hear me. The town limit sign's a hundred feet ahead of us. I turn the knob on the stereo, but the music goes up instead, the car jolts, black ice, then thrums onto the shoulder. She centres us, slips a bit more. Headlights. A car goes by in the other lane.

She turns down the music. "What?"

The sign sails by. I turn around, but I can't see it. "You know what," I say.

"You're not eighteen."

She's using me. She doesn't have anyone else to go with, so she's forcing me.

"Chris, it's not far and I'll be careful."

Careful. She is a good driver.

I think of Ty standing by the fire, us talking. He likes art, I bet. Likes reading. *What do you read?* I'd say. Maybe his favourite book is *Brave New World*. I haven't read it yet but I'd have to act like I had so we could keep talking. I'd ask if he's having a good night. *Better, now,* he'd say, smiling, *How about you?*

I want to like parties. How many more will I get to go to? My birthday's in seven months. I should be filling my life with experiences. And what if Trina shows up? Maybe she's been going to parties all along and I've been missing her. Or maybe it would be her first in months, and she has fun, remembers how great it is, and stays. What if she wound up somewhere nearby? She could come in every week or every other, and we could go for coffee and ·poutine at Petro-Can. We'd talk till late — they're open twenty-four hours — and she'd tell me what was new and I'd take it all in. *So you're living with someone now. So you're pregnant?* I'd keep trying to get her to come home. *I miss you,* I would say. Or, *Dad and Mom miss you.* Or, *things haven't been quite the same since you left. If you come home I'll do whatever you want.* I'd say something like that every ten minutes, every hangout at least. I wouldn't be able to help myself. And she'd get tired of the weekly sermon, all my promises, and eventually stop agreeing to meet.

"Are you okay?" Kay asks.

"I guess," I say. "Who all do you think'll be there?"

"I dunno. Kat, Carcadian, Kevin, Mike Brown ..."

"Mike Brown." I'm thrilled.

"Van Duysen," she says, a little quieter.

"Van Duysen," I say. "You mean Chiggers? Is he someone you wanna see or someone you're trying to avoid?"

She smiles and shrugs.

"You got weird taste in guys," I say. Chiggers is a nature boy. On weekends, he camps out on Taimi Road. You can see his fire if you're driving by. Mondays at school, you'll see him scratching, hear him in the back when it's quiet, during exams. Little red bumps on his arms, his legs, who knows where else? I see her and Chiggers going a couple of different ways. Maybe they fall in love and spend the rest of their days outside, scratching themselves. What kind of guy is he, though? "You know, if he hurts you —"

"Why would he hurt me?"

"Just be careful, okay? It's not the same for girls."

"He's better than that skank magnet Ty Rodriguez," she says, then starts telling me something she heard about Ty and Aimee Jessop.

I look out at the trees. Whenever I'm on the highway and see a clump of trees, I imagine something running out from it, some kind of ultra-fast humanoid monster who'll tear through the field between us and rip off the car door to get me. He looks like the Grinch who stole Christmas, only scarier. I check to make sure all the doors are locked.

Kay turns down a gravel side road and slows down. She follows the road a few kilometres, past farmhouses, before turning off into an open field. Tall thistleheads with little piles of snow on top pock on the car like rain, depositing their loads. When we find the path — two strips of tamped down snow that lead into the woods — she turns down the lights. The path snakes around an obstacle course of trees, we rock up and down over moguls and molehills and under low-lying branches, going twenty. I open my mouth and say *ahh*, and it sounds like I'm having a seizure.

"Are we close yet?" I say.

"It's still a little ways."

We can only see ten feet ahead of us. I think again of that thing leaping out of the woods onto the windshield, and just then, something big appears in the headlights. I jump, cover my eyes, but instead of going faster, Kay slows down even more.

"Kay! What the fuck! Go!"

"Chris," she says, real quiet.

"I'm scared."

"Chrysler, it's okay."

"What is it?" My eyes are still closed. A windy sound. "What?"

"Moose," she says, louder. I open my eyes, turn to look. I don't see much, it might be shadow. I turn around all the way and see nothing. The car is a parcel of moving light and heat leaving dark and cold in its wake.

There's a faint orange light up ahead. We go towards it and the path opens up to another field. Kay hunches over the wheel, trying to keep control of the car over ruts.

As we get closer, we see the party is in full swing. It's huge, about a hundred people, all yelling, laughing, talking, getting into and out of cars parked in a wide circle like protective buffalo around the fire. Beer and cigarettes, muffled music, cinders popping and twisting up.

We pull in, and right away, some guys fall onto the hood, roll up onto the windshield, fighting. "Put *this* in one of your stories," I hear one of them say — to me, I guess. Mike Brown. Pretty soon they're on the ground outside my door. I open it on them, as hard as I can, and there's a sound like a big snowball pelting the car. A blast of cold comes in. One of them groans. Nasal. Mike Brown. I hope it hurt. "Sorry," I say to them.

Kay puts on her coat and we get out. I peel the plastic off my smokes, shove one, my first-ever cigarette, into my mouth like a message in a bottle, light it, and right away there's a nicotine buzz. A ripple in the crowd as someone totters up. He's small and stooped over, his arms hang down, and he's got a wide gait like a monkey. Curt Mayhew. He's had more than a few. A blinding light — a flashlight — and he slurs a confirmation: "Dead Girl!" A couple of others join in.

Kay's checking my side of the car for dents. I climb onto her back and hoot and a whole crowd of drunks hollers back. She gets up, starts running, and I hold on tight as we go between pallets around the fire. Kay's normally shy when she's on her own, but she's happy now to make a scene. "Oh, my god!" she says, freaked out. Some people cheer us on as she runs through the crowd to the far end of the clearing. I tell her to go faster, she does, and I grip harder. She trips when I start coughing but then recovers and saves my life.

We end up in the woods, trees too thick to run. Kay sets me on a stump. "I'm gonna have a beer," she says, eyes flitting over the crowd. "You want one?"

"Okay," I say, though I hate the way it tastes and the prospect scares me. Smoking is slow suicide, but drinking too much can kill you in just one night.

We go back to her car, where she gives me a vodka cooler before going off to pee. I walk my drink to the fire, take a look around. I've always been impressed by the people at these things. Here and now, we're in the midst of a social experiment. Skids, skaters, jocks, and cowboys, all together in a non-school environment. What will happen? Will they mix? You don't know who anyone is until the firelight shows you, and you forget again when they leave it. There aren't enough strangers. Chiggers is here. Ty isn't but it's early. I look for Trina, too. I can't help it.

Then a hand on my back — "Hey, Chrysler" — and I turn. Tight shirt, low cut. Cleavage. She smells like candy. Maddy Hawkes. She once had a thing for Gene. Fifteen-year-old lusting after my eighteen-year-old brother. I felt protective. She wanted to know what he looked like in his underwear.

She puts her arms around me — I've never even hugged my dad. She squeezes tight, and her breasts nudge in. She's brought her boyfriend, too, some older guy in a Lee Stormrider. Bryce from Sifton. We shake hands, joke around, clink bottles, move on. I go from person to person. Everyone knows my name, and a couple of them give me booze. How much can I drink before it kills me? Do I care? It's a good night.

At one point, Curt Mayhew, a jock, comes up and asks if I want to buy drugs. He deals? Probably does them, too. Curt's sister Jocelyn is in Grade Nine. She's a straight-A student. I hope she's not here. It's weird seeing your drunk and fucked-up older sibling at a party. I should know. I saw Trina swaying around in someone's backyard once. I didn't know it was her at first. She danced with a lot of arm and didn't notice all the guys watching her. Didn't see me, either, and I walked away, acted like I didn't know her, but I checked back a couple of times to make sure she was okay. What else could I do — embarrass her with a glass of water? Ask her to stop? I was fifteen.

"What kind?" I have to ask. It's like when you're at a concert in the city. Even if you have a ticket, you ask the scalpers how much, just to see what they'll say. I could do something. It'd be fun. How many more chances will I have to do drugs?

"I got pot, acid, shrooms, uppers, coke ..."

Coke. You can die from doing that.

A guy comes up to me and starts talking. He's dressed like a Hutterite in a fisherman's sweater. Collar of a green button-up peeking out. Wool pants. I don't know what he's saying. I interrupt: "Nice outfit."

He looks at me like *come on*. "My whole school beat you to that one," he says.

"I'm clever. You just don't know me." He's a bucket of water. Sobers me up some.

"Come sit," he says.

"Why?"

"I don't know anyone here."

"You must know someone."

"Yeah," he says. "He's over there trying to pick up."

"Why would I talk to you? I don't know you."

"'Cause I'm fun to talk to and you seem friendly. Plus, I like your shirt."

I look down. My unzipped coat, NASA shirt underneath. I zip up. "Thanks," I say.

"Are you okay?"

"I'm woozy."

"All the more reason to sit," he says, and holds out a bottle. "Want some water?"

I smile. "You're like a reverse St. Bernard."

"It was for me, but you can have it. I've got more in my car."

"Thanks!" An unopened bottle, the only kind to accept from a stranger. I open it and take a sip. He sips, too, from a flask. "What's your poison?" I say.

"Pretty girls."

"Won't be a problem dying here, then."

"Not for you. You can't be poisoned by them."

"Huh?" I try to focus.

"You're immune to pretty girls. Ever heard of lead getting lead poisoning?"

"Huh?" I say, then after some thought, add: "Screw off!"

"Gosh. Compliment someone and —"

"I gotta go," I say. "Nice talkin' to you."

"Let's talk about something else. What's the worst thing that's ever happened to you?"

"You're really, uhh, forward." I want to get up but can't.

"Well?" It's like he really wants to know.

"Really, I gotta go." Just push off from your knees. Hands on your knees and push. Go. I find Maddy and her boyfriend Bryce from Sifton, and ask, "Do you know that guy over there?" They don't. They introduce me to their friends, and I teach them all a dance for fun. All you need to get a group of people to dance is a leader, a few followers, and a lot of alcohol. It starts slow, at first only a few people want to do it, but in the end, everyone is dancing slowly, watching their feet as they go, little cloud trails trickling from their mouths. "That's my having to pee dance," I say. I duck out of their circle and into the bushes, deep enough for privacy, not so deep there's danger.

When I come out, Kay's standing by the fire. I ask if she's seen Chiggers, and her eyes shine. "Talk to him," I say. "If you don't, I'll do it for you." He's on the other side of the fire, by himself on a pallet, casually scratching his knee. He'd be cute if he weren't so dirty.

"What should I say?" She's beaming, covering her mouth with her hands like she's ashamed of her own happiness. Her shy laugh.

"Ask him if he wants to make out."

"No! Look at him." She says it despairingly. What she means is, *why would he want me?* Why wouldn't he? He's wearing a Beastie Boys shirt. They like the same music. And camping. It's a start.

"You should do it," I say, then my gaze shifts and voila, there he is, Ty Rodriguez, one of a group of guys in army coats by the fire. He's drinking beer, I can't see what kind. The fire makes his skin glow. He's handsome, wearing a checked shirt and work pants, he's the centre of his group, strong and assertive, talking and gesturing with a cigarette bobbing in his mouth. He points at something, and his friends turn to look and shout-laugh. Now he holds his hands a foot apart to show the size of something. I hear him say the word *plastic*. It's the only word I make out. I want to know: *what about plastic?*

I take a sip of my drink, fast, eyes up like I'm doing a shot because I can't look at him, and when I'm done, he's looking my way through the fire, head at a little angle, a little smile, not talking anymore. I turn around to see who he's looking at and there's no one there. I look up, stars, whizzing cinders. He's still looking. The ground by the fire the same colour as Mars. I kick one shoe with the other. "He's looking at us," I say without turning to Kay.

"Looking at you, more like," she says. "Now he's coming over."

"Here? He's coming here? I have to go. Can I have your keys?"

"Where you goin'?" she says.

"To the car. Don't feel good."

"The guy you like —"

"Shh!"

Kay, whispering: "Sorry. The guy you like is coming over and you wanna go?"

"What am I gonna say?"

"You'll think of something."

He's ten feet away. What do you say to someone you've never talked to before? *I saw you biking on the highway. At night. You looked happy. I think we're soulmates. Wanna get some coffee?* Or at the Co-op. *Do you have any more niblets? This can is kind of dented. Hey, don't you go to my school?* "Listen, if he talks to you, don't say anything about me, 'kay?"

Her hand on my arm. "Chris."

I get out of there, my heart pounding. I'm fast, too fast, I trip and fall into some guys. "Sorry," I say.

Mike Brown's squeaky voice. "You better watch out. She'll kill you."

I run, slipping and sliding on tamped down snow. No keys, nowhere to go. I'll freeze to death, I know it. More than thirty cars. Red, brown, old truck, new truck, white car. Kay's car? No. Where's the car? When I find it, I drop to the ground beside it and heave, the snow cold on my knees and melting into my jeans, heave, wheels and the bottoms of cars beside me, the sound of heaving so pathetic, heave. My stomach. "Are you okay, Chris?" someone says. I nod big enough for them to see in the half-dark — "Yeah, fine," I say — they walk away, my eyes wet, heave, and a curtain of liquid splatters on the snow, my jeans. Will it leave a stain on my clothes? I don't want to move, I feel like shit, but I'm dirty. I take some snow, rub it between my hands till they're clean and ice cold, then go into my pockets for tissue. I've got a napkin. I wipe my eyes, hands, and face, try to get the puke off my jeans, but the napkin's too small. I get up and try the door to Kay's car. It's open. She's a country person — it's a matter of trust and convenience. The doors in my house are always locked.

Is there a way to salvage the situation with Ty? *I was running because I had to pee.* No. *Because I needed to puke.* No. *Because I saw my friend was leaving and I wanted to say goodbye.* Yeah. That'd be okay. And how about if I invent a memory-erasing machine so we could start over? I sit in Kay's car and imagine Ty and me on a hilltop or riverbank. It's my fantasy, so it's warm outside. I'd tell him the constellations I know, and he'd hold me, and I'd smell his smell, musk and stale cigarettes, and I'd have to break it to him, tell him I'll probably die soon. He would say it's the saddest thing he's ever heard. *You don't deserve that*, he would say, and suggest we spend every day together these next seven months to make up for our lack of a future. *Are you crazy?* I'd say. *I got stuff to do. Plus, I can't settle down that fast.* But who am I kidding? I'd be with him if he'd have me. Of course, I would.

I WAKE UP COLD and needing to pee. I'm still at the party. Can't believe I missed out. People probably saw me sleeping, too. Whatever. I get out of the car. Dying embers. I must have been asleep for hours. Almost everyone is gone. No Ty, no Kay, but Maddy and Bryce are there with a couple of people I know from school. The guy in Hutterite clothes is there, too. He waves me over, his motions big, and he'd be funny if I were in a different mood.

"What are you guys still doing here?" I say. "It's fucking freezing!"

"Talking about you," the Hutterite says when I'm close enough.

"Really," I say, looking around for Kay. "It's true: I do have a tail."

"My kind of girl," he fake-whispers to Maddy and Bryce.

I raise my voice to the people left. "Has anyone seen Kay Berringer? Girl with the coiled up hair?" I draw circles with my finger by my head like I'm crazy.

A few people look up. Some shake their heads and shift a bit.

"It'd be really, really good if someone knew where she was," I say. "You know, in case something bad's happening to her?"

Silence.

"Okay, well, g'night, guys," I say to Maddy and Bryce. I start heading for the bush to piss. Movement behind me: the Hutterite. I keep walking.

"Hey," he says, catching up. "Were you gonna look for your friend? 'Cause —"

"I'm guessing she'll turn up. But thanks." My guard's up.

"It's good of you to be concerned."

"Thanks."

"I'll keep an eye out. Hey, maybe I'm being a little forward here, but ... can I give you my number?"

I turn at him. *Why*, I almost say.

"If you say no, I'll just keep asking," he says, holding out a slip of paper.

I don't want it. *Be a good person. He wants you to take it.* So I do. "Thanks."

I keep walking, but five seconds later, hear his voice behind me: "So I guess I should expect a call in, what, a couple of days, tops?"

I turn to him, then tilt my head up as if it were set in motion by the enormous force of my rolling eyes. My gaze arcs off, making stops at Orion, Andromeda, the Pleiades. I rubberneck all the way to the edge of the clearing, then walk into the woods, pick through for a place to pee, and squat. The sound of my piss in the snow, some wind in the trees, and clapping — clapping? A rhythmic shifting nearby. I look over. One big jostling shape, part standing, part pushed up against a tree. *Slap slap.*

We're in the middle of the woods where who knows what can hide, and I'm scared, even after I find a path, even after I find a road. Death is more likely at night. Some things are just too much. Some people's singing voices, the looks of strangers' faces when they cry, the sounds you make when you're doing it.

Clack. Behind me. What the? *Crunk crunk.* My shoes on gravel. It'd be great if you could will yourself not to make any sounds at all. Black sky, moon and hundreds of stars, pine trees as far as you can see. It would all be beautiful if I weren't so scared. I walk, panicked, till I find the clearing and Kay's car.

A little while later, she shows up. My eyes closed, my breathing slow, I nestle into my seat. We pull out, make the whole trip backwards. Field, rutted path, gravel road, highway. I keep my eyes closed but I can tell where we are from the feel of the road, and a couple of times I sneak a peek at her. Kay's eyes point straight ahead, her hands are sure on the wheel. White skin — like, actually white — with short braids hanging down like a

1920s fringe cap, and she's frowning the way you do when you don't think anyone's watching. Frowns take less energy. We pull into town, streetlights through my eyelids. We turn, turn again. The third turn is illegal, across the solid line that runs down Main. She parks in front of my house.

I make a show of waking up, opening my eyes. "What time is it?" I ask. The clock says 2:57. 2+5=7. I yawn. "Y'ave fun?"

"Yeah," she says, lightly.

"Cool. See you Monday?"

She nods and I get out, walk up the sidewalk steps, get my key. The lock clacks open, a familiar sound. One big step and I'm inside, a familiar smell. Dust, food, my mom's natural baby scent. I'm safe. Kay's headlights arc away as she backs out. I wave, turn, and climb the stairs.

7

❁

I DREAM I WRITE the saddest story in the world. I write it all in
the library based on stuff I learn from the encyclopedia and
Time Magazine. It's so sad and funny that lexicographers have
to make up a new term to describe it, and a Hollywood pro-
ducer calls and asks me to adapt it for him. The film is not a
commercial success, not critically acclaimed, either, but one
girl in Tallahassee with cotton-candy pink hair watches it, likes
it, and writes me a letter. I don't remember what it says.

I dream I'm driving in the country, with Ty or someone else,
some other guy, and the sun is coming in. We go down highways and through rutted fields and there's music and birds —
so many birds — and I love him. We stop in a field and I play
the ukulele, I'm wearing this beautiful dress even though I never
wear dresses, and there's food. Garlic mashed potatoes and
apricots and key lime pie and fried chicken made from chicken
plucked from trees so no one had to die.

I dream that Trina shows up at the back door with suitcases.
Blue, red, white, green stickers on them from different countries. *I'm home*, she says. We go upstairs, through my bedroom
closet, to another world where we can do what we want, since
we're still technically in Spring Hills.

And then I wake up. Saturday morning. I open the door

— bright light — and my mom's in the hall with the dresser drawers open. TV on in behind.

"Jo sun," I say. "What are you doing?" Nothing in the drawers but pictures, awards, and report cards, old purses, coins, and bugs. My mom's not one for housework.

She doesn't say, but I see when I get closer. Pictures of Trina. She's put them in the drawer. Trina with my dad at the car, her in a cap and gown, him in a suit, happy on graduation day. Trina and me on the rollercoaster at West Ed, her flirting with the camera, me wincing, eyes and mouth squeezed shut like I just sucked on a lemon. An early party picture, her and friends. Kirk's there, too, on the edge of the group.

"What are you doing?" I repeat.

Scattered in with pictures of Trina: Young Reggie with a bowl haircut, no smile, holding an award. A somewhat recent one of Gene, his arms wrapping twice around my grandma, a crazy love look on his face. A close-up of Stef and my dad at the lake, giant smiles, life vests over T-shirts. She taught him how to fish, maybe even that day.

My mom closes the drawer and shuffles away. The only photos up now are of me and my parents, a couple of bad ones I haven't seen in years. Me with buckteeth and a home haircut. A picture I drew in Grade Eight art class of Mr. Berkson's house.

"You know she's not dead, right?"

My mom looks back at me. Sad eyes, a cold sore on her droopy mouth. In her hand, the remote, the volume going up.

"Well, she's not," I say louder, pulling down the ugly pictures and replacing them with ones of Trina from the drawer. I follow my mom to kitchen. "I don't know how you do that," I say.

She puts fruit in the blender. Apple, watermelon, grapefruit. The TV on way too loud.

"Well? Say something."

She bites the end of a banana, peels it, puts it in. My dad comes into the kitchen, the toilet still flushing. Orange hunting vest over an old cowboy shirt.

Me to my dad: "Nei yao mo sai sao?" *Did you wash your hands?* And to my mom: "Why do you eat that? Don't you care about how it tastes?"

"Yeah!" my dad says, washing his hands. Contempt in his voice.

She pushes a button on the blender. On TV, two men in suits shaking hands, flags and more suits in behind.

"Watermelon, grapefruit, apple, and banana," I say. That's fucking gross. "Why don't you put in some honey?"

My dad takes something from the toaster, starts to assemble bacon sandwiches. My mom spoons fruit paste the same colour as raw chicken into a bowl. Did she hear me?

"Want some honey?"

She's rinsing out the blender.

"Mom. Do. You. Want. Some. Honey."

She starts walking away.

"Mom!"

"Talk talk talk talk talk," my dad sneers, turning to me. He cuts his sandwich without looking, I wince, but he doesn't hurt himself. "I hate you. Always talk! Think you smart, you so goddamn dumb."

"Fuck you," I say, and go down to the store.

The whole first hour of work I think of how I could screw him over by doing a bad job, show him how stupid I really am, but all the customers wanting something bring me back. It's a game. There are at least four times as many customers as there are people working here. The goal is to serve them all. Family businesses are team efforts. You run extra hard, you can go without lunch, close late if you have to. You do up the pants of some fat guy who acts like he can't figure out button-fly when all he wants is your hands near his crotch. It's okay because everyone else, your entire family, is running, too. I sell a pair of boots. My mom, at the counter, gives me the thumbs up. Go Wongs. Lunch, then a busy afternoon. Some lady tries on twenty pairs of jeans and doesn't buy a single one. A big shipment of shirts comes in. I sell seven pairs of shoes in three hours. I go up and down the hollow basement stairs, my head pounding — a hangover, I guess.

When it's quiet, I try to start on homework, but then my mom comes and hovers around me, eating from her bowl of fruit paste, trying to get the dirt on last night. It's awkward. We're not close, she's not the mothering kind, and not subtle. "What time you come home last night?" she asks. "Did you smoke? Did you drink? Did you do drug?" With every question comes a bit of nervous laughter.

I can't keep a straight face either. Her cold sore. I can't stop looking at it. We all have them, but my mom's are always coming to the surface. Must be stress. My dad tells us to burn them off with hot rice.

What if I tell her? *Mom, I got wasted last night. It was fun. The guy I like was there, but I didn't talk to him. Later on, people were having sex in the woods.* I tell her I didn't do anything crazy, but that's not enough. She wants details. She's playful about it, too, her hands on my arm, her voice melodramatic on purpose. What was she like when she was young?

"What does it matter if I did? As long as I was safe, and as long as I can work today ..."

"Aiyaa!"

"I didn't say I did anything."

"I can tell."

It's like her cold sore's talking. "Tell what?" I say.

"If you did."

"So did I?"

She doesn't say anything. She probably doesn't know.

I ask if I can take a break and she says yeah, peels a twenty off the roll in her pocket, doesn't ask when I'll be home. I go past my dad, who's making coffee, and up the back steps out to the alley. The steel door shuts behind me. Warm wind, a chinook, the smell of wet pavement. Little piles of melting snow. Cars make *shrik shrik* sounds as they go by.

I grab my trike from the shed. Weird-looking thing, same as what a kid rides — two wheels in the back, one out front — but five times bigger. I walk it to the top of the alley then ride on the sidewalk. It's a struggle in the wind and over patches of ice. Someone honks. Biking for transportation is not a thing people do. I think of Ty. Why didn't I talk to him?

My mom must think Trina's dead, putting her pictures away like that. What if we all die when we're eighteen? If so, I've got seven months, maybe more, maybe less if I'm extra unlucky. Still enough time to travel, or at least live in a city. But what if I'll only die if I leave? Is it worth living here for the next one, two, five, ten, twenty, eighty years? How long could I do it? Is it possible to die of unhappiness? And what if I'm no safer in town?

Cars go by. I'm on the street now, passing houses from the seventies, a trailer park, fields. I pull in to Pudgee's, chain my trike to a sign a hundred feet away. Imagine eighty years more of biking there for a slush and beef jerky, eighty years of dust and the railroad tracks and the thin strip of mountains on the horizon. It's mildly pretty here, more tantalizing and disappointing than anything, like a sign that says *There's more to life, if only you leave — these mountains are ones you could climb*.

The tracks right here. Ten paces. How much more should I tempt fate? I step onto them. It's exciting and scary, and there's so much wrong with my life. I start walking, my eyes on the ground. Fifty feet in front of me, the track crosses the river valley before turning and disappearing into the trees. How long would it take for a train to cross that gap? The ground under the bridge tapers off, and forty feet down, the Clearwater River runs fast over rocks. All around me, trees are nodding in the wind, and I start to run, sloppily. I'm a kid again, chasing Trina and Gene as they go off to buy snacks or try on jeans or just hang out. *Wait for me! Wait!* Gene making fun of the way I run, me ashamed but laughing a little bit, too, and glad to be included in the joke. I find a rhythm. Blood pounding in my ears, breath catching in my throat. In elementary, this nerdy Jesus freak John Stevenson ran everywhere. To and from home, between classes. I see now why he ran.

Halfway across the river, though, I'm wheezing. I say I'm a partial asthmatic when all I really am is out of shape. Hands on my knees, I kick gravel through the ties and watch it fall. It's a long drop, the water hard as cement from this height. I trot out to the lookout point, wood planks and a tall guardrail offset from the tracks. Across the way another bridge, the green one, where people have spraypainted *Grad '80*, *Grad '86*, and *Grad '97* — Trina's year — in white.

Trina. Stef. The river. Them in it. I turn around.

On the way back, I see someone coming towards me. Some kid, probably. Or kids? It's hard to see that far. What's a train look like from that distance? A hundred feet. Trees. *Walk faster. You don't wanna be hit by a train. Yeah. And I don't want to trip and fall off the railroad, either.*

This person's still coming. How much money do I have? What can I use as a weapon? Keys. My little Leatherman with tweezers and a toothpick. Birds fly by, birds chirp in the woods. Something moves in the trees. No train. This person is skinny, dark hair. Trina? But how'd she know I was here? She wouldn't, or would she? Walking on the train bridge is just like me. Is it Ty? No, but wouldn't that be awkward? Maybe they're here to kill me. *Don't be paranoid.* They could push me off, or do it some other way, no witnesses.

I start walking fast, back to the lookout. Adrenaline rising through my body. A person can lift a car with enough adrenaline. I could sit to lower my centre of gravity, make it harder to push me off, but that's just asking for trouble. Instead I lean against the rail like I'm taking in the view. I open my Leatherman to the knife, then put it back in my pocket, still gripping it.

The person stops a couple of feet away and leans, too. "It's nice," he says. "Didn't think I'd see you here."

I turn to look. It's the Hutterite guy from last night, wearing old man pants and a thick grey-blue cardigan over a T-shirt with a whale on it.

"Didn't think I'd see anyone here," I say.

"There's always another weirdo," he says. "How ya feelin'?"

"Huh?"

"The party."

"Okay. Tough day at work. You? D'y'ave fun?"

"It was fine. Not something I do very much."

"Square."

"You were pretty wasted."

"Life is short. I gotta go." I turn to leave. "Sorry to be abrupt."

"Some people called you Dead Girl. Last night."

"The nerve!" I say, start walking to my bike backwards on the track. One, two, three …

He follows me. I've never seen grey eyes before. "Sounds like you've got an interesting story," he says.

"I'm a regular Oliver Twist." Nine, ten, eleven, twelve, don't trip.

"You're an orphan working in a factory during the Industrial Revolution?"

"Something like that. Sadder and less sad."

"How about we grab a coffee and you tell me all about it?"

"Why are you here?"

"My mom met my dad at bingo in 1978. She liked him right away."

"Very funny," I say. "I meant why walk here. You don't live here. Aren't you from … I don't know." Twenty-six, twenty-seven, twenty-eight. Thirty feet down, twenty feet to go. I'm still walking backwards.

His eyes shift. "Eckville. I'm killing time."

Killing.

"My mom lives here," he says.

"Without you."

"Yeah. I live with my dad."

"You don't seemed thrilled by that. What, you don't like him? Or her?"

"I want to have coffee, not give my whole life story."

"So don't." We reach land, my trike. I unlock it. "Guess I'll see you around."

"What?"

"You don't wanna talk, you want one-sided sharing. Don't waste my fucking time."

"Okay, yeah. I can dish out questions, but sometimes I can't take 'em. Is that what you want me to say?"

"I don't want you to say anything." I get on my trike.

"Come on," he says.

"Come on what?" Why am I so mad?

"I like my mom, okay?" It takes effort for him to say. "I don't like my dad."

I shrug. "Whatever."

"So," he says, "the Leonids happen tonight. Supposed to be great this year. Reports from Asia are showing lots of fireballs."

The Leonids. "Really. You're what, some kind of brainiac?"

"Just a guy with a telescope. I've seen pretty much all the 'ids' for the past five years."

"All the 'ids'?"

"Leonids, Perseids, Geminids, Quadrantids, Lyrids, Orionids. It makes for a busy social life. You've got a pretty smile. Can I buy you a coffee yet?"

I'm not sure why I say yes. I guess because the back and forth is fun.

We go to Marlene's, keep it light over bowls of broccoli and cheddar soup. I say nothing about my siblings, he says nothing about his mom and dad. We have things in common. Of course we do. His name is Conrad. We're both nerds who like science and books. While he's telling me about the *Rafflesia*, this flower in Malaysia that straddles the line between plant and fungus, I check my watch and see two hours have gone by in what felt like five minutes. I wait for him to finish talking, then say, "I'm sorry but I have to go. My dad is gonna kill me."

He says he has to go, too. "But that was good, right?" he says. "The hangout?"

Surprisingly good. It was fun, exciting. I do a reluctant diagonal nod, all cool like a breakdancer.

"You gonna call me?" he says.

He had to wreck it. I shrug, but Conrad keeps asking in different ways, like an enemy in wartime. Airplanes, soldiers, U-boats, tanks, and bombs.

"Okay! Okay! Fine!" I say. "Are you happy?"

"Do you promise?"

I throw up my hands. "Okay! Whatever! Fine!"

WHEN I GET HOME, sadness creeps back in. It's dead downstairs, so I go up to take a nap and read. Peter Pan's just lost his shadow when I hear the door and my dad's footsteps. There's something comforting about those sounds. He's in the kitchen by himself. No cupboards slamming, no chopping today. It occurs to me that when he's not yelling or turning up the TV because he's half-deaf, my dad is quiet. I like it.

Pretty soon, he calls me to help with dinner. Walking down the hall to the dining room, I see: Trina's pictures gone again. I rummage through the first few layers of stuff in the drawers and find nothing. I check the hallway shelves. Books, papers, and clothes, no pictures.

My mom comes up, and I ask her where she's put them. She walks by, acts like she didn't hear me. I follow her to the kitchen, where she's all excited, telling my dad about the German tourists who came in just now, what they said about the store, how much they spent. He pulls a plate of steaming fish from the wok. Fish is the only thing my mom can eat an entire portion of.

I stop asking about the pictures. An unwritten rule: don't talk about stuff with my dad around. He overhears and gets confused, tries to participate, gets mad sometimes. Doesn't know that some talks don't concern him. I grab bowls from the cupboard, start scooping rice, a heaping bowl for my mom, less for me, even less for my dad.

My mom goes by with bone plates and chopsticks and I say, "Mom, wanna burn off your cold sore?" She doesn't. Stef or Trina could've convinced her, though. *It'll make you feel better*, Stef would've said. *Do it. You'll look better*, Trina would've said. *And it won't hurt that much.* "You'll feel better," I say. "Look better."

"No, thank you," she says, overenunciating.

After dinner, I check for Trina's pictures in places I didn't before. The garbage. The shelves in my room, the dresser in the girls' room. Between and under mattresses, in the guest room. I find a few, amass a little pile, but there aren't as many as there were before, and I can't find any of the ones that were hanging. I check the downstairs garbage, the dumpster outside, my mom's office, the filing cabinet. I go back upstairs, check my parents' bedroom. No dice.

My parents are in the living room with the TV on. That mini-series about the family, that one with Fei Fei. She's fat, bold, funny — Hong Kong's sweetheart. My dad's asleep on the couch, unaware. I crouch down beside my mom, my voice low: "Mom, don't mess around. What'd you do with the pictures?"

"I'm keeping them."

"Why? So no one else can see them?"

Her eyes back on the TV, but she's not watching.

"Where are they?"

Fei Fei's at a restaurant table, talking to a young couple, imparting a lesson with her forefinger raised.

"Mom, where are they?"

Jaunty music. Food has arrived. Fei Fei is sampling soup.

"Did you throw them away?"

Wow, it tastes really good! Fei Fei says.

"Mom!"

"Yes! I threw them away!"

I go back to the hallway drawer, dump out the rest of the photos. I linger and find a few more of Trina. One of them was taken when she was a kid — like, seven or eight. We looked the same when we were younger. It's like I'm holding a picture of myself. Trina. When you're that age, do you have any idea who you're going to be when you grow up, how much you'll devastate other people by what you'll end up doing?

I take the pictures of Trina to my room and lock the door, put on my headphones, look through them. Trina and her friends at a studio shoot, glamorous, she in white shorts and a red silk shirt, permed hair. Trina in a pink wig and vintage dress in a park in Edmonton, last year. Trina at the wheel, on a road trip to Vancouver to see New Order. It's sunny. She's wearing a tank top, her new tattoo out for all to see. Squiggles in a frame. Birds. So many bruised and bleeding birds, all flying together.

SOMETIMES A BAND CAN change your life. That's the way it was for me with New Order. Before I got into them, I liked mostly bad music, cheesy eighties hits I'd learned from my siblings and things I'd heard on the radio. Tears for Fears, Eurythmics — that kind of stuff. Only three stations here, not including the CBC, and two of them feature an identical mix of heartsick tear-in-my-beer ballads and whose-bed-have-your-boots-been-under anthems. The third station plays mediocre rock.

A few years ago, Trina and I were getting snacks, driving around. It was Sunday, our day off. The tape player was broken, which left the radio. I was riding shotgun eating cheese fries when this song came on that felt like spring. I opened my window and stuck my head out, filled my lungs with melty air. The song made me happy, sad, and nostalgic for a time I never had. It made me want to dance. Most songs don't make me feel anything.

It was "Regret" by New Order. To this day, I don't know how it got on that station. A few weeks after I heard it, we were in Edmonton, and I bought some of their music as well as a British magazine that had them on the cover. That's where I learned about Joy Division, the band New Order used to be.

We left to see them on the morning of my sixteenth birthday. Trina woke me up at five a.m. and asked if I wanted to go on a road trip.

"What?" I was annoyed.

"Road trip. You and me. Wanna go?"

"When?"

"Now."

It wasn't long after Gene had died. Eight months. I didn't really wanna go, but I also kind of did. Trina and I hadn't hung out in a while, so I was surprised she invited me. We packed bags and music for a couple of days, then woke our mom up to tell her we were going. I didn't know about the New Order concert till we pulled up to the theatre. Trina wasn't a fan of theirs. I still can't believe she would do something like that for me.

She made me drive a couple of times, even though I didn't have a licence. I was scared, but it was great, fun, and the responsibility made me feel closer to her. She sat with me for twenty minutes the first time before going to sleep.

It's eleven hours to Vancouver if you don't stop. Mountains. It was hard to keep my eyes on the road. And she didn't just sleep the whole time. We ended up talking a fair bit about our parents, our siblings, ourselves — old stories we loved, our hopes for the future. I told her not to smoke and she said, "There's nothing I can do about that." We were quiet sometimes, and sometimes there was music. We took a walk through the Kootenay Plains. Weird patchy grass, mountains rising around us like we were standing in a massive bowl, cars zooming by, a terrible, menacing sound when you're outside and twenty feet away. "Stef died around here," Trina said. We stopped at fruit stands, diners, and roadside monuments. Radium Hot Springs. She met and hung out with some guy there for, like, an hour. I thought, *What about Kirk?* We saw clouds on the horizon and drove towards them. Vancouver.

The concert was great. She bought me a shirt. I thought things were going to be good after that. Looking back I wonder, why did I think that?

JOY DIVISION COMES ON through my headphones. "Atmosphere." A perfect song for now. I fuck everything up. Ty at the party, me on the bridge. What did I wanna do there? Who walks on the train tracks? Will I ever find Trina? She left, after all. Wanted to leave. My mom got rid of her pictures. Maybe she was onto something.

The song changes to "Disorder." Sparse, echoing drums, high, fast bass. It makes me wanna dance. Shimmering, dirty guitar like an organ. My shoulders and hips tick to the drums like I'm being electrocuted. Ian Curtis, the singer, was known for the way he danced. He had epilepsy, sometimes he had fits onstage. People watching thought he was crazy, dying. My head thrashes side to side like I'm refusing everything, like I'm some ugly, hated punk rock kid in a dirty, little club in the seventies. Hair swinging in my eyes. No future. This is my crazy dance. He sings about disconnection, but when I hear it, I feel connected to everything. Guitars like rain dripping on cobblestones at night somewhere in Europe and you've just arrived. The song starts on a high point, gets higher, and I dance harder, spin around as I sing along, loud. I thrash around like everything depended on it instead of nothing, I kick and spin faster and faster, my limbs everywhere like I'm not in control of my body. Around and around and around and around.

Then no music. Did it finish? Someone's banging on the door. My head hurts. Hard. I feel around with my hands. Hard and dirty. I'm on the floor. "Yeah?" I yell half-heartedly, but the banging keeps on. I lay my head back down. Screaming headache. I touch the back of my head and there's blood on my hand. Pounding on the door. "WHAT!"

Muffled voice, my mom. "Chrysler?" Lighter knocking. "Chrysler?"

"Mom?"

She keeps knocking so I get to my knees, lightheaded, grip the side of the mattress and haul myself up. Collapse on the bed. Toilet paper on the nightstand because we're too cheap for Kleenex. I grab some, hold it to the back of my head. "Just a sec!" I call out and look at it. Lots of blood. I limp to the door — my hip hurts — and open it. My mom with a worried look on her face. "What's up?" I ask, aiming for alert but casual. It's hard to stand.

"Everything okay?" she asks.

Hide the damage. "Uh, yeah. I just fell." But the ache in my head is like my tongue on a battery. I try resting on the doorframe but miss, slip, end up crashing into her. She almost falls, but she's stronger than she looks. Tissue on the lino floor, red blotch like a Rorschach test. Her hand on her mouth. I pull myself back up. "Mom, it's nothing," I say. "Just a nosebleed."

She's usually gullible, but the lie is bad. She calls my dad, who looks in my nose, finds the split in my head instead. He half-supports, half-drags me down the outside hall past the clothing room, where my mom tries to share a bit of the load by pulling up on my belt loops and giving me a wedgie.

At the top of the stairs, weak and whiny, I tell my dad I'm cold and my mom runs to get me a coat. My dad and I try to navigate the stairs but they're not wide enough for two. I take more of my own weight because I don't want to push him down, but it's killing my hip. "I'll meet you down there," I say, and sit. Old wood. Tired. I close my eyes, lean back, and the angles dig in. My head. Silence for a while, then creaking. It gets louder. Something on my stomach, on my back, and then I'm being hoisted in the air, light like a leaf in the wind.

It's cold for a while and then there are voices. Movement. Something goes around my arm, squeezing tighter and tighter. Something on me, blankets, but it's still cold. Voices. I'm on my stomach. Something's touching my head, wrapping around it. Then I'm being rolled onto my back — my hip — something's in my mouth, around my finger, biting at my arm.

I wake up in a dark room, head heavy, a doorway lit yellow, white figures walking by. Am I dead? I lift my legs and arms, wiggle my fingers and toes. I can move.

A woman with a pen and clipboard walks in. "Oh. You're awake." Light goes on, blinds me. She says they've put stitches in my head, asks me what my name is, how old I am, what town I was born in, what I did on Friday.

"Went to a party."

"How many fingers am I holding up?"

"Is this some kind of test?" I say.

"We're just checking your cognitive skills."

"Three, then."

"Good." She holds up a finger, tells me to follow it with my eyes. She draws a cross, then drops her pen. I catch it. She doesn't even say thanks. "I'm going to say three words," she says. "I want you to remember them."

"Okay."

"*Random. Faith. Pronunciate.*" She says it with a straight face.

"You mean *pronounce*?"

"*Pronunciate.*"

"I hate to be a smartypants," I say, "but I don't think *pronunciate*'s a word. It's either *pronounce* or *enunciate*."

The corners of her mouth pull back. It's not a smile. "Congratulations, Chrysler," she says. "You just made a doctor feel stupid."

Doctor. "Where are my parents?"

"I sent them home. You're gonna spend the night here."

I've never spent a night at the hospital before. When the doctor leaves, fear sets in. The building's public, open twenty-four hours, anyone can come in. There's no security. I check the closet, under the bed. No one there, so I lock the door — then unlock it again. What if there's something still in here? I go back to the bed, then tell myself a story to stay awake.

8
✺

MY OLDEST BROTHER REGGIE was odd. He had an existence I now know was typical of child geniuses, but back then, we had no explanation.

He did things like win the National Math Award and the science fair four years in a row. There were stories in the newspaper about him — some of them even had pictures. We taped them up on the fridge. One, from May 19, 1991, shows a seventeen-year-old Reggie holding up this giant check with some tall guy in a suit, who the caption says is a representative of the Power Corporation. Reggie's got this serious look on his face, like they forgot to tell him to smile before taking the picture.

"Why didn't you smile?" we asked.

"Aren't I smiling?" he replied.

Gene's finger on the newsprint photo. "No, man. You're not smiling at all."

We were a family of jokers. We'd do things like surprise each other on the can with a camera, put chicken bums and heads on each other's dinner plates, leave weird things in each other's stockings on Christmas Eve — a black banana, some dusty toy found abandoned on a shelf, crumpled pages from a porno. Reg hardly ever laughed. He'd just pull a thawed fish or whatever from his stocking, say *What's this?* and move on to the next thing. Either that or he'd get mad. Reg had a temper. He once threw a set of keys at Stef when she came home late one night while my parents were away. Left a triangle of holes in the drywall. And where each of us had our little obsessions — Stef with the outdoors and our family; Gene with girls, art, and basketball; Trina with boys, clothes, and music; and me with reading and being weird — all Reggie had as outside interests were the dictionary and advanced science texts, and he probably only read those for academic benefit.

How do you know when the quiet person in your family starts feeling sad about life? His unhappiness crept up like cancer, unseen at first, then visibly manifesting the year he turned seventeen. Cheering Reggie up became the big family project. We each made a point of saying something nice to him every day, things like *Reggie, you're going to do so much someday*, or *Have you been working out?* We bought him weekly lime misties from the Dairy Burger — his favourite — and over Christmas we let him win all the games, even our favourites like Crazy Eights and Taboo.

We kept on with our practical jokes, though, we just didn't play them on Reggie. We put a fake cockroach under the covers of Trina's bed four nights in a row, and pretended Old Rick Jones had the hots for Gene. We cracked ourselves up and even made our parents laugh. Reggie just watched us, though, like *who are these people and where is my real family of astrophysicists and Model UN participants?*

I've tried to figure out why he was like that. Birth order, maybe. We all had our theories about what was wrong with him. Trina thought it was about school ending, thought he might be sad about leaving town for university. Stef worried he wasn't doing as well as he wanted to academically. "You're a high achiever already," she'd say. "You've got the best marks in your year. What else do you want?"

Gene's idea was simpler. He thought Reggie was lonely, so he drew up a plan he called "stud coaching." It was a twelve-step program tailor-made to get girls to like Reggie. We didn't think he could pull it off, though, since it was obvious that Gene got girls' attention without actually trying — even after he got sick and began occasionally walking with a limp. It's amazing how popular he was despite that. It could have been because he was handsome and tall and used his weight machine religiously when he was feeling well. Plus, he had a real talent for art — these chaotic pencil and ink drawings of skulls, needles, and shards of glass — and a brash confidence only sometimes shaken by his health problems. If I wasn't so scared for him, I'd have thought the way his limp transformed his walk looked cool.

Unlike Gene, Reggie was pale, skinny, and socially awkward — things that took us a while to realize. Love and familiarity are strange that way: they blind you to a person's flaws.

Still, according to Gene, the twelve-step plan was about "distilling the essence." Steps one to six related to hygiene. Gene tried hard to be tactful about the benefits of regular showering and tooth-brushing. One morning before school, I saw them in the bathroom together. Reggie was taking notes, engrossed in Gene's every move like he was the younger brother. Gene raised his arms one at a time, spraying his pits with Preferred Stock. "See that, my man? Chicks love it. Pheromones! Works for butterflies, it'll work for you." It sounded like a bad sales pitch, but Reggie wrote wildly, underlined and drew asterisks in his notebook. He came home from school that day with a bottle of Old Spice, and Stef let him reek like the high seas for half a week before she intervened.

"Don't look now," she said as he came towards us, "but Captain Highliner's coming."

Each Monday for three months, a new theme was unveiled. Gene's lessons ran the gamut from working out, dancing skills, and the use of money, to possible topics of conversation, confidence-building, and appreciating the inner you. From time to time, as each was doing his own thing — carrying freight or serving customers or whatever — they would see each other from across the room, and Gene would gesture as if to say *I'm watching you*, pointing two fingers at his eyes then one back at Reggie.

Reggie changed slowly, but in the end seemed like a totally different person. He started going outside, he tanned his face and hands though it was the dead of winter. He smelled better, too, like Hawaiian Tropics. His body got thicker, and he started talking in a lower voice, he practised his conversation skills on us, and asked me what I thought about nuclear arms and whether or not I'd seen the new Duran Duran video. I was eleven.

That spring, while in the library after school, I spotted Reggie outside through the window. Just his head and shoulders. He was there, then he wasn't, then he was. I thought he might have been playing a game like peek-a-boo, but he wasn't the playing kind and I was too old for baby stuff. I waved, but he didn't acknowledge me, just kept going up and down. Nancy was sitting beside me, but she and everyone else were too busy playing MASH and writing ghost stories to see what was going on. I got up, went to the window, and saw the full picture: Reggie squatting with a loaded barbell balanced across his shoulders, all alone on the school lawn with this weird faraway look of concentration on his face.

I wonder now if his mind wasn't just on bearing the load. Was he thinking about something Mr. Calhoun had said earlier that day in Physics, or the revenge he'd take on Adam Lougheed, a C student who'd crushed him against lockers, calling him fag, chink, and worse since they started school together? Maybe he was registering the absurdity of lifting weights — didn't we invent machines so we wouldn't have to exert ourselves that way? Isn't the body just a vessel for the mind? Maybe his thoughts were on what was waiting for him on the other side of all that work.

What was waiting was Peggy McInnes. Her brother Steve was a math and music geek a year ahead of me in school, in Trina's year. I liked his big brown eyes, his slept-on brown hair that accidentally looked cool. I didn't know anything about him. Trina said he was awkward. That was fine by me. I didn't know Steve had a sister until Reg started dropping her name in conversation. She went to a different school, and kids in one school rarely know what's going on in the others, even if they're just down the street. Reggie started requesting things like tuna casserole and boiled peas for dinner, quietly explaining to us that those were Peggy McInnes's favourite foods. He started saying things like, "Peggy's dad is a doctor. She thinks I could be one, too."

It wasn't long before I met her. I agreed to a hangout at her house because I thought I might see Steve and because I was curious to see if she and Reg really were dating, and if so, what kind of girl he could attract.

Peggy was beautiful, though, a real charmer with green eyes and long blond hair. She giggled a lot, had a cute way of glancing around without moving her head when she was acting faux-suspicious. The first thing she did when we showed up at her place was compliment me. "You have beautiful hair," she said. "I could braid it for you if you want."

I'd never had a braid in my hair. Of course I wanted it.

Reg went to the living room to work on math puzzles with Steve while Peggy and I went to her room. It was pretty — big, pink, and clean. She sat on her canopy bed and asked me to sit in front of her. "Come on, closer," she said, her voice like warm bread, and I moved up and thought about Steve in the next room and wondered if he thought about me. Peggy's bedspread was a blanket made from bits of fabric with different flowery patterns on them. She started brushing, was really gentle about it, but I imagined her and Reggie kissing and it irked me. Years later, I realized that I always felt this kind of jealousy towards all the people my siblings ever dated. There was no one good enough for them. Peggy was close, though.

She had these weird-looking small guitars on her wall. I asked her about them. The bigger one was a mandolin and the smaller a ukulele. She told me about how she played them sometimes at out-of-town festivals and local seniors' homes. There were ribbons tacked up near the window. I knew what they were for. Reggie had told me she trained her wiener dog Schweigen for dog shows.

When Peggy was done braiding my hair, we went out to the living room to rejoin Reggie and Steve. Out in the hall, framed awards hung on the walls. Peggy and Steve had another sister, Kathy, in Grade Nine. All of them got awards for achievement and attendance. Peggy had a few for excellence in science. Steve had two for math and one for trumpet-playing. Kathy had Home Ec awards. There were cookies on the table that Kathy had made. Peggy offered some to us. They were delicious.

I was amazed by how different our families were. We didn't bake — we went for treat runs. And we had a lot of awards, too, but they were all stuffed in the drawer across the hall from the reading room. Stef had a guitar, but was terrible at playing. Paint was peeling from our walls, and a lot of our doors had holes covered over with brown-painted drywall from when Reggie and Gene, in separate fits of anger, had punched them. In comparison, Peggy's house was pristine, clean as a baby's stomach. I could tell that they dusted. I wondered if they'd ever cooked anything in a frying pan, since there was no grease on the walls.

AROUND THAT TIME, REGGIE'S scholarship offers started pouring in. He had some pretty hefty ones, full rides to the University of Michigan and the University of California in Berkeley. He was especially excited about the California scholarship. He said he wanted to practise his surfing. When I said he'd never surfed before in his whole life, he said that was beside the point.

One day the head of town operations, Bob Paquette, came into the store to tell Reggie to consider working for him after graduation.

"I don't know," Reggie said, scratching the back of his head. "I was thinking about going to university."

"You're eighteen," Mr. Paquette said, "so don't let me say what you can and can't do. But you got a future ahead of you here. I can't offer anything special, but I've got an opening for a meter reader. Say you do that, I could find some special projects, if they come up, keep things interesting. You keep at that long enough, you get promoted. It's not a bad wage. Lots of people go to university and waste four years of their lives getting a piece of paper saying they can do something they could've done before if they'd had the connections. Well, here's your connection."

Reggie said he'd consider it, but he never really did. He and Peggy sounded like they were planning on going to the same university — I listened in some nights, when he snuck off downstairs to phone her. He told me he wanted to live with her, and we both knew he couldn't do that in town.

My dad was always going on about the purity of the
Chinese race, about how Chinese couples never divorced but
white ones always did, about how our friends were just our
friends because we had a bit of money. Whenever Stef or Trina's
guy friends came into the store and my dad saw, there'd be
screaming fights after they left — between my dad and my mom,
or my dad and Stef or Trina — even if the guys came in with
their families. In the middle of one of those fights, my dad
clutched his chest and we had to call an ambulance. No one
wanted to see how he'd react to his first-born son living with a
white girl.

In the end, Reggie chose the University of Michigan because
they'd offered Peggy a scholarship, too. He told our parents
what he'd decided one night after supper, and my mom started
crying. My dad was sad, too, but back then, I'd only ever seen
him cry twice, both times at the funerals of his brothers. He
didn't cry about Reggie. What he said was, "I'll support you."
That meant he'd pay for anything the university didn't.

"Oh, Ba. You don't have to do that," Reg said. "I've got a full
scholarship. That means they're paying for everything."

"Room and board?"

"Yep." Reggie looked really proud of himself.

"What about fees?"

"Those, too. That's the most expensive part."

My dad bent over a bit then, like a part of his stomach had
suddenly gone missing and he was looking down at where it
had been.

Reggie sat our parents down and explained all of the logistics,
like the fact that the University of Michigan was in Ann Arbor,
a city whose crime rate was forty-eight per cent lower than the
American national average, and that he would live in dorm,
though he didn't mention his room would be next door to

Peggy's. He told them he'd start in their general studies program and then transfer either to pre-med, law, or engineering, he couldn't quite decide which. My mom thought he had some good ideas. Years later, she would pressure each of us into applying to programs in those same fields.

Reggie's grades had slipped a bit that year, but he still made valedictorian. It was a strange feeling, seeing someone you know up on stage giving a speech. We were one long line of fancy, in the centre towards the front, trussed up in our most uncomfortable clothes. Us girls were in dresses, nylons, and jewellery borrowed from my mom, solid gold necklaces and pendants weighing on our chests. My dress was beautiful, black with dark red short sleeves, sash, and crinoline. The boys were in suits and stiff leather-soled shoes. Stef bought corsages for the girls and boutonnieres for the guys. My dad was surprised and happy she'd made the effort. Gene didn't want to wear his but he did — "Just for Reg," he said. I'd never worn a flower before, besides the daisy tiara I'd made in art class in Grade Three. When Stef put my corsage on me, it made me feel special.

I listened to Reggie's speech, curious about what he'd say in front of all those people he didn't know, all those people he did. I kept turning around to look at all the people behind us, expecting them all to be blown away by his brilliance. My dad kept talking in the middle of the speech, reminding everyone around us that was his son. I saw Peggy in the stands behind Reg, blending into the crowd of graduates. Earlier, she'd given the salute to teachers. Did she and Reg share any momentous looks or nods? Had they, at any point, walked past each other, brushing together? Did either of them make reference to the other in their speeches? There was nothing I saw. Knowledge of their relationship was like a line you were about to draw on a connect-the-dots puzzle.

After the ceremony, teachers, parents, and other graduates flocked around Reggie to offer conspiratorial small talk and congratulations. He looked at ease with them, in part, I think, because of Gene's stud coaching. Then we took some pictures, some with just us and some with Reggie and his classmates. One group photo shows Reggie and Peggy crouching side by side in formless black gowns, shit-eating grins on their faces.

We left to have dinner at Giorgio's, a family restaurant on the highway that we'd only gone to once or twice before, on really special occasions. After ordering, Trina asked Reggie when he was going to Grad Campout. He hadn't said a word about it to my parents at that point, but we were all still thinking about what he'd told us the night before. His plan was to meet Peggy at the old coal shaft in Nordegg, and they'd be going to the campsite together. Two secret lovers meeting in the dark, with just the moon and two sets of headlights to guide them.

"Isn't it romantic?" Trina said.

A thump under the table.

My mom perked up. "What's so romantic?" she said.

"*I am very romantic*," I said in overemphatic Cantonese, like I was a character in a kung fu period piece. "*And you, you are also very romantic.*" Everyone laughed.

The boys made small talk about the restaurant and the food other people were eating, while our parents asked Reg the same set of questions they'd asked many times before, ever since he'd announced his plans to leave the country.

My dad: "Are you sure you'll have enough money?"

"Yes, Ba," Reg replied, contemplating the door. "Look at how many people there are."

"It's a Thursday," Gene reminded us.

"And look at how fancy everyone looks." Reg sipped a beer, his face red as an apple. Normally my dad would freak out if we even so much as joked about ordering alcohol at a restaurant, but tonight was special. He even let the rest of us drink pop. We went home. Reggie changed out of his suit and loaded a big old backpack and duffle bag into the back of my dad's truck. I went to see him off. Outside, the night was warm and the sun still on the horizon, though it was well past nine, the sky in a fancy dress of colourful ribbons — pink, purple, yellow, orange. "Peggy looked really pretty tonight," I said.

"Yes," he said, and drove away. That was the last any of us saw of him alive.

THE COPS SAID THAT Reggie went full speed through the guard-rail out on Five K Corner. It was a stretch of highway he'd driven on dozens of times. The truck was found by Darren Bigchild and a bunch of other Grade Elevens going out that way for Grad Campout. Some in that situation wouldn't have stopped, but these guys did. They drove back to Spring Hills and alerted the cops, who came back with them and pronounced Reggie dead on the scene, while forties and Bacardi Breezers warmed in the trunk of Darren Bigchild's dad's Cavalier and cherries flashed through its windshield in the dark.

At the time I couldn't figure out how Reggie died on a road he'd been on so many times. He'd been careful for eighteen years, never jaywalked, didn't take risks, never even broke a bone, and he'd only ever gone to the hospital to visit other people. I brought up the Chinese fortune teller in conversation once, but Stef said it couldn't be that. It was carelessness and random chance and about a million other factors, and she was mad at me for suggesting otherwise. Well, I'm not sure if I agree with her now, but I've thought about it, and there are other explanations, including two that are pretty convincing. The first is the beer at Giorgio's — probably the first one Reg had ever had, and he was probably a little drunk. The second is desire. At the time of the accident, both Reggie and Peggy were probably still virgins — Trina said she could tell by the way they interacted — but a few hours later, maybe they wouldn't have been. Now I'm no expert on male psychology, but you have to wonder what the anticipation of first-time sex with a beautiful girl does to a guy who'd been a geek for most of his life.

Still, I can't help but think that Reggie picked a fine time to die. Most of his life was a dull, diligent investment in an impossibly bright future. He'd seen signs of it coming, all the scholarships, that town job offer, being valedictorian, Peggy. Reggie had never failed at a single thing he put his mind to, but to live is to fail, isn't it, at least some of the time? It's almost as if he'd spent his whole life building a house of cards. Painstaking, time-consuming work. The house got bigger and bigger, got palatial rooms with little card chairs and little card tapestries — and the bigger and more elaborate it got, the more devastating it would've been when it all fell down. And at some point it had to. He didn't live long enough for that to happen. It's a kind of blessing.

Once, on the CBC, I heard about a mobile abattoir. Basically it's run by this guy who drives around southwestern Ontario with a rifle. Farmers book appointments with him, and he tells them not to feed their chosen cow or pig for twelve hours — long enough to make them hungry, not so long that they're suffering. At the end of those twelve hours, he comes and puts some feed in front of them. Comfortable, at home, with their head in a bucket and all their needs taken care of, they hardly notice the buckshot going through their brains.

9

IN THE MORNING, DR. SPADE comes in and asks me how I am. I say great. I'm not ready to die, though it would have been nice to miss some school. Nothing like being in the hospital on a school day to make you feel like a hero among your friends.

"You hit your head pretty hard," she says. "Your hip, too. You're lucky it isn't worse."

"I don't feel lucky."

She helps me out of bed and administers Check Stop tests, shows me leg exercises, and gives me a prescription for the pain and an antiseptic cream for my stitches. They're starting to hurt a lot. She wraps new bandages around my head, tells me I'll need to change them a couple of times a day and to keep the area around the stitches clean and dry.

"Can I wash my hair?" I ask.

"It's better if you don't, but if you do, you need to do it carefully. It's best if you get someone to help."

Like who? I want to ask, but don't.

She says I may have trouble keeping balance over the next few days and that I should call her if anything weird happens before sending me home. Luckily, Spring Hills is practically deserted most Sundays, and nobody I know sees me when I walk into the pharmacy with bandages around my head like

I'm five per cent mummy. It's a post-apocalyptic film inside, everything glossy, white, and quiet. Only one other person shopping here, a short woman with long dark hair. I approach but the look on her face like *get the fuck away* is like a shot to the brain and I wobble off, get bandages and gauze and my prescription filled, and go home.

The sounds of my key in the front door, and the slide click of the lock opening, are two of the better ones I've heard in a while. I go up the stairs, and for a second, I see the way my parents are when I'm not there. My pockmarked, grey-haired dad on the couch, clutching his glasses, his angry sleep face. My mom slouched in her armchair, looking bored, her black and white hair standing up and her legs curled out like crooked plants on the ottoman, huge flaking corns on her feet. She's feeble, like he is, but lacks his medical record, just has a heart that goes too fast when she runs from one end of the store to the other, so fast I'm afraid it'll pop. She'd literally rather die than see a doctor — the last time she went was probably to have me. My dad, on the other hand, has so many problems with his body and has had so many near-misses, including car accidents, being a victim of armed robbery three times, falling into a rice field when he was a boy, getting lost in storms, the Sino-Japanese War.

Some people my age spend time thinking about what they'd call a band, if they had one. Me, I think my family circus act, if we'd had one, would have been called Invincible Jack Wong and His Fabulous Diers. Just think of it: my brothers and sisters in amazing, star-spangled uniforms wrestling bears, juggling knives, shooting through flaming hoops on motorcycles, valiantly defying death, though also occasionally accepting it. My dad parading around in an old-fashioned swimsuit showing off his scars as I read out his medical records — *Diabetes! Vision problems!*

Kidney problems! Heart problems! Very high blood pressure! — and regaled the crowd with stories of times this very young and healthy-looking man almost died. Some in attendance would not have known there are so many ways for a life to end, or that it is possible to be so close to death so often without succumbing. But what would my mom do for the show? Take tickets? She lacks the exhibitionism of my father, lacks his stories.

I'm thinking about what side my mom would be on in the circus — invincibility or fabulous death — when she turns and looks at me, and my heart stops with an unexpected surge of love. I go to her, say a silent *hi*, crouch down and kiss her on the cheek, taking in her baby scent. She accepts it because she is one to accept her lot in life. When she starts talking, I hold an upright finger to my mouth, then point at my dad. She follows me to the other side of the house, to the laundry machines. I hug her — again, she accepts it — then we sit down, rest our shoulders against a cupboard her mom made from a cardboard box. My grandmother used to live here half the year, grew up poor in China. She's dead now.

"What did the doctor say?" my mom asks.

"I got some stitches. I sprained my hip. Otherwise, I'm okay. Tired. It hurts."

The next question she asks in Cantonese. Its direct translation is *How did you do that?* which implies blame. It's a Chinese thing. Here, if someone got murdered, you'd say, *He got murdered.* There, you would say, *He let someone kill him.* What she wants to know is how it happened.

The last thing I remember is spinning around dancing. If I had to guess, I'd say I tripped. Not something you want to tell someone. "I don't know," I say. "Can't remember."

"You must be more careful," she says, this look of pained worry on her face. My mom only has a couple of facial expressions.

Most of them look like pain. "You must be more careful," she repeats.

"Okay."

"So nothing else wrong?"

I shake my head. My stitches.

"No. Just tired." And alone. I'm talking slow. "Is there anything else you want to talk about? 'Cause I'd really like to sleep now." Why am I saying this? I need her, but I don't know how to talk about that, how to say it.

"I just want to see how you are," she says. Her elbows are up and her hands are on the armrests. She's gonna leave.

"Mom?"

She looks at me, eyebrows raised. She's slouching forward now, her thin, bony, defeated hands on her knees. My mom's probably more afraid of the world than me, but it wasn't always that way, I'm sure of it. My dad's life was sad before he came here. He's used to tragedy, maybe even thinks he brought bad luck with him. But my mom is from Hong Kong, a fucking first-world city. She went to university, read books. Nothing bad had happened to her until her husband ended up being mean, and her first three kids died, and her fourth kid ran away. What the fuck am I doing, putting myself at risk?

"I'm sorry," I say.

"It's okay."

"You don't even know what I'm sorry for. I'll be careful. I promise. Really careful. Your life is hard enough."

"It happened," she says. She's strong, scared but strong. I don't know where it comes from. "That is life. What can I do?" It's not a question. Or if it is, the answer would be *nothing*.

"Mom, what do you think happens after we die?"

She shrinks away.

"Well?" I say.

She says, "Die is die."

"You don't think there's anything else? We don't become ghosts or start another life somewhere else?"

"Some believe that."

"Do you?"

"No," she says, but in a way that makes me wonder if she's ever thought about it before.

I don't need to ask my dad what he thinks of the afterlife. He thinks we become ghosts, the kind of ghosts that can bring on bad shit if they're unhappy with the kind or amount of praying you've been doing. That's why we had an ancestor shrine, this table in the corner of the living room with red candles and little red place settings no one ever used, it's why he used to bring us to the cemetery — because he was born and raised into a culture where people pay their respects that way. There's something really nice about that way of doing it. Even though we've never done it, I like the idea of the ritual. You go out of your way to buy the cemetery food and paper and incense, then you drive to the cemetery, find their grave, and sit by it, and the whole time you're doing that, you're probably thinking about the person who died. Love becomes duty, and as long as you keep going, you'll keep remembering.

I don't know what I believe. Is it really true that we go somewhere when we die, that if people don't burn money for us in the human world, we're fucked? Maybe heaven is real or maybe the spirits of people you love roam the earth looking out for you. Maybe Gene got reborn into one of the mice in the hall. There's no way to know, but I need to think there's something, or at least be unsure about what happens, because the thought that there is nothing at the end of this — that some of the people I love most in the world are just gone, just like that, even though they were so alive and full and real when they were here, and

that all this bad shit happened to us for absolutely no reason —
is the saddest, most unbearable thought there is for me, even
worse than all the bad shit that really did happen.

My mom sits there, looking at her hands, sick with worry and
pain because she doesn't think her first three kids are anywhere
other than in the ground in Edmonton and because her last two
don't give a shit about living and because she left the city and
a family that she loved for this and the only permanent respite
from pain is nothingness, and it makes me even more tired.

"I'm sorry, Mom," I say, getting up, "but I have to go to sleep
now." I stumble to my room and into bed where I lie on my
front, my face pushed into the pillow. Black are the insides of
my eyelids, and black is this room without windows.

I WAKE TO A sore neck and exhaustion, but the doctor said to
change the bandages twice a day so I get up. I start unravelling
in the bathroom, but the bathroom's dirty and stinks like rotting
washcloths, so for the first time in five months, I go to my old
room to use the mirror there. I unwind the rest of the bandage
and see they shaved a bit of my head. I take the gauze off slow.
It feels like skin is coming off with it. A yellow stain, orange
crumbs that I touch with a hairpin. I smell it, then twist and strain
to see the stitches in the mirror. Trina's compact is on the dresser.
I open it and angle it behind me, and I'm both grossed out and
impressed by that black string threaded through my skin.

My dad comes in wearing just his underwear and an old
cream-coloured cowboy shirt. "Hey, Ba," I say, tired and cheerful. He puts his hand on my head and shoves it around, and I
jerk back. "Ow!" I say. He looks confused, so I show him the
stitches. My dad hurts himself a lot at work. He knows pain.

"Everything okay?" he asks. It's the closest he gets to empathy.
I nod humbly, smile like it's just another day at the office,

but I'm thankful for his concern. "Yeah. What time is it?"

"Twel o'clo," he says.

"Do you think I can call Mom?"

"Why?"

"I want someone to help me put the cream on."

"I'll help you," he says.

My love turns to fear on a dime. My dad is unpredictable. How much can you ask of him and how much can you push him? It changes by the minute. Gene spat soup out at dinner one time — it was beautiful, the defiance, it looked like a fountain, he got it in all the food — and my dad just playfully swore like it wasn't anything, but one time I accidentally spilled soup, he hit me. He's hit me lots of other times, too. There's no pattern.

"Your hands are dirty and you'll do it too hard," I say.

"*I'll* wash *them!*" He sounds incredulous, playful. But still.

I cup my hand around my stitches, careful not to touch them, and we limp to the bathroom together. Dirty knobs, black grime around the sink, dripping faucet. "You have to use soap and hot water," I say. "If you don't, it'll get infected."

So he turns on the hot water and lathers to his elbows. My dad's not a soap kind of guy. When he's done, I turn the hot tap back on and put my finger in the stream. Lukewarm, not hot like I asked. War zone. Mines. Still, an infection is bad news — maybe worse than anger. "This water is cold," I say. "Can you do it again when it warms up?" He looks at me and swears some. What's gonna happen? When? He turns the water back on, waits, then washes his hands again. I hold out my towel and pass him the ointment. It's small in his hands, like glue for a dollhouse. I think of Trina, that grease she had to put on her tattoo. "Do it lightly," I say, "or it'll really hurt."

I barely feel his fingers on my head. He's never done anything so soft in his life. I'm watching him in the mirror, the concentration on his face. I open the pack of gauze. He puts some on and wraps the bandage over top of it, skillfully, like he's tying up a chicken, then fastens it with metal clips, those flat ones with teeth. Even that doesn't hurt. I wish he were slightly less skilled, so it wouldn't be over so fast, but he's been fixing shoes for thirty years. He's good with his hands. I'm safe.

"Thanks, Ba," I say and bite his arm. He whacks me on the ass, toddles off to his room, leaves me standing there alone.

Only two lights on in the house, one long, dark hall in between. How is it that I'm scared even at home? There's nothing for it. Turn on the lights but it still feels spooky, so I go, fast, get into my room.

An envelope, handwritten, addressed to me, sits on my desk. I never get mail.

Trina.

Is it possible? Is it really? Who put it there? Not my dad — he would have opened it. Probably my mom, because she's too busy popping out babies and working to know what her kids' writing looks like. I find scissors, cut the envelope, take the letter out.

She wrote, just like she said she would. Water in my eyes.

10

※

THE NEXT DAY AT school all anyone can talk about is my bandage. That and what Kay did at the party. She wants to talk, keeps bringing it up. My heart's not in it, but I ask about it anyway. "What's this I hear about you and Curt?" I say, as we're walking down the hall.

Mike Brown jogs by, shouts, "Mummyhead!"

"Yep!" I yell back. "One foot in the grave. Better not let me touch you!"

"Yeah, you know," Kay says, all casual. "The party?" People talking, lockers slamming. Some jock girls whisper and look at us as they go by. She says it's fine, it's what happens when you drink. No one got hurt.

"I thought you liked Chiggers," I say. I'm tired of this. Nine a.m. and I'm already tired.

"He left early. It was a party," she says. "That's what you do at parties."

"What, get fucked by random guys?"

First period is Math, we have it together. It's as bad as you'd expect. People talk about us like we're not even there. At one point, I instinctively turn around, and Carrie Pratt pretends she didn't just pass a note. Kay pays attention in Math for the first time in her life. We're the two class freaks, conveniently positioned so that no one has to swivel to look at us both. I probably shouldn't have come, but I needed to get my mind off things.

Trina's in Whitehorse, or she was last week. She took the long way — took the 16 through two chains of mountains, then stopped in Prince Rupert to stare into the Hecate Strait before taking the 37 up. She said she felt the islands there all the way in the west — the same way you feel a twin, how far away they are or if they are in trouble — and that the drive was long and sometimes boring, but to combat that, she'd been picking up hitchhikers. She chronicled her life — she ran low on money and had to stop for months to work as a waitress in Dease Lake, she said there was something clean about it, working for a wage, and then when you go outside, whoa — and there were misadventures, too, like fishtailing in the mountains, having to pull over when eighteen-wheelers passed because of the dust, and running out of gas on the Alaska Highway. When I read that I thought, *serves you right* and also *for fuck sakes, be careful, will you?* She enclosed pictures and I could barely look at them. A big wooden cowboy beside a teeny little diner. A picture of herself at the wheel, a serious look on her face, she looked both different and the same. The Northern Lights. A bird off in the distance — a juvenile eagle, she said. She apologized for taking so long to write. She said she thought of me every day, and that she was having an amazing time, but that I couldn't tell my parents where she was. *They've already made their peace. If I come back, let it be a surprise, but if I don't …*

It's 9:08. Another seventy-two minutes left in class. An eternity. I shouldn't be here. I could take off now, fake the flu. People laugh. There's something on me, a spitball? I don't check to see. I think, *Please, God, Allah, Buddha, whoever, if you're there,* and the PA blips. Mr. Anderson stands there holding a piece of chalk like a chess piece, but when nothing happens, he keeps writing.

Second period is a spare, so I go home. I stay in my room, come out for lunch, then skip the rest of the day. Her letter under my pillow is like a fly in the room: no matter what else I'm doing, my mind is on it. I take a nap, change my bandage, work on my contest entry. Every time I hear my dad coming, I shut the light so he won't know I'm here. I try to relax, and read. Peter Pan takes the Darlings to Mermaids' Lagoon, they rescue Tiger Lily, then I put the book aside.

"You win," I say to the letter, slipping my hand under the pillow. I open the envelope, and read it for what seems like the twentieth time. It doesn't help. It does nothing good for me. I can't help myself.

I leave the house, go for a walk. I should buy some cigarettes or smoke the ones I already have, but I even fail at being bad, so I wind up at school. No one but stragglers here. I'm getting my Biology textbook so I can bring it home and study when Nancy shows up and asks me if I'll go with her to the basketball game. A guy she likes is playing. I want to tell her to forget it, that he either doesn't like her or is just a big fucking asshole who'll use her and leave if he gets the chance, but she looks at me with these pleading eyes. "Chris," she says. She's simple and happy. I wish some of that could wear off on me.

When we get to the gym, the game has already started. Dribbling, squeaking high tops on the floor. Carrie Pratt and five other cheerleaders in tight black pants and white sweaters strike unconvincing fuck-me poses, and it shows. No one's cheering at all, and I'm glad. The other team's mascot is wearing a bee costume, doing the Worm with no music in front of bleachers of bused-in fans.

"So who's the guy?" I ask.

Nancy points. "Jamie Aaronson," she says. "He's got the ball."

"Him?" I ask. Tall blond with a ponytail and glasses. He's butt ugly, but a good shot. Everyone loves a hero. "You'll have toothpick babies."

"Yeah," she says, sighing.

The game is boring, but it's hard not to watch the bee. It's like a train wreck. He's dancing with someone's mom — she's getting a kick out of it — then he's picking up a kid for airplane spins. The kid loves it. The quarter ends, halftime, with the away team winning. The bee sets the kid down, and takes his giant fuzzy head off. He looks familiar. It's Conrad. He crosses the floor, head underneath his fuzzy bee arm, carrying a duffle bag with one small heavy thing inside. When he sees me, he changes course, comes over.

Nancy looks at me, but there's no time to explain as he approaches the bleachers.

"You didn't call me," he says loudly. Luke Carcadian, Laurie LeMay, pretty much everyone turns to see who he's talking to. When he gets closer, this sad look comes onto his face. My bandage. "Oh, my god. What happened?" he says, like he owns me. It makes my skin crawl. But he's the only one who's asked besides Kay and Nancy.

I wave him over, whisper into his ear: "If you come outside, you can see the stitches." Why I say this I don't know.

He whispers back. "I've never wanted anything so much. I'm big on medical procedures."

Nancy's watching us so I can't back out. I tell her I'll see her in a bit, then get down from the bleachers on my own, even though he tries to help. We head up the ramp from the gym and hang a right.

"You're really forward," I say. The school looks different with half the lights out.

He screws up his eyes, tilts his head, says, "What do you mean?"

"Don't you worry what people think? Coming up to me like that. You don't even know what I'm gonna say."

He seems confused.

"People don't know much about me, and I'd like to keep it that way."

"I get it. So what happened?" He gestures at my head.

I cup the side of my mouth like I'm telling a secret. "Dancing accident," I say quietly.

"Dancing." His face alive with the possibilities.

"Yeah, there's this band Joy Division?"

"Yeah, right. Highly danceable. And?"

"And ... I just ... fell. I think."

He nods gravely, then says, "You're gonna be more careful, though, right? You got parents and a, uhh ... boyfriend? What does he think of it?"

"Boyfriend?"

"Ty."

"Ty's not my boyfriend. How do you know about him?"

"From your friend Kay. 'Member she got lost during the party? I found her, told her you were looking for her. We started talking about you and she mentions this guy, Ty. Turns out, I'd already talked to him earlier in the night. Tall skid guy in an army coat. He was, uhh ... charming."

"Charming?"

"Not really. He's a bit of a pig."

"Oh?"

"Kept pointing at different girls, saying which ones he wanted to fuck, which ones he could fuck — ends up being the same for a guy like that. Yeah, then he points at this cute girl in a NASA t-shirt, and ..." He breathes deep. "So I guess he likes you or you like him or maybe something's gonna happen?"

"Yeah, maybe."

"You can do a lot better, though. Just saying." He pulls up his sleeve, looks at his watch. The bee head under his arm looks out into space. "Did you maybe wanna go somewhere?" He starts taking his bee suit off. I turn away, but he says, "It's okay. I've got clothes on under here."

"Don't you have to go back to the game?"

"Nah," he says. "Some benchwarmers owe me a favour. A couple of them asked about being the bee." He sees me smile. "Yeah, some guys are good at sports, others want love however they get it. Any good places to eat around here?"

WE TALK ALL THE way down the highway. When we get to town limits I stay back, saying I have an errand to run, before sending him off to Perry's. We pick it because he's vegetarian.

"You don't eat meat?" I say.

"No."

"Never?"

"No."

"That's huge. My dad would lose his shit if I stopped eating meat."

"What's it to him?"

I shrug and tell him to meet me at the Dairy Burger. Fifteen minutes later, he comes in with a steaming box of pizza. We go back to school, where I buy us Cokes at a machine, then take us to sit in the far stairwell. It's cold but no one ever goes here. I try giving him money for my share of the pizza, he doesn't want it, so I sneak it into his bag when he goes to the bathroom. When he comes back, he says, "That pizza's the best thing I've eaten in a fifty-mile radius."

I ask if I can tell him about butterflies. For some reason, I think he'll understand or appreciate the knowledge. He says sure, so I start telling him about how, most often, flight is the thing that kills them. "Most butterflies live between a day and a week, and with every beat of their wings, they tear little holes in them — 'cause, like, wind resistance causes lift, right? — and that's fine, but eventually, a butterfly's wings are so full of holes that they can't fly anymore. When that happens, they spend all their energy trying to fly or they can't get food, or a predator gets them, and that's the end."

"That's pretty intense," he says. Then he starts talking about what it's like to be the weird kid in his town. "If I lived here, too, no one would know which of us to hate more. Or maybe all the other science geeks would start coming out of the woodwork. We'd make this whole new social group."

"People don't hate me," I say. "Yeah, a couple of people don't like me, but mostly they leave me alone. Except for, well ..." I gesture at my bandage. "People are used to my family being weird." He asks me how and I start telling him, cautiously, about my parents, how in their own way they're individuals who don't give a fuck about what other people think.

I'm not much of a talker normally, but Conrad laughs when things are funny, he listens, he keeps asking questions. Still, it feels weird talking about my parents with Trina's letter on my mind. I don't know if I want to tell him, but it ends up coming out anyway. I didn't know it would feel so good, like I just stopped holding my breath. I tell him more: about how Trina ran away and how I can't find her, about Mike Brown's dad at the cop shop being a dick, about how sad we all are, about how Trina told me not to tell my parents and how it's going to be hard to lie to them.

"That sucks," he says.

"Remember at the party when you asked me what the worst thing that ever happened to me was?"

"Yeah."

"What's the worst thing that ever happened to you?"

He doesn't say anything.

"Is it maybe, like, your parents splitting up?"

A mocking look. "No," he says. "Not even close."

"I'm listening."

He takes a swig of Coke. "The worst, and best, thing that ever happened to me was three summers ago when my dog died." He sees my face. "Chrysler, hear me out. Her name was Checkers. She was a golden retriever, husky mix. She came when you called and she had, like, the nicest bark. We had her for eight years. One day I was on my way home from my summer job when I saw something in the road near my house. When I got closer, I got a weird feeling, it told me to run, so I ran to it and it was her. That whole fucking summer I was distraught, but the bigger thing was that it made me think about death. I mean, I'd thought about it before, but this was the first time I seriously contemplated my own end. It made me think, *All of this right here?*" A finger to his temple. "*All of this, everything — my personality, everything I am and everything I've seen, all my memories — will be gone.* Even worse, I won't be able to see, touch, taste, smell, hear anything. I will be nothing. My dog died, and I realized I'd die, too. Chrysler, someday we will die and we will be nothing. Can you imagine that?"

"No," I say because I can't. I've spent years thinking about this, wondering what happens, but I can't imagine how any of it would actually feel.

"See, I couldn't, either, the first few times I thought about it. It's scary as fuck. But it's motivating, too."

"And sad."

He's looking at me in this grave way. "It's just you and your sister in your family?"

I ask him for a walk.

Outside, far from anyone else's ears and in the comforting cold, I tell him, not the details, but the broad strokes, about my siblings, the curse, how careful I have to be. It seems to knock the wind out of him.

"I can't imagine," he says.

"I'm the life of the party."

"You don't have to joke about it," he says, and it's a blow to the head, those words.

Don't cry, I think. *Don't cry.* We're stopped on the shoulder in front of Fas Gas, and Conrad's looking at me so concerned, and no one ever asks me how I am or how things were, and no one knows I've had the best years of my life already and that I'll never feel that good again. I used to be able to cry in front of Stef or Trina. I've cried in front of Gene, even Reg. The more I try not to, the sadder I feel.

I shake my head, see the blue whale on his shirt. "Do you think the barnacles on a blue whale die soon after the whale does?"

"What?"

"Do the barnacles benefit from coming up for air sometimes, or is there a certain pressure level they need to live at? Or maybe whatever scavenger fish that eat the blue whale accidentally eat some of the barnacles, too?"

"I don't know."

"I thought you'd know since you have one on your shirt."

"That's, umm, some pretty specialized information."

I look at my watch. Five-sixteen. 5+1=6. "Yeah, I should probably go. My dad gets weird if he doesn't know where I am every minute of the day. He might be shitting bricks as we speak. I'll have to pretend I didn't already eat."

"I have half an hour before the bus leaves. I could, uhh ... walk you home?"

"Maybe partway," I say.

We walk on the south service road, parallel to the highway. Light is fading, cars go by with their red and white lights. We turn at the school, pass the KFC and Tomboy, the hospital and the furniture shop where IGA used to be. We don't talk much. The sky is dark and pretty. Cars and trucks pull up and down Main, loud without their mufflers. Ten feet in from my corner, in front of the bar and out of view of the store, I stop walking, and so does he.

"This is gonna sound ridiculous," I say, "but my friend Nancy likes Jamie Aaronson. Do you think you could get his number for her?"

"It might emasculate him, but I'll try."

"That's my store right there." I point. "Jack's Western Wear. I'm sorry, but you can't come in." He looks confused. "It's hard to explain."

"Can I at least call you?"

A boxy brown beater goes by, then a souped-up truck going the other way with the bass up high.

"I'm not special," I say. "Not that pretty, not that smart."

He gives me a look.

I shrug. "I guess I don't understand why you'd want to talk to me."

"Why wouldn't I want that? We just talked for two hours. Again. You're smart and weird in a good way and we care about the same things, and I think I understand some things about you."

What's the problem? *You're gonna die. You can't get close to anyone. You're gonna die, and soon.* "You seem nice," I say.

"I *am* nice."

"So meet someone this summer or next year at university or tomorrow." I stick my hand out. "I had fun."

He takes it. "Me too."

"I'll see you," I say, then start walking.

"But your friend wants Jamie's number."

"Right." The store glows yellow out the front windows. Dark blue sky. "Right." I take a pen from my back pocket. "I shouldn't be doing this. You can call me, but only for this."

"You're seriously saying that?"

"Do you want my number or not?"

"I want it," he says.

I write it on a receipt, hand it to him. "You can only call after eight or on Sundays. Otherwise, my dad'll pick up."

"And he'll shit bricks."

"Yes."

"Okay," he says. "Goodnight." His eyes are big and dark like the woods at sundown. The store is a beacon of light. I'm there in time to help my mom close. Supper is a can of salmon with fried bacon on top and stir fried greens on the side. I push the food around my bowl and think about how flying kills a butterfly.

11

※

WHEN I GET UP for school I feel stronger somehow. In the hall at lunch, I see Ty and remember what Conrad said about him maybe liking me when he turns his head as I pass. Then I think, *God, you're fucking high on yourself.*

In third period, Mr. Birch says to me, as he's handing back exams, "I've been disappointed by some of your siblings, Chrysler, but with you, we get another Reggie Wong." He proudly places my exam on my desk, a 94 scrawled in red at the top. "Highest mark in the class," he says, and for a second, I smile like a keener, though that's just reflex.

Ninety-four. When I get home, my mom'll get all excited and ask if I've applied to Harvard yet. My dad won't care. No one will ask if I even like chemistry. I don't, it's hard and boring. The night before the exam, instead of studying, I typed out the words to my favourite Ray Bradbury story, "One Night in Your Life." I had my mom read it out to me. She over-pronounced most of the words, and when I watched her read, I saw that she moved her mouth a lot. It was the first story she ever read to me. I guess I wasn't sorry it was.

The store is busy after school so there's no time to tell her about the test. You can't always predict it. A Tuesday that feels like a Saturday afternoon, and then at 8:01, the phone rings. I pick up. "Jack's Western Wear," I say in my chipper work voice.

"Umm, hi. Can I talk to Chrysler?" It's Conrad.

"Is this the bee?" I say. My mom's right there, cashing somebody out.

"Is this the apiary?"

"You don't waste time."

"I got the … uhh … stuff you wanted." His voice is playful.

"Oh, the stuff. Uhh … meet you in the alley?" My mom perks up. "It's busy today."

"Should I let you go?"

"Maybe. We can talk later, though."

"I'll call you tonight?"

Say no. Say no. "Sure."

"Good luck today."

"Thanks. Bye."

After I hang up, my mom says, in Cantonese, "What's in the alley?"

I look at her slyly and shrug.

Pretty soon the rush ends. We count up, cook, eat, do dishes. I do homework, watch TV with my parents. They go to bed and I go to my room, and at ten-thirty, the phone rings.

"Hello?"

"Guess what I learned today."

"Did you learn that pirates wore eye patches so that one eye would be adjusted to see below deck?"

"Is that real?"

"Yeah. Also not the thing you learned today."

"You got a pen?"

"Yeah."

"Seven two nine seven one five four." Jamie Aaronson's number.

"Thanks! Goodnight!" A smile on my face.

"I'll bet you look really pretty right now, even if you're mean."

"Can you believe this guy? Complimenting me and tearing me down all in one sentence." *Pretty?* No one's ever said that.

"I'm a real wordsmith," he says. "How was your day?"

I tell him about my Chem test, how Mr. Birch and probably all my other teachers taught my siblings and know what happened to them.

"Small town life is an aquarium," he says. "Teachers were extra-easy on me while my parents were splitting up. Also? You're fucking smart."

"No, I'm not."

"Uhh … ninety-four? Yes, you are. Chem is hard."

THE NEXT DAY, I pass Jamie's number on to Nancy, and she looks at me all starry-eyed like that slip of paper is a winning lottery ticket.

Conrad calls again — I should've known he would — and he tells me about Belize, how he wants to go, how Pakistan has nuclear capabilities now and what that means. I tell him about Northern BC and the Yukon. He tells me about whale falls, whole ecosystems based on whale carcasses drifting down to the bottom of the ocean. I try to keep our talk short, maybe half an hour, but one evening becomes two, which becomes three, which at the end of the week becomes him asking if I want to hang out on Sunday.

"I don't know," I say.

"Why not? Store's closed."

"I tend to spend the day with my folks, though. Plus, I have to finish this thing I'm working on for that writing contest."

"Well, my mom likes me to spend weekends with her and Larry."

"Yeah?"

"So I'll be in Spring Hills, if you wanna meet up."

TRINA ALWAYS WANTED TO go somewhere. Could be why she got that tattoo of all those birds. Imagine a way of life that forced you to fly halfway around the world twice every year. I wanted to go somewhere, too. Sometimes she'd bring home pamphlets from Destiny Vacations, brochures about Acapulco and Cuba, New York City, and we'd read them together. Black sand, white sand, the Lower East Side. She'd talk about the things she'd wear in each place, about how good the shopping was in New York, how fun it would be to learn to surf or sail. One time I went with her to look at brochures. That's when I saw it: a scene of soft, snowy peaks and two small trees, sky dark purple like I'd never seen, with alien streaks of cool green light winding through. Yukon. It sounded magic. I took the brochure home with me and read about the Gold Rush, arts festivals, dogsledding, hiking trails, whitewater rafting. I saw pictures of desolation, bears, the warm yellow lights of a chalet town at night, and the unclimbed peaks, glacier caves, and vast ice fields of Kluane National Park.

It became a joke for us. "Just think, Triny," I'd said. "Twenty-four hours of darkness or light. Glaciers! The Northern Lights! We've been to Vancouver. We could go there, too. It's just, like, ten hours more."

"Vancouver is Vancouver," she'd said. "Why would I wanna go to the Yukon? It's fucking cold. It's all brown and white, and everyone wears a parka all the time."

It's still sinking in that she's alive, really alive and out there. I spend lunches and after schools in the library looking at wildlife guides, a history of the Yukon and Northern BC, a book of photos of the Coast Mountains. I look at the atlas, trace her path to the Alaska Highway, and speculate. She took the 16 because it's beautiful, it's random, and it goes west. All those mountains — did she feel hemmed in? And what was the view from Prince Rupert? Water, a thousand miles' worth, she wouldn't have known it was the Gulf of Alaska unless she'd looked at a map.

Though I don't really want to admit it, I think it's cool she went. What she's doing? Holy shit. Unbelievably cool, she's so alive, doing and seeing as much awe-inspiring stuff as she can before she — you know. I picture her driving, seeing ptarmigan and tundra swans, stopping at the side of the road to walk into the woods with a pair of binoculars. But don't forget: there are also bears there, muskox that can go crazy and stampede. She could fall through thin ice, get run off the road, have a run-in with some miners who want their way with her. There are so many ways to die out there, even more than there are here.

SATURDAY COMES WITH ANOTHER rush at the store. It's the middle of the month, and people come in with their loud families in tow, their reserve cheques in hand. We cash them if they buy something. There's a couple of dozen people in the store right now, lots of native families and some people without cheques, too. My mom and I each have to serve more than one person at once.

I'm running a pair of toddler cowboy boots to the counter for Darren Bigchild, making a mental note to hire someone on part-time, when my dad calls down on the intercom, oblivious, telling me to come up and help with dinner. I look at my mom. She says go like she's the one noble soldier left behind on the battlefield in a war movie.

Upstairs, he has Chinavision on, some talk show about what to eat and wear when your kids get married. He doesn't know how to work the TV even though I've shown him like a billion times. I find him a show about sharks, start rolling out dough for barbecue pork buns. It's a personality test. Who pulls for the predator and who for the prey? Dramatic music, near misses, then a seal pops out of the sea like a champagne cork, flapping its fins as it lands in the mouth of a shark.

"Wow!" my dad says, a piece of dough in hand. "What he eating?"

"A seal," I say. "It weighs four hundred pounds."

"Waa." He's mesmerized.

I pinch the top of a bun till it's closed. One time on TV I saw a shark with a four-foot wide mouth — a filter feeder, the biggest fish in the ocean, they said. Its mouth was fleshy inside, reminded me of my dad when he takes his dentures out at night and you can finally see how old he is.

When the store closes, my mom comes up to help with the buns. She's short of breath, excited, bragging about how busy it was today as she joins us at the table. I ask what they want to do tomorrow.

"No-thing!" my dad says, sing-song incredulous.

"I thought you might wanna go to Edmonton."

"What I leave for?" Loud and proud agoraphobic.

"Why'd you used to leave?" I say. "Get a good supper, bring Mom to the mall, get some Chinese groceries."

On the other side of him my mom shakes her head wildly, waving and mouthing something at me. My dad doesn't notice even though it's like she's trying to signal an airplane. "Naw," he says. "You go out there, get char siu bow from factory! What's good for?" It's the final word on the subject.

In the past I would've pushed for it, talked to him about seafood and Peking duck, talked to her about the preppy stores and the place with the little cottages at the mall. It's not like I wanted to go — I just wanted to remind them of how their lives used to be, how they still could be. But things are different. A stack of cheques in the cash register, a nature documentary when you're expecting a talk show. This is what constitutes happiness for them now.

12
※

I USED TO LOVE when my parents left town without us. My parents not being around was not a new thing. They were always like that, too busy at the store or, occasionally, away from home. Stef wanted for someone to be there for us, so when they went to see a salesman or visit relatives and we stayed home, she would make Hamburger Helper and Betty Crocker cake, stuff my dad never made. Stef in an apron, long hands ripping apart a head of lettuce, me asking if I could help. She made my lunches, too — every day she did that — and she was there for me when I was mad or sad. I used to sit on her back in our room, braid her hair and write poems for her. *I hope you never go deaf.* I took her for granted. I wish I'd said thanks, or taken care of *her* some Sunday.

Stef loved animals, always wanted a pet, but we never had one. Too dirty, our parents said, and it was fine by me. You love them like family and they inevitably die on you, so why bother? Gene said Stef saw the family as her little hobby farm, this collection of animals who couldn't live without her, but I knew all along that she took care of us because she loved us, because of some idea she had about what family was and what siblings do for each other — points she drove home in the days after Reggie died.

Rodeo was a bad time for tragedy. Busy. My mom kept breaking down when people asked about Reg, so one of us was always near the counter just in case. My dad was the same as always, making meals and fixing shoes in the back. He never mentioned Reggie once. We couldn't imagine our parents discussing terms with the casket and tombstone suppliers. They're just not that kind of people. But we were all still kids, way too young for that kind of responsibility. We didn't know how to book a funeral home, didn't know that we needed a picture for the service, little pamphlets with details of his life and death, an obituary.

Eventually, Stef took a stand. She should have been mad, but instead she quietly got all the necessary catalogues. It was settled. Daytimes we spent rushing to our mom's aid, getting sizes, shaping hats, cashing people out, trying not to look too sad. Nights we girls spent in our room going through the catalogues.

"What do you think of this one?" Stef asked Trina and me. She was lying on her stomach in bed, holding a pen, one foot dangling in the air. The catalogue was open to a page that could've been any other, and the one she'd circled wasn't anything special, but there's not a whole lot you can do with a casket. Different handles, different colours of wood. Twenty to a page. It was like we were picking the new fall shoes.

"I like this one," Trina said, her finger on one called Matt Pecan. Matt Pecan like a nut with a name.

"Not bad," Stef said. "But it's more than a thousand dollars."

I picked one called Oxford Tweed. It was full of character, covered in cloth. Stef said it seemed inappropriate. I wondered who it was appropriate for.

In the end, we went with a cherry casket and a mottled grey stone. We also decided on Edmonton. It wasn't Ann Arbor, but at least it was out of town. None of us wanted to live in Spring

Hills after high school or stay here longer than we absolutely needed to, not even Reggie. Stef was looking at the Conservation Sciences program at U of A, and we all saw ourselves living in Edmonton, too. We went to the library, huddled around a phonebook, and chose the cemetery by the west end museum. There were dinosaurs there, a bug room and scientific exhibits. Stef thought Reggie would have liked it.

The flowers started coming around then. We were as surprised as ugly girls being asked to dance when the first arrangement came. Back then — Trina and I were thirteen and twelve — flowers meant romance and popularity. With every arrangement we got, we felt jolts of confusion — sadness, excitement, and duty intermingled. The guys from Current Electric pooled together money for carnations, and one of them, Ed Burns, walked them up in his coveralls. For some reason all of us kids were at the counter. He didn't know which of us he should talk to, so he addressed the wallets and bandanas under the glass. "Would you accept these?" he asked them, slack-jawed, cap off his greasy, grey head and in his hand like this were an old movie and we were the love interest. The carnations were red and white and stuck in green foam. Trina took them, and we all went to the back together to put them on the same work bench we had placed the ones Stef got from Josh McMurtry and all the other guys who liked her.

By the end of that first day, we'd received more than half a dozen arrangements. By the third day, there were at least twenty more. We ran out of space for them, started putting them on the floor. Most of them ended up upstairs, in the office and in our rooms, on the sideboard, coffee table, and ancestor shrine. I'd never seen so many different kinds of flowers all at once. My dad kept knocking them over. He poured a coffee and a vase would tip — whoa — same thing when he hemmed jeans or plugged in the rice or tried sewing a tarp. He made us clean up after him.

On the fourth day, with flowers on the coffee table blocking his view of the TV and signals from the remote, he blew a fit. He shoved some onto the ground, sent lilies, tulips, roses flying. He interrupted dinner to make us throw them all out. We tried to reason with him, but that only made things worse. I'd never seen him so mad.

I was mad, too, so mad I went to my room, but the sounds of everyone working and talking in the hall drew me back out. He'd calmed down by then, fast as usual. I didn't have the heart to help throw the flowers out, so instead, while Carol Burnett floated around in a big white bell of a dress on TV, trying to seduce a man in a southern accent, I cleaned, scooped up water, broken stems, and glass. Meanwhile, the jungle of flowers retreated. We cleared the living room, kitchen, and dining room, but left as many as we could in our rooms.

One at a time, Stef, Trina, and everyone else came upstairs to take another bouquet away. It seemed weird, not being a part of that. Stef said it wasn't that bad. She said it'd be worth it for me to come down and just hang out if I wanted to, so I went. I'm not sure what I thought I'd see. Maybe flowers spilling out of the trash, or an assembly line: my dad by the dumpster, everyone else offloading their bouquet for him to chuck in. Instead I saw flowers everywhere, arranged neatly on the landing outside the back door, on the concrete ledge where the dumpster was, on the little dirt pile below. There were even some on the crabgrass hill across the alley. My dad and Gene were placing vases. My mom was positioning individual flowers. Trina was adding water.

It was a pretty nice scene, but as soon as I saw it I imagined a stranger coming that night to wreck it. Broken flowers, vases, leaves, a huge mess for us to clean up. Stef said there was nothing we could do short of camping out on the concrete pad. The next morning Gene and I saw that even though some flowers had been taken and one of the vases had tipped over, leaving a drying wet mark down the alley, for the most part things were fine. Gene took the tipped vase inside, filled it in the workshop sink, then brought it back out and set it where it was. "There," he said, after arranging the flowers.

On Saturday, the day before the service, Mr. Gustafson, the funeral director, called. He wanted to pick up the flowers we'd received so that each attendee could throw one onto the casket at the graveyard. But vases had been steadily disappearing from the alley — all that were left were some bundles of carnations, sick and wilted in the heat, despite our tending to them in the evenings. A crowd was expected and Mr. Gustafson needed more.

The main events of the Caroline Rodeo — barrel racing, pony chariots, and chuckwagons — were always held on the third Saturday in June, and the store was extra busy that day. Lines were forming at the till and our mom could barely keep up with all the sales. But we had our priorities in place. When Mr. Gustafson showed up in his van, we climbed the stairs single file and came back down with the offerings for Reggie. We'd kept them in our rooms. We gave him every last arrangement, even favourites we'd hoped to keep, till the house was empty, till there was no sign of Reggie being gone at all.

We took up most of the front row at the service. No one else sat with us, which was right. In attendance were teachers, some classmates, their parents, people from the town, good customers. I only had one dress that fit — the same one I'd worn nine days before at Reggie's graduation.

Mr. Gustafson stood at the podium and talked about youth and potential, about how much sadder it was when a person died young. The speech dragged. Reggie didn't know Mr. Gustafson at all. Neither did we. I slouched down with my elbows on my thighs and my chin in my hand. My mom nudged me, wanted me to straighten up, but I didn't. I turned to my dad. His eyes looked slimy. He swept his meaty fingers across them. Crying is like laughter or coughing: contagious. Before I knew it, our whole family was at it — all of us but Gene, though he still looked pretty sorry as he passed a pack of tissue down the row. Somewhere else in the room, someone was sobbing. Peggy.

The casket sat on a raised platform at the front of the room. I couldn't see Reg from where I was, but I'd seen him a few days before in a different part of the funeral home, this small, dark, yellow room. I remembered the shock of seeing him, his face caked with powdery makeup. I remembered prying his hand open, how it settled back in place around mine, like we were holding hands. When it warmed up, I put my arms around him. He felt hard and more muscular than he'd ever been in life. Stef said he smelled like the frog she dissected that year in Bio.

When the eulogy was over, we stood, and immediately a long line of people snaked behind us. There wasn't time to look at him the way we wanted to. I started counting when it was my turn, stared into his face like I never had while he was alive — I felt really bad about that, I missed my chance to know him — and when I got to thirty, I walked away. My mom came up next. She opened her mouth to cry, and threads of spit stretched between her lips. She collapsed and Stef was there to catch her.

Being in this family made you strong. When it was quiet in the store, we flexed our biceps for each other, bulges like balled up socks. We hauled boxes at the post office, went down stairs with teetering stacks of jeans on our shoulders, opened crates with our bare hands. Every summer, we threw ourselves under a dusty, old air conditioner, lifted it into the living room window. It's how we could pile into the car and head for Edmonton, treat guests to a banquet lunch, then watch the casket sink into the ground.

I saw Stef and Peggy talking by Reg's grave. My parents still didn't know about Reggie's girlfriend and probably never would. She wore a pillbox hat and veil, a fitted knee-length skirt, and showed a sliver of chest. Trina and I had our arms around each other, Gene was dabbing at his eyes. We ate dinner at Panda Garden. Some guests from the funeral came, too. They tried to share in our grief, but they weren't Reggie's friends or ours, and eventually it was just us again, a new family made from old parts.

I remember the drive home on that pretty little road we'd convinced our dad to take in memory of Reg — how I imagined a dirt-covered Reggie on the doorstep smelling like chemicals after my dad wondered aloud, "What if he not dead?" — and I also remember deer, they came suddenly, first one then another, then boom in the air legs up. Someone screamed. The car shook, then slowed to a stop. Was I okay? I felt jittery. A couple of seconds passed and we didn't say anything. Then Stef asked if we were all okay. I had my seatbelt on. My mom and dad did, too. I turned around. Stef and Trina seemed fine. Gene, too. All those times he refused to wear a seat belt. We were fucking lucky.

The deer was limp and brown. My dad got out and pulled it to the ditch by its hind legs. He came back in and tried to start the car. It wheezed, wouldn't start. He tried again.

"You're flooding the engine," Stef said.

He tried another four or five times, then yelled and hit the steering wheel.

"Ba, stop. It's not working." Stef said it without emotion. Or maybe out of sympathy. The deer lying in the ditch like it was sleeping.

My dad and Gene got out of the car, still in their suits. They tried the hood awhile, another tantrum from my dad when it wouldn't open. Finally, it came and they fiddled with the engine, but they didn't know a thing about cars. An hour went by. Still nothing had happened with the car, and it was getting dark, and no one had driven by. It was a bad idea going on that road. We didn't know then how little traffic there'd be. My dad got up and walked to the ditch. His feet were near the deer and I was afraid he was gonna fall in. "Hey Stef," he called, "why not I go?"

Stef had gone out to the field, we thought to take a piss, and after a while I'd forgotten she was there. "Where?" she said.

He said he thought there was a house a few miles back.

"When did you last eat?"

"Well, suppertime."

"And how long ago was that?"

"Yah, I know, but otherwise we just sit here do nothing. No use."

My mom's lips moved like she wanted to say something, but she never did, and my dad kept offering to go to that house, as if it were a new idea. Knowing him, I guessed he was forecasting to a time when there wouldn't be food when he was hungry. Still, Stef shut him down when he offered, and other times, too, when he didn't.

"You better not be going, Ba!" Stef yelled from the field from time to time. Stef wouldn't let any of us go — the reason was, she'd recently seen on the news about a guy whose head got lopped off while he was walking on the side of the road at night. It seemed reasonable enough. Still, we were antsy. "What's your rush?" she said, when Gene tried sneaking off. It was like she had sonar. "It's a nice night. Plus, this has never happened before, us sleeping outside." She said it like it was some epic thing.

"You do it all the time," Trina said.

"Yeah, but we've never done it together. It'd be fun if you didn't stress. Forage some food, eat off the land ..."

"What if we went through the fields instead?" Gene said.

"Are you crazy?" Stef said. "You can't see a thing out here. There could be bear traps or electric fences. You could trip. May as well wait till morning."

I agreed. I thought it might be fun to stay the night, and hard times were part of the experience.

Stef told us about the flashlights in the trunk. "Shine one around," she said. "Someone will see it and get us." We did what she said — I went first — and it was awkward. I stood with the dead deer a couple of feet away. Everyone yelled out the car doors, telling me how to do it like I was a little kid who didn't know anything. But *I* knew what to do. I started screaming for help, so loud they closed the doors. Then I was alone.

I thought of Reggie. I wondered where he was — his mind or soul, I mean — and if he'd had a good life. The night was both opening and closing around me, my arms were getting tired. Highway 117 was a quiet way to go. Too quiet. I kept half-expecting, half-fearing headlights approaching on the horizon or someone else with a flashlight. Sometimes I thought I saw these things, but it never panned out. It was always some illusion instead, a car at the junction too far away to see us. I imagined us killed by wolves, murderers, monsters, wondered if Reggie had a ghost, and if so, would it want to talk. I thought I should be tough — I was in Grade Seven then, junior high — and told myself I wasn't scared, but there was no denying I was.

When everyone but Stef had had a go with the flashlight, people were saying it was my turn again, and my dad was grumbling about food. He had this idea to cut up the deer, but he didn't have a knife. "I'll bet Stef has one," I said, and went to find her. It didn't take long. She had a flashlight, too. "Stef!" I yelled when I was close enough.

"Shh!" she said.

"Dad wants a knife to cut the deer open." She was crouching on the ground. I got a little closer. "What are you doing?"

Stef started to walk again. She had something that looked like grass in her hand. I followed her for a little while till she bent down and started ripping things out of the ground.

"What are you doing?"

"Getting salad."

I wanted to ask what kind but didn't want to sound dumb. Soon we came upon a bush. She was excited. She picked something from it, then put it directly into her mouth.

"What's that?" I asked.

"Berries."

"How do you know they're not poison?"

"I just do," she said. Wanted me to eat some, too, but I wasn't sure.

"I'll have one," I said. It was smaller than a pea and sweet. I was scared but I ate more. Later, she told me that blue berries are usually good, white berries are usually poison, and with red berries, you have a fifty-fifty chance. She had me hold the greens while she picked berries. I was uneasy, thought the greens could've been poison. What if they were poison ivy? "Are you sure this stuff is okay to eat?" I said.

"Chris, it's sweet gale and wood sorrel. I've been taking Outdoor Ed for two years. I got a hundred per cent in foraging. Will you relax?"

We went back to the car with a hat full of berries and two handfuls of greens. No one would touch her salad, not even me, but she, my dad, and I ate the berries. I was proud of my sense of adventure. Stef said it felt great to eat something you foraged for yourself, and I could see she had a point. My dad, though, made a fuss about the lack of food. He thought it'd be easy to make a fire and cook the whole deer.

"If you want to stay up for another few hours, okay," Stef said. "But we'd have to find enough wood, cut a leg off, make a spit, then start a fire. It'd probably take a couple hours to cook. I don't think we should do all that, do you? This isn't crown land. You can't just start fires wherever you want."

"Oh?" my dad said, surprised.

Stef didn't say how she knew how long it'd take to cook the deer, but later she told me that she and Josh McMurtry had spit-roasted them quite a few times while camping. My dad found a jar of nuts in the trunk and calmed down, got tired, lost the gumption to walk alone on the highway at night. Still not a single car had passed.

Stef collected branches from a nearby thicket of trees and made a lean-to in the field. I helped, but went back to the car when we were done. "There's room for two or three more," she called out, but no one got out of the car to join her. I sat in the front between my parents, thinking of Reg and the deer on the road. I watched the spot in the field where Stef lay. She didn't seem to be afraid of anything. Hard to believe that there are people like that. Quite a few of them. It's kind of inspiring.

13

✳

SUNDAY MORNING, MY DAD wakes me up by turning on the light, finding my leg under the blankets, and yanking.

Bolt upright. "What do you want?!" I yell without thinking.

"Want to learn to drive?" he asks.

No, I don't. Not at all. But he's grinning.

"Fine. Yeah. Okay," I say.

DRIVING IS A BIG deal in my family. We all learned how, even my mom, which is weird, since she's so afraid of everything. You know I've never even seen her drive?

My dad made her learn five years ago, after he'd hit black ice and the guardrail on Taimi Road Turn. He was on his way home from delivering stuff to Mary-Beth Erickson, a customer who was too fat to walk, and was lucky no one else was in the car. My dad came home frazzled, rubbing his head and suggesting my mom learn to drive. "For future," he said.

My mom said, "I don't have to learn. You're here. Why would I learn?"

That shut him up then, but he brought it up again every chance he got: during dinner, while she washed the dishes, while they watched TV, while reading a story in the newspaper with stats on women drivers, on weekend trips to Edmonton, during a TV show where a woman was driving, and sometimes in bed for no reason at all. Their voices in the dark, us laughing. *Give it a rest, Ba.*

It took three months but eventually she caved. She started going to classes at the high school every Wednesday afternoon and was the oldest person there by decades. My dad drove her there, paid for Stef to go, too, even though she'd already passed the test. Stef was there to help out — all those strangers — and also so my mom wouldn't cut class or get lost. That's how important it was for him that she learn to drive.

I wish I could have been there. Her first class in anything in close to thirty years, her writing faster and messier than I've ever seen it, her awkwardness with the high school kids that made up the rest of the class, her not knowing what to do when she didn't understand the teacher — and Stef a skinny security blanket who looked like my mom, only forty years younger and ten times more social. I picture her easy grace in those classes, think of her slouching and not paying attention, making small talk with kids a year younger than her, kids she might not have even known. Having a bit of fun. She was one year away from the end of her life. Imagine being that close and not knowing.

Stef sometimes went when my mom practised driving, reminding her of things they'd learned in class like the hours of a playground zone and how you're supposed to stop three seconds at a stop sign. But mostly my mom practised after dinner with my dad. I kept trying to come along, but I wasn't allowed. My mom can be real proud of herself. She goes on about how quick her hands and eyes are, about the classics she read in high school, she gets excited talking about her school days, about all her classmates who became professors or lawyers. She wanted us to be doctors, wanted each of us to have the best marks in our year, as if all it took was will. But it's easy to succeed at everything when you never try anything new, let alone something you might fail at. It would have been nice to see her be worse than one of us at something for a change.

MY DAD AND I meet outside five minutes later. Eight a.m. I'm still half-asleep. It's windy and too warm for November. Low grey clouds you could reach up and touch. Across the alley, cinder block apartments painted white. Crabgrass, puke, wild roses.

I wake as soon as I get behind the wheel, the car enclosing us like the fist of a giant. I do what my dad says, back straight out, turn sharp, then go. Dread in every move — but also delight. There's an arena parking lot four blocks from our house where all the kids in my family — and probably my mom — learned how to drive. It's closed for construction, though, so we drive away, end up in a field near the bike path. I try a parallel park by the trees. He doesn't ask me to, I just think it'd be fun to know how. I get it wrong twice, and when I get it right, he gets out. I open the window. "What are you doin'?" I say.

"Well, I go home." The car's still running.

"Home?" I say. "But you asked if I wanted to learn to drive."

"Wah, I go home, watch de news, make breakfast. Yo mudder —"

"What, you're just going to leave me here?"

"Sure! I come back long about elaven." And with that he walks away. I watch him shrink with distance. Why learn to drive when you can walk everywhere you need to go?

I put the seat back and pop a tape in. The car is a mobile karaoke unit. New Order's *Substance* came out when I was seven years old, but it still sounds fresh. "Blue Monday" comes on, a driving song if there ever was one. I bring the seat up, shift the car back into drive. An empty field — what could go wrong? I press the gas and lurch into trees, turn hard and the back end slides pinging into low-hanging twigs. I right the car somehow and cruise the edge of the field, bob my head to the music. The first two minutes of the song are artificial, synths and drum machines, sad and happy at the same time. I'm driving, like Trina is driving. I whip another shitty — it's deliberate this time, something she does, too. Ice in the Yukon. While I'm singing, I whip another shitty, and something thunks against the car. Oh no. Shit. I shift to reverse, back up, and it thumps again. Ruts? I get out. Grey. The forecast calls for rain. On the ground is a twitching red thing. Behind me, a different red thing. Fur on both. I used to be fascinated by dead animals — roadkill, dead squirrels on the sidewalk — but it's different when you killed it. I get back in the car and try to collect my thoughts. I press the gas and poof, something else dies. Impossible but true.

Is there someone to call in the event of half-dead animals? I get out and start walking. Walking can't kill anyone, can it? Fuck. Bugs. Stef would have known what to do. I walk fast. The path: asphalt paved, trees on both sides, winding. It's busy. People keep saying hi to me. They don't know I'm a danger. I turn at the junction, cross the highway to the north service road. Fuck. I watch my feet for bugs, look up, see the Petro-Can sign, walk towards it.

He told me to call him. Phone book. What was his last name? Marsch. Four rings, then a woman answers. "Hello?" she says. Her voice is groggy.

"I'm sorry to bother you so early in the morning, but is Conrad home?"

"Yeah. It's fine. We should be getting up for church, anyway. I'll go get him."

A minute passes, then, "Hello?" His voice even sleepier than hers.

"Umm ..." I say.

"Hi!" he says energetically, though his voice is still gravelly. We laugh. "Just had a dream about you, I think."

I don't want to see him. *You need to talk to someone.* "How soon can you leave the house?"

"Uhh ... pretty soon?"

"Can you meet me at Petro-Can?"

"Yeah. My mom lives down the road. I can be there in, like, ten minutes?"

"See you. And fuck, I have a story to tell."

I grab a corner table, order an orange pop, and look out the window as I drink. Grey. A few cars and trucks go up and down the highway. Little bells on the door. Every time they ring I turn to look.

Eventually he shows. His face lights up when he sees me, not in an obvious way, but you can tell by someone's eyes if they like you. "Hi, Chrysler," he says when he's close enough, all gentle. He chucks me lightly on the arm, then sees my face. "What's wrong?"

Sorrow makes a hollow in my chest. "I don't want to talk about it," I say.

I get the bill and pay. We go outside, start walking. "What should we do?" he says.

"We just left the only good place that's open. How much time you got?"

"A few hours."

"What, you're not going to church?" I'm teasing, my smile and tone of voice. I do everything but laugh in his face. Church.

"Look at me like that again," he says.

It's actually kind of cool, this science geek loyal to his church-going mom. I ask about his parents, and he tells me his dad cheated for more than two years, and that it really fucked up his mom. She tried to bring him in for couples counselling, but he wouldn't go, kept cheating.

"Uhh, but you live with your dad. That's … weird, isn't it?"

He nods. "My dad's rich. He got a good lawyer."

"Sorry," I say.

"Why are you sorry?"

"I guess it can't be easy." He shrugs.

We stop at the Red Mart for snacks — Josh McMurtry isn't there — then we go through the industrial area, past the water tower, down the hill of Fifty-Third, through Old Town and the new subdivision. It doesn't take long to see most of it. At some point, we wind back up on the highway.

Conrad points and says, "What's that?"

It's Joe Play's, a half-finished amusement park built by the Meers. When Gary Brown sued them for food poisoning, they ran out of money, stopped construction in the middle, though I hear the rides work. An amusement park is a good idea in theory — people love the midway when it comes to town with the rodeo — but Spring Hills is cold nine months of twelve and too close to the mountains for tourists to want to stay long.

Conrad and I walk in the gate, past a cracked red booth with yellow marquee bulbs and white plastic signs reading TICKETS in old-timey letters. Behind it are three and a half unloved and rusty monsters — a Ferris wheel, some bumper cars, a roller coaster, and an unfinished ride we called the Arms — about to be abused by more rain. They're all pastel coloured and covered in pathetic graffiti: *BLOOD KILLER, COP KILLER, CRIPS*. Garbage cans on their sides, chip bags and beer bottles, abandoned clothes half-hidden in tall grass. Near the Ferris wheel we see Mo Meer and his daughter Aabidah, who I know from school. Mo hauls up a lumpy garbage bag and stuffs it into the trunk of his Chevette. Aabidah sweeps at the dirt and grass, picks up a crumpled pop can with two gloved fingertips and tosses it into a bag.

"It's a mess down here, eh, Mr. Meer?" I say.

He looks up, says to Conrad, "Have you come to mess up my park?"

"No, Mr. Meer," I say. "We're just passing through."

"Please leave," he says, and Aabidah looks at me apologetically. Her dark eyes and thick lashes — she's pretty, even though she looks like her dad.

"See ya," I say to her.

At the edge of the park, Conrad vaults over the metal bar fence, a character in a video game, while I squat down and squeeze through. After ten feet, he crouches down, digs into the snow to uncover some plants, then lovingly cradles some in his hand and says, "This is edible."

I look at him.

"Well, it won't taste great now," he says, "but when it's alive? White sweet clover. Put some in a salad. You will fucking love it."

I tell him about Stef, how they probably had some things in common, then quiz him on the names of all the plants that will grow here come spring. For all I know he could be making them up: shepherd's purse, lamb's quarters, woolly lousewort. Cows in a nearby field, trees further away. Wind messing up our hair. Cold, wet, red hands.

"So what do you think of Spring Hills?" I say.

"Eckville doesn't have a half-finished amusement park."

"What's it like there?"

"I don't know. Like any small town. Nothing to write home about."

"Yeah, but every place has a story, don't you think? Like, the place we went to last week, Marlene's, has amazing soup, better than anything I've ever had in Edmonton."

"Yeah. Nothing like that in Eckville."

"But every town has a feeling. What's Eckville feel like?"

"Boring, shitty, depressing. I've been in Eckville my whole life. It's like, close your eyes."

I do what he says.

"Okay, now describe your hands."

"They're small, a little bony. I like the lines on my palms, on the fronts and backs of my fingers. I like my nails. The one on my left ring finger curves weird. I've got scars, cooking accidents. I could go on."

"But you like your hands, right?"

"Yeah."

"See, I don't like mine at all. You know them well enough, they become boring. I like seeing new things. All these towns are the same."

"I wanna see new things, too, but this town is a part of me. If I woke up tomorrow in some other place and someone said I couldn't come back here, it'd mess me up."

"Couldn't you leave, then come back, then leave again, then come back again?"

"If I live past the first time I leave."

We walk towards the cows. I'm excited — never petted a cow before — till I see the electric fence, and we turn around.

When we pass Joe Play's again, Aabidah's there all alone. "Sorry about my dad," she says, glancing at graffiti on the roller coaster. "I know you're not a Crip."

"Yeah. Blue's not my colour," I say. "Uhh, we should probably go."

But she's introducing herself to Conrad now, looking into his eyes as she shakes his hand. I bet they're soft. Every time she comes back from the bathroom at school, she reapplies lotion. "My dad went to the dump," she says. "I could let you guys ride if you want."

"Really?" Conrad says.

"Well, the bumper cars are outta commission, but that still leaves the Ferris wheel and the roller coaster."

I ask Conrad which one he wants to ride. He says Ferris wheel. I look at the sky. "Could be lightning soon," I say. He says the more excitement the better and gets in. I don't.

"Don't make me ride by myself, Chrysler." He gives me this look, goofy and pleading. There's something about it.

"Okay. Fine." There's no recourse. I check the hinges. They look strong, but what do I know? I get in the car with him. It's cramped and cold.

"I'll hold your hand if you're scared," he says.

"I can hold my own hand, thanks."

Aabidah takes something from her pocket, a key, and starts the engine. The Ferris wheel rumbles and vibrates.

"Are you sure it's safe?" I say.

"Yeah," she says, casual.

We start moving, it keeps shaking. It gets windier as we go up. I look at the hinges again, the floor and sides of our car, check the safety bar. When I look out, I can see the whole town, the thick, dark stripe of highway and the roads coming off it like branches, the trashy businesses, all that white. "Cool, hey?"

"Yeah," he says, shifting in his seat.

"What's wrong?"

He's looking at his hands. "Umm. Kind of afraid of heights."

You're the one who wanted this, I almost say. "Umm, well, it was probably a thing back in caveman days to be afraid of heights, right? Like, don't go too high because you'll probably die. It's survival. We'll be fine, I think — but if we die, it was nice knowing you."

The wheel groans, slows as it reaches the top. I think of us in a movie, bits of colour in the sky, a grey backdrop. Far away, my dad's car in the field by the bike path. He might be waiting, blowing a shit fit. Or he might not have come back yet. Quarter to eleven right now.

Conrad says, "What if we get stuck up here?"

"Then someone'll have to throw sandwiches at us."

The wheel keeps going and Conrad eases up. A crow flies by really close. When I reach out for it, it caws and poos. I watch the poo drop till it's too far down to see.

"Why'd you pick the Ferris wheel if you're so afraid of heights?"

"'Cause I knew it'd look different from up here," he says, peering out. "It's cool up here, it's like we're part of the sky. All those cars down there look like they're going really slow, but they're going at least fifty, more like eighty or a hundred over there. Like, I can barely look at them, but I can't be afraid of heights forever. I gotta push myself, you know?"

We get a long ride, close to five minutes. When it's over, Aabidah asks if we wanna go for ice cream, but I've never hung out with her in my life, and three is a bad number for a hangout. "Sounds good," I say, "but I gotta meet my dad."

"Conrad?" Aabidah asks.

"Nah, I should go, too," he says. "Maybe next time?"

"Sure," she says. "Anytime."

Our arms swing as we walk down the south service road. When we graze against each other our coats make *zjoop zjoop* sounds.

"That was fun," he says. The wind in his hair.

"Yeah. That was my first time on that thing. You know, you could've stayed with her if you wanted."

"What, and miss hanging out with you? You're, like, the

best inspirational speaker I've ever met. That caveman stuff? It didn't really help, but it was interesting."

"Thanks," I say. "I really do have to meet my dad, though."

"Were you ever gonna tell me what was wrong? Seems like before you were having a bad day."

No one ever asks how my day has gone. People say, *How are you?* Most of them don't mean it. "I hit some animals in a field with my dad's car."

"Animals."

"Yeah." I tell him how it felt to hit them, what they looked like after, how I had to get out of there as soon as it happened. The whole time, he's got this real sorry look on his face.

"Did you see what kind they were?"

"I don't know. Maybe rabbits? As I said, I couldn't stay."

And then somehow, without speaking, we decide to stop walking. I close my eyes and feel him coming near but I don't move, feel his arms around me, and I can't let him, but I do. I'm afraid, so afraid, can he feel it? He draws me in deep, I should like it, they did studies on this. Without physical contact, people die. Still, I'm stiff, clenching, my arms are at my sides. Think of something else, not his smell because that's scary, maybe think of Trina, think of someone being carried by the wind, a little magic bird that's come to bring us something good, think of the wind, that thing that just fell on your head.

It's water, a drop of it. Rain.

We start running, even though my hip still hurts. We're at least a mile from the car. The sky cracks and it starts coming down in cold buckets. We pretend it's acid rain. The object of the game is to stay as dry as possible. I run under the lips of buildings, avoiding ice piles, while Conrad splashes through puddles, unafraid. Closer to the car, he asks if he can see me next Sunday. He can.

Once he leaves, the day starts to drag. I think of him as I wait. When my dad gets back he makes me drive home. I'm shaking, going extra slow, but he doesn't notice.

We stop at the post office on the way. Another letter from Trina in our box. I sneak it into my pocket, put everything else — the newspaper, junk mail, other envelopes — under my arm. As soon as we get home, we have lunch, then my parents go for their daily walk. Normally I'd go with them, but this time I stay back to read the letter. It tells me things I both do and don't want to know.

Trina's having the time of her life. She had spent a mind-bending time in Kluane, where the harshness of the terrain showed her, more than anything she'd ever seen in her life, just how small she was, how magnificent the world. After that, she walked into a terrible Chinese-place-slash-pizzeria in Haines Junction, and walked out with a travelling companion. She's going to Dawson City with her now. Her name is Billy. Apparently, she's fun — troubled but good company. And smart. *She knows random facts just like you do, Chris*, Trina writes.

I feel my stomach fall out of my body.

14

I'VE OFTEN THOUGHT I had an attractive family. Trina's bold and in your face. She has nice eyes, good style, this smile she practised in the mirror but didn't have to. Gene was funny, wild, and dangerous. He had these really intense eyes and a tall, lean, strong build. Me and Reggie were the worst: plain, I guess, a little nerdy. Not bad, though.

Stef was somewhere in the middle — smart without being a geek, pretty without the mass appeal. Good personality, too. Her friend Josh McMurtry was crazy about her, used to send flowers every few months with those little cards attached. His pathetic handwriting and skipping ballpoint pen. Merry Christmas. Happy birthday. Happy Thanksgiving. Stef took the cards off the flowers as soon as they arrived. My dad asked me a few times where they came from, but I'd seen enough of him yelling at all of us for no reason to tell him.

She didn't like Josh back. He was just a friend. Old Josh McMurtry, whose parents own the Red Mart. A sweet guy, all in all, but I guess Stef just never saw him that way. Nature and her family were her real loves. Most of her time she spent working in the store, studying, reading wilderness and survival guides, and hanging out with us. The rest of the time, whenever she could get away without rousing suspicion, she was camping. Josh McMurtry was a camper, too. They'd bring their guitars to the mountains and sing country duets by the fire. "Louisiana Woman, Mississippi Man." "Sweet Thang." "Islands in the Stream." At home, she'd sing along to Trina's tapes in that *la la la* way you do when you don't know a song so well. She especially liked boy-girl songs. "The harmonies are sweeter when a guy and girl sing together," she said. I agreed.

The summer after she graduated, Stef, Josh, and a bunch of their friends went on a trip to Bull River to pitch tents a few miles before the falls. There's a campground near there, but Stef was known to say campgrounds were worse than cheap motels. She was all about the authentic experience. I think of them hiking and fishing, Stef with her pocket plant guide, Josh hunting with his crossbow, a deer, giant Flintstone drumsticks. We had to lie to our dad about it. She said she was going for school, which didn't make sense, since the trip was after graduation, but my dad still doesn't know how school works here, and that's a thing you can exploit if you have to.

When we got the call about Stef, I was scooping rice for supper. Black things in the pot of white rice, little skinny brown bugs that found their way into the bag in the hall. My dad made beef and greens that night, lots of leftovers. Trina answered the phone, didn't know who it was at first. Then she figured out. My dad told her to set the table. She didn't even flinch.

"When'd it happen?" she said, then listened, hand curved around the mouthpiece.

What was going on? I filled the bowls little by little so I could take out all the bugs, and my dad brought a pot of soup to the table. Gene funky-danced into the room, past Trina, past me, but I wasn't feeling it. He stopped at the table, picked a strip of beef from the plate, dangled it into his mouth, and sat down.

"Lui la," my dad said to Trina. *Come on.*

I grabbed chopsticks, bone plates, and spoons, everything in multiples of five, and set the table. Trina still on the phone. My mom — fresh out of the shower, extra-long strands of hair poised to drop into her food — sat down, the grunt-squeak of her chair.

My dad turned to Trina. "Kut cheng hee," he said. His impatience. "Talk talk talk."

"Did you call the cops?" Trina said. "Is everyone else still at the river?"

I finished scooping the last bowl — mine — and sat down, ears on her conversation. She wasn't saying much. I took some beef, shovelled rice into my mouth and my mouth was instantly itchy. Allergies, I guess. "Wow. It's good," I said to my dad. "You want some water?" He didn't answer, he was stewing, so I got up and came back with water, then went back to the kitchen for more.

When Trina asked how far their campsite was from the falls, my dad started freaking out. It's funny when you think of what he's actually saying — *I'll stone your entire family to death, I'll stab you* — but in the moment, it was a pile of shit. Put us all on edge, and why?

Trina covered the mouthpiece. "Can you shut the fuck up? They lost Stef in the river."

Gene stood up. "What do you mean?"

"Josh McMurtry threw her in the river."

"Is she —"

"I don't know. They called Search and Rescue."

I put the water down, and Gene and I went for the door. My mom stood, too, lost in her own little world. Who knows what she was thinking? My dad was confused. We had to explain a few times before he understood.

"Where are you now?" Trina said into the phone. A pause.

"Okay. We'll meet you." She hung up. "Come on, Ba," she said. We all went downstairs. Gene insisted on driving, said my dad would go too slow. Gene's brand new licence.

At the bottom of the stairs, my dad said, "If Gene drive, I not go."

"You don't want to go?" I said. I was worried about Gene. He was okay then — in retrospect it'd be weeks till his next bout — but you never knew. Plus, two hours each way is a lot of driving.

My dad shook his head. His red face. He looked like how he does when he's in insulin shock.

"How about you, Mom?"

She was quiet, looked down, held her thin right arm with her bony left hand, maybe thinking *Why the fuck is my life so sad?* as she followed us out.

We burned down Highway 11, met the guy who'd called — Josh's friend Mark Jorgenson — in Nordegg, and followed him to the river. A loud *fip fip fip* noise when we got out of the car. A helicopter. Sunshine. It was a nice place — trees, boulders, mountains, water, sky. We walked downstream till we saw guys in helmets and coveralls, zip lines. A cop there said there wasn't much for us to do besides look out for her on shore. They gave us supplies, split us into groups of two — my mom and Trina, Gene and me — and told us to head downstream.

Along the way there were guys in T-shirts and shorts. One of them was screaming Stef's name, pacing up and down the bank. It was Josh. Gene ran at him, lunged, pinned him down, started punching. My mom stood off at the side as Trina and I and some of Josh's friends jumped in, tried holding them apart. Josh had a few inches and thirty pounds on him, but wasn't fighting back. A bunch of us were hanging off Gene, but he kept at it. Josh had it coming. I let go. Trina went between them. "Gene!" she said, her voice higher than mine. "That's not gonna help us find her. Gene!" He shoved her out of the way, but Trina — who was fourteen then, and small and strong like my mom — is brave when she wants to be. All it took was one kick and Gene fell to the ground. "Fucking idiot," she said. Then, to Josh: "You're fucking dead if something happened to her." She stormed off with my mom, who walked behind her, uneasy.

I DOUBT ANYONE SOBER would have done what Josh did. Maybe they were horsing around. Was Stef kicking and screaming? Was she laughing? At what point did it stop being fun? She didn't love Josh. He loved her. He threw her in. Stef once told me they used to have swimming contests to see who could go fastest or furthest, and usually she won. She could have been a Barracuda — her long hands and height. But the current still swept her up.

From where Gene and I stood, I could hear the falls in the distance. Besides a couple of tubing and canoeing trips with Nancy, I'd never spent much time near the water. I couldn't tell if it was going fast or slow and I didn't know a thing about rescue protocol. Five minutes in, I saw something float by and was sure it was her. "Did you see that?" I asked Gene. He hadn't. I called in on my walkie-talkie. "Hi," I said into it. "I'm at Checkpoint D, and I just saw something go by."

The guy on the other end said they'd alert some of the guys downstream from us, and he'd tell me whether or not my lead checked out. It didn't. Your eyes can play tricks on you in a situation like that. Before long, I started seeing more things that looked like her. Something would go by, I would stare at it, and it would end up being a piece of driftwood or an optical illusion in the water, a drawn-out current. Wishful thinking.

One time I saw something sleek and long. It had to be her. No, it was brown and had a tail. I didn't know what it was, maybe a beaver. I'd never seen a beaver before.

There was a path behind us. I kept my eye on that, too. I wanted to know what the workers were up to and in what ways they were prepared to find my sister. Around ten minutes after I'd called in on my walkie-talkie, one of the hardhat guys came walking down the path soaking wet. He looked up, saw I was watching, didn't change his expression at all. I thought of Stef in the water clutching a rock, guys in hardhats swimming out to her, tossing her a rope like a lasso.

A couple of minutes later I saw something in the corner of my eye, someone familiar with long dark hair. It was only Trina, coming up to me to switch spots. The plan was to trade off every twenty minutes, one by one, to keep our eyes fresh. I looked for something in her face, some hidden happiness. *I've got a secret for you*, I wanted her to say, like maybe she'd found Stef and for some reason hadn't said anything to the guys, like maybe Stef was sitting on a stump somewhere, wrapped in a blanket, shivering but fine. Trina put her arms around me. I wanted her to say something.

She said, "Chris, what are we gonna do?"

I didn't know. I got on the path and walked downstream. The falls got louder and louder. Up close, they were amazing, white and hard like ice, a one hundred foot drop. My mom was there, a good four feet from the edge of the valley. It was just like her not to take a risk, even in the hopes of saving her own kid. But I understood her point.

I went past her and peered down. She said, "Mo kei gum mai," *Don't stand so close*, but I couldn't obey. I could see the river had been way bigger once, or that there had been a glacier. The bottom of the falls was surrounded by a deep round crevasse like a bowl. The sound of the water was clear, like thousands of crisp sheets of paper being crumpled all at once, over and over through an amp, or marbles clattering while someone made K and C noises – *kuh kuh kuh kuh kuh*. I thought the sound would make me crazy, but you can get used to anything, even danger.

I imagined Stef being carried by the water. Would she be alive or dead? I'd heard of people going over Niagara Falls in a barrel. Had they lived? I didn't know.

They wanted us to stay at the top of the falls. It wasn't a bad place to be, but it seemed too far from the action, so when Gene showed up, we climbed down together. I've always been bad at going down hills, so I held his hand as we went. I thought he'd say something to make me feel bad — I was thirteen and old enough to take care of myself — but he didn't. The mist was like backwards rain, upsplash from the falls, and it pelted us so hard I thought I'd lose my balance. It was all slope and no flat bank at the bottom. It was slippery. Gene with his arm out across the front of my shoulders so I wouldn't fall in. It was kind of an asshole thing to do — patronizing, plus he wasn't as strong as he used to be — but it made me feel safer.

Through the mist, I saw something move that wasn't water. I walked around a bit on the slope, changed my angle to get a better view. It took a minute to understand: rescue workers going in and out of the cave behind the falls. How many of them were there and what were they doing? I felt a tap on my shoulder and turned around. "You shouldn't be down here," the worker said. "It's dangerous."

"Sorry," I said. "I wanted a better view."

Back at the top of the falls, Gene and I stared out at the water, not talking because the falls were loud. Sometimes it seemed like he wasn't present, like the things he saw weren't penetrating. This dull-eyed look on his face sometimes. We waited for news but nothing came, and soon went back upstream to switch places with our mom and Trina. They looked tired. We went back and forth seven or eight more times, we set up camping chairs at our lookout stations and ate our cookies and energy bars.

Dusk fell and they still hadn't found her.

After two more changeovers, the workers started telling us we should leave. I asked one of them how much longer the search would go. He said you can't really see much in the dark.

"So you're gonna leave?" I said.

"A couple of us will stay behind. We might get lucky. Occasionally, it happens that a person goes missing for a while then turns up alive. But at this point — I'm not gonna lie to you — at this point, it's more likely retrieval."

"What do you mean?"

"I mean we're probably looking for a body. You can't survive long in water this cold. A couple of hours if you're lucky."

I didn't move. Grey light on my shoes, on the rocks.

"It's dark," he said. "There's a better chance of you falling in, and it'd be hard for us to pull you out."

So we sat in the car. I shut my eyes thinking about the chances, but Trina said that anything was possible. Gene, in the driver's seat, kept flipping the sun visor, kept putting his hands through his hair and gripping like he wanted to rip it out. Waterfall sound in the night, the clock said 9:28.

"She's a good swimmer," Trina said from the front seat.

"Yeah," I said. "Could've made the Barracudas."

"Still can. Tryouts in September. Kirk's sister said." Only Stef was supposed to be moving to Edmonton in under two weeks.

The workers set up a few lights outside. I saw silhouettes coming towards us, the nubby tops of hard hats, two people carrying toolboxes and backpacks with lengths of rope looped over their shoulders. They stopped at their truck, next to our car. I heard one of them laugh. He talked friendly to the other guy, said something about Cancun as he threw his rope in the back of the truck.

"So Gene," Trina said. "Tracy Lawson?" Kirk's sister had a thing for Gene.

Extended cab. Internal lights on. The Cancun guy was young and in his twenties, cute.

"It's pretty nice out here," Trina said. "They picked a good spot."

"Yeah," I said. "I heard Stef talk about this place a few times. She said there'd been bear attacks." I looked at my mom. She was looking out the window, hands in her lap. I put my hand on top of hers. Hot bones. "They said the chances weren't great," I said to Trina. "I don't think they think she's —"

"She was in Outdoor Ed for four years. You know, they teach survival in that class — how to make a fire without matches, what plants to eat." Trina popped her seat back. "You got enough room?" she asked.

"Yah," my mom said. "Yah, I do."

"Those energy bars were weird," I said. I asked my mom if she ate one. She said she had a bite. I said, "Lei ho noi mo sic yeh."

"I don't have mood to eat," she said.

Gene: "Do you think we're gonna find anything out tonight?"

Trina: "I don't know. Kind of thought we'd stay the night."

"Maybe we should eat," he said. "Anyone hungry?"

I pictured Stef in the river in the dark. She was probably less than ten miles from where we were. I rolled the window down, and the water got louder. I rolled the window back up.

Gene said, "Dad's probably worried."

No one replied. The clock said 9:34. I looked out the window and locked the door.

Trina said, "Do you remember the time Stef got lost?" That was more than ten years before, when Trina was three or four, but she asked like she remembered. Maybe she did.

I'd heard the story before from Gene. When Stef was seven she started wandering off, going on adventures. First time it happened, my parents lost their shit. My dad frantically searched the store, house, and basement before driving off to search town. He was gone for hours and had forgotten to eat so his sugar level dropped. He almost collapsed in the Dairy Burger parking lot on his way to a bacon double cheese and cone. The whole time he was gone, my mom ran around the store, fretting and serving customers, worried and useless, not looking for Stef at all. A cop came and started questioning everyone, and it was in the middle of that that Stef walked in, wondering what the fuss was about.

"I'll never forget," Gene said. "She was holding this bag of chips, only it wasn't chips, it was ants."

They were those big ones. She kept them in a box with sand and sugar, but within a day or two, they all got free.

"Yeah," Trina said. "They were on me. You know how sometimes you feel something on you, and you look and there's nothing there? This time there was. A big fucking ant. It freaked me out. I had to sleep on the couch."

My mom was looking down, but you could tell she was listening. Gene's soft eyes in the rearview. He was smiling. "That was the first time," he said. "She kept going after that, she'd come back and tell me about a bird she saw or a flat squirrel in the middle of the street. We got used to her leaving. She left during a —"

There was tapping at the window. Josh McMurtry. The nerve

of that guy, showing his face. He brought friends with him, held something in his hands. It was football-sized, shiny, multi-faceted like a metal gemstone.

Gene cracked his window. "Yeah?"

It was foil. "We thought you guys would be hungry," Josh said. "We got some leftover meat and potatoes. Thought we'd bring some over."

Gene didn't say anything. Three or four guys, two girls, all of them expecting some kind of response, but he just let them hang.

"Gene," Trina said.

Josh: "Well, do you want it?"

"Gene, I'm hungry," Trina said.

The closest town was Nordegg. We could've been there in forty-five minutes. But the restaurant would be closed, if there was a restaurant. Two hundred people.

I rolled down my window. "I'll take it," I said, and Josh passed the package to me. It was cold. "Thanks," I said.

Trina called out the window. "Are you sure you guys have enough?"

"Yeah," one of them said. "It was a big doe. There's lots."

That was a joke. We didn't laugh. Trina asked if they were staying the night.

"Yeah," Josh said. "There might be something for us to do."

Gene thanked him for the food, then closed his window and said something under his breath I couldn't hear. They were still standing there.

"Thanks," I said again out my window. "Really. Thanks." I was mad at Josh, worse than mad, but hunger has a way of making you do things you wouldn't normally do. The meat was tough but tasted okay. For a while, the only sounds, besides the river and the wind, were of chewing. I watched Trina in the dark. She's a dainty eater, held her sandwich with her finger-tips. I gave my mom my potatoes because she doesn't like meat. We borrowed one of the rescue workers' phones and called my dad, told him we'd be staying the night. His voice was faraway and quiet. He never sounded that way in his whole life. What a night to be alone.

We fell asleep. When I woke for good it was dawn. My mom, closed eyes, open mouth, leaned against the door. Trina's head was back, her sleeping face exposed in the yellow morning light.

I got out of the car. The door whined, and I closed it behind me as softly as I could and went down to the river. Gene was there. He looked out at the water, arms crossed, holding himself. It was cold. I walked towards him and he saw me.

"They showed me this chart," he said over the river. "It was a graph, the amount of time someone has been missing against the chance of recovery."

"What do you think we should do?" I said.

"Eighteen hours she's been gone. The river only goes one way. There's nothing to do. She's either gone or has reached land and is waiting to be found. I say leave it to the pros."

I didn't want to do that, but it made sense. None of us had the survival or tracking skills needed to find someone in the woods. We'd probably just get lost ourselves.

"If anyone could survive out here, it's Stef," Gene said, look-ing at my feet. "You, Reg, and her — you're the smart ones in the family." It was like he was thinking out loud. I wondered if he'd miss me if I were the one who was gone. He picked up a stone and threw it into the water. "The only thing I can fault her on is her friends."

What do you say in a situation like that? *Sorry* is weak, you need something at least four or five times stronger. *I can't believe it*? No. That's for when you're buying gas and you see it's ten cents more than you thought it'd be. *I can't believe it's not butter.* If only there was a word that could bring someone back, a word that could turn back time.

"You never know," I said.

He looked at me, then at the water. We found a spot and sat. I looked at the sky and imagined flying away, then realized I didn't want to do that, so then I thought about why the sky was blue. I'd read the explanation recently. The bushes moved. Stef? Hope rose in me, but it was only Trina and my mom. I looked at Gene and knew he had felt the exact same thing. When they got closer he told them what he told me, that we should go, but Trina refused. We went on a twisty little walk in the woods and ended up upstream fifty feet from where we started, trees on one side, water on the other. It was quiet, birds, early morning sun. We didn't say much. There wasn't much to say.

Sometime in the late morning, we decided to leave. Checked in with a couple of rescue guys still at the site, who said there was no news and that we could go. We were quiet the whole way home, gliding down the highway in my dad's Oldsmobile, edging away from the mountains, the trees, the bighorn sheep and deer on the sides of roads that cut through rocks, the little waterfalls you pass on your way to wherever you're going, the natural sounds and peace, the beavers, otters, weasels, whatever, the birds and the green lake, the river that had taken Stef, all the beautiful things that continue on when you leave, that don't care if you're gone, back to your town in the middle of nowhere of autobody shops and farmers and fast food joints and convenience stores and drugs, only it's not nowhere because you stop there, you live there, you belong there, so it's somewhere. Close to the mountains, not close enough. I vowed to move to the mountains as soon as I could. After university, I guessed.

It was a Monday, and we still had school. We got back in time for last period. Gene and Trina both went to John Palliser, so they could walk, but I was in Grade Eight, going to Ridgemore, so my dad gave me a ride. In the car, he was quiet, but the quiet felt different. He didn't talk about Stef that day, and almost never did after that, even though she was his favourite, she and Trina. Who knows what was going on for him? It had also been more than a year since he last mentioned Reg around me. Over time, I came to realize that as soon as someone was gone, my dad stopped talking about them.

When I showed up at school, everyone already knew. Someone's dad or brother might have been a part of the rescue crew, or knew someone who was. What a thing, people knowing something like that without you ever having told them, without you even knowing how they know. In Social Studies, while Ms. Jesperson told us about Japan — the honesty and pride of people there, the low crime rate, kids killing themselves if they didn't get into the right school — people whispered. "Two in a row," I heard somebody say.

No one talked to me on the bus ride home, and I walked home alone from my stop. Cars drove by oblivious, or else the drivers knew and were unsympathetic, or they were sympathetic, just not in the way I wanted them to be. How did I want them to be? No way, I just wanted my sister back. I went upstairs, tired. I wanted company. I used to lie on the couch after school, watching TV, *Today's Special* or *The Urban Peasant*. I'd fall asleep and wake in time for dinner, but it struck me then as a lonely way to spend time.

We'd all been through a lot and I thought we'd bonded, or had gotten through it because we were close-knit, but when I passed the boys' room, I saw a new knob. A lock. I knocked. Through the door, Gene told me to go away.

"Y'okay, Gene?"

"Go away," he said again.

But I needed someone to be with. Trina was out somewhere. My dad hadn't been at the river, and he wouldn't know how to be. Neither would my mom. Stef would have been great. She was good company, often lent a new perspective on things and gave good advice. Sometimes we'd just sit and not talk at all, or just very little, about things unrelated to what was bothering me. Usually, though, I'd pour it all out. She'd comfort me, maybe take me out for ice cream.

Music started playing behind Gene's door. Industrial music: loud, fast guitars, shouting. Our rooms were right beside each other and when I went to bed, his music pounded through the wall. Gene didn't come out for dinner that night, though one by one we all tried to convince him. My dad started yelling, banged on the door for five minutes. Gene opened up and growled back, "Leave me alone!" then shoved my dad, who fell into some chairs. Gene should have had some sympathy — my dad was sixty-seven, old, and there was all that stuff with Stef — but my dad should've had some, too. Years of dishing it out, I guess it was time for him to take it.

TWO WEEKS AFTER STEF went missing, we got a call. They found a body, and had to check dental records to figure out who it was.

"Sorry we didn't find her earlier," the guy on the other side said.

Of course, we sort of knew by then, but we had our hopes. That she was walking home from the falls and would come in the front door, the same way she did as a kid. Or that she'd gone rogue, was tired of taking care of us all and needed a break. That she was living off the land. But we knew, and I felt bad. Her whole life she spent taking care of us, she only needed one thing in return, and we couldn't give it.

Still, I wonder how she felt about dying. I don't mean, *Did she want to die?* Of course she didn't. But I wonder if she feared it, if she was okay with it. Some people aren't afraid. They say things like, *Well, if it's my time, I guess I have no choice,* or *I've lived a full life. If I had to go, at least I have no regrets.* I could see Stef being that way. At least, I hope she was.

15

✳

MONDAY MORNING, I FINISH my contest essay and drop it off with Mac before heading to Math. In the end, I wrote a lot about Trina. I hadn't actually used her name, I made up a character, then imagined her in a variety of travel destinations. New York, China, a tropical beach, the North. A cool first-person sort of thing. I wrote that travel changes your perspective on things, but perspective is all it changes. You're still the same person inside, and you'd be a fool to think you can go somewhere new and try to be someone else. It'll always come out, who you really are. Mostly I sugar-coated my opinion on things. I'm not dumb. I want to win, and winning essays go in the travel section of the newspaper, which exists to sell fantasies and plane tickets and resort and tour packages. You have to make travel sound appealing. *The sky is the limit.*

My real feelings: travel, leaving, is a kind of betrayal. What about the people you leave behind? You go off and they miss you, or you go and they're left to lead their boring lives and guess at what things you're experiencing that they cannot, and worry about how you're going to be crushed by an elephant or muskox, or how you're going to go off and never come back or that you'll replace the people who love you with others you could grow to love.

After class, Aabidah Meer comes prancing up asking about Conrad. *Who gives a shit?* I almost say, but instead, I walk away.

"Yeah, so," she says, following me, "I think he likes me?"

We're not friends. I'm not here. "Yeah, maybe," I say to get her off my back.

Conrad calls later that day and knows right away that something's wrong. When I don't want to talk about it, he starts guessing at what it is. He asks how school is, if my parents are okay. We agree that narwhals *are* a mindfuck. The Winter Formal is soon: I don't have a date?

"We could go," he says.

I don't say anything.

"Come on," he says. "You know you want me."

"Okay. You know what? Stop."

"I was only kidding," he says.

"Saying the same bullshit thing over and over will not make it true."

"What?"

"Nothing," I say. "I got another letter. From Trina."

"Why are you mad?"

"I have to go. I can't keep trying to talk to someone who can't relate."

"No offence, but I don't think anyone can."

He's right. She's the only one alive who'd know how it feels. Not even her — she wasn't betrayed.

Dusty stucco ceiling, bare bulb, mint green wall with a hole covered over with duct tape. Henry Rollins, Tool, Bruce Lee posters. Gene's clothes in the closet, Reg's shirts in the dresser.

"She's with someone. This girl."

"What, travelling with her?"

"Yes. They're together. Travelling."

"Huh."

"Everything we've been through, and she abandons me to go traipsing around someplace I've always wanted to go to with some random girl. She chose her. After all we've been through."

Trina and Billy looking up at Northern Lights that take up half the sky. Good colours: purple, blue. That spooky, lonely glow. I've never seen ones like that in my life.

"Yeah, but, like," he says, then pauses, "you know you can't take it personally, right?"

"Why not?"

"It's not like she's thinking *What is the way I can hurt Chrysler the most?* before she acts, is it?"

Trina having an adventure, walking out onto ice with Billy in the half-dark like it's part of a montage scene in a romantic comedy. Trina driving up to a snow-covered lodge, the Northern Lights in the back. She gets out of the car. No one else in sight. No cars, no sounds of anyone. Lights are off in the lodge. She takes a cigarette and her little yellow lighter from her pack of DuMaurier, makes a little snowdrop of fire, melts the end of the filter, then lights the business end. She's been jonesing for a smoke, and there's no better feeling than slaking addiction. The first drag is something magic, a yes yes yes kind of moment, she starts to twirl the way she does sometimes when she's really enjoying something. She gets to a hundred and eighty degrees when she sees someone in her peripheral. She turns all the way. *Billy!* she says. *God, you're a fucking ghost or something, sneaking up on me. Or a ninja. You're a ninja.*

Yeah, sorry, Billy says, and the knife comes out of nowhere.

"Hello?" Conrad says.

Trina on the ground, motionless. Blood leaking onto snow. Billy gets in on the driver's side, almost hits Trina's body as she backs out of the parking spot.

"Hello?" he says again.

"It doesn't make sense. It's dangerous. She shouldn't have left."

"What?"

"She had everything here," I say. "My parents, money, clothes, me, good food. I understood her. Do you think Billy understands?"

"Okay, one, you can't fulfill all of a person's needs and, two, you can't compete with the world. We live in Buttfuck, Alberta. The smallest towns ever. There are six billion people out there, two hundred countries. Can you see why she'd wanna take a look?"

"*I* don't wanna leave. My parents are here. They're all I have."

"Shouldn't you try to have the world?"

"Have it?"

"I mean see it, experience it."

My eyes close.

His voice in my ear: "I wanna see you."

What am I feeling? What do I say? What? "That girl you saw yesterday? Aabidah Meer? She thinks you're cute." Relief and pain when I say it.

"You're gonna tell me that?" he says. "Seriously? You're gonna tell me that some random girl likes me? You? Are you stupid? I like you."

"I'm gonna go now," I say.

"Because I like you?"

"I'm just really confused. And overwhelmed. Also, I'm not stupid."

"I didn't mean it."

"I'm gonna go now. Sorry." I hang up, close my eyes, reach under the pillow. The letter. No energy or desire to read, so I just look at it. The date. Her writing — perky, appealing, familiar. But no return address. The phone rings. It rings again, keeps ringing, both in the bedroom and in the hall. It'll wake my parents. I put the letter away, then disconnect the phones.

16

✳

IT'S QUIET AT THE store. People come in one at a time and mostly leave empty-handed, or with a ten-dollar toque or cheap mitts. Small beans considering we also sell saddles and cowboy boots, running shoes and jeans. One guy does buy a few pairs of deerskin gloves, though. When he leaves, it's just my mom and me, Country Christmas playing to an empty store. A dead evening look on her face. December 1. It should be busy. Is she blasé or sad? Either way, it's hard to handle. What did she look like before it all fell apart? I don't remember.

Trina's alive, though. I've known for more than a week. My mom would want to know, and I want to tell her, but I can't. She's standing there drawing eyebrows on a piece of scrap paper. I'm thinking, *I could change your life in five seconds.* For the better or for the worse, though? Who can say? It's not like me to hide things. Well, big things, at least.

I haven't told her about the letters because Trina told me not to. Because my mom's already made her peace about Trina being gone. Because if Trina's not coming back, she's going to die out there. Because it's unkind to tell someone their daughter was alive all this time but never called and continues not to call for no good reason. Because the letters were for me and they're private.

I start walking to the back. There's something about lying to someone that makes you not want to be around them, like if they spend enough time with you, they will catch you out. Plus, guilt.

The phone rings when I get there. It's 8:01. *I wanna see you. I like you.* I pick up the phone and hang up. Coffee machine, sewing machines, a stack of pants waiting to be hemmed. I wait. The phone rings again. I pick it up this time.

"Hi," I say.

"Hi," he says. His voice.

"I can't talk to you." It hurts to say.

"Why?"

"Doesn't feel right." The phone jiggling against my face.

"We can go slow," he says.

"Why would you want to be with someone who resists you so much?"

"Maybe I shouldn't."

I don't know what to say. I should say something. "Yeah, maybe," I say. Do I mean it?

"Okay. Well, I'm gonna go, then," he says. He sounds sad. He hangs up and the sound goes hollow.

AT SCHOOL A COUPLE of days later, Kay comes to my locker to walk me to Math.

"Are you okay?" she says.

"Yeah."

"You know, I've been talking to Carcadian. We're worried about you. Haven't seen or heard much from you lately."

There's nothing to say. I just nod. She starts asking about my weekend plans and university, starts talking about Chiggers, this new rap album, and it's boring, her talking at me for five minutes that feel like forever. All class, I can feel her there, feel everyone around me, and it just feels wrong. Kay's flipping through papers, puzzling through a quadratic equation like it's the proof of Fermat's Last Theorem. Erasing, scribbling, erasing. Effort. If I look at her, I'll wanna help. I don't look. When the bell rings, she turns to me and says, "Wanna go to KFC?"

"Sounds good," I say, "but I'm busy."

After school, I'm in the library again. I get the atlas and trace possible paths to Whitehorse, and from there to Dawson City. I can't drive, though. I'd have to thumb for a ride. What would she do if I showed up? She'd abandon Billy, or would she? I stay with a stack of books — wildlife guides, someone's old meteorology textbook, something from the sixties about the northern peoples of the world — not reading any of them, till they turn out the lights at six.

On the way home, I see her car. I don't realize it at first, but when I do, I wave my arms and start running. "Trina!" I yell. "Trina!"

But she doesn't stop. She goes fast, up Fiftieth Ave., before turning down Fifty-Second Street and disappearing altogether. I walk around for an hour but don't know where she's gone. When I get home I tell my dad I don't feel well enough to eat, then go to my room and have crackers and cheese.

She'll come when she's ready. She wouldn't be here unless she wanted to see us. She's just not ready. She'll be here tomorrow. Guess I'll just have to wait. Maybe Kirk knows something. I dial his number, hear his mom's ghosty voice calling his name. It takes a while for him to come on.

"What's up?" I say.

"Not much."

Not much, except I've seen him with Miranda Lewis, and he's working at the car wash now. I saw him there the other day on the way to the Co-op. Dirty blue coveralls, holding the wand.

What thoughts can you come up with at that job? How much water he's using, how cold it is, how much his skin is rotting? I don't tell him he's too smart to wash cars. "Guess you haven't heard anything."

A pause. "No," he says.

"I think I saw her car today."

Silence on his end.

"I have a good feeling," I say. "I got some letters from her."

"Really?" he says.

"It makes sense she'd be back now. She's thinking about us, she wrote me letters. It makes sense, right?"

"I guess," he says, like he's tired of all her shit. I am, too, but you don't give up on a person you love. "I don't know, Chris," he says. "She wanted to see the world. So let her see it."

THE NEXT DAY, I sleep in, stay home. My dad comes up around ten while I'm making toast — nowhere for me to hide — and asks me why I'm not at school.

"No school today," I say. But then someone from school calls around eleven, asking where I am, and I don't want trouble with my dad, so I sneak out the back door and go.

I'm there in time for third period, Bio, and when I walk in, I seize up. That smell. Throat, stomach, nose, dry heave. A small white pail — garbage — I run towards it. Little grey pigs inside. The smell is formalin, the universal chemical preserver of dead things. I make a show of holding in my puke, and people laugh. I should've known this was coming. Last year, Trina came in to Bio early, stole the bucket of pigs and hid them because she didn't want to see them all cut up.

I tell Ms. Germaine I won't participate on ethical grounds. Something in her eyes I can't read, but she lets me go. I have an hour and fifteen minutes. After that, there's an anatomy quiz.

I go to the library, look at the picture of a split open pig in my Bio textbook and read that pigs have all the same organs as humans. That's interesting. So I find a book about pigs. It says they have personalities and are smarter than dogs and as smart as three-year-old children, that the way they're normally raised is cruel. Kept in little pens, separated from their moms. I study the anatomy a while, then go outside. Blue sky, sunshine, playground, highway. I walk west, past the woods and track, and on the far end, coming out of the woods like the Sasquatch, is Trina.

Finally.

I run ahead. It's really her. Black ponytail, red coat, black jeans. Simple and still so cool. How has the road treated her? Maybe bad, maybe okay. Where's Billy? I knew that she'd come back. She's couldn't stay away. Has she seen me? What if she hasn't?

I start yelling her name. "Trina!" Then, "Katrina!" Then, "Katrina Wong!" Variety makes it fun. She'll think I'm fucking loony by the time I get there. The people outside for gym are staring, but who the fuck cares? It's her. "Trina!"

She's looking at me. What has she seen? Is she home to stay? Friday, which means at least a weekend full of talks — I hope. How much money do I have? Enough for a pizza?

"Trina!"

Dirt on her face, a dark tan. Twenty feet away, I see it's not her. Sometimes you want something so much, you see what isn't there. It's Carson Bigchild, a short, thin Native guy I know from the store. Long hair. Probably wondering why I was yelling. What's he doing in the woods?

"Sorry, man," I yell. "Thought you were someone else." *Fucking idiot.*

"It's okay," he shouts back.

LATER, I'M IN A cold bathroom stall with my feet propped up so no one can see I'm here. Brown metal door and walls, little tiles with dirt in between. It smells like shit, crotch, piss, someone's tampon, but there's nowhere else to go to be alone.

The bathroom door whines open as someone says, "That fucking nutso Chrysler Wong." It's Carrie Pratt, I think. "She's on the track after lunch yelling at this Indian guy, and he's just looking at her."

"Oh my god," someone else says. Meaghan Kennedy? "She's always been weird. Got even worse when her sister died or whatever."

Doors slam, zippers, shimmying, pissing. I wanna kick them, keep kicking till they pass out, bruises, internal bleeding, but I just sit there, make as little noise as possible, my feet against the door. I picture it springing open. I can't fight them, but I could go to a good school, go be a doctor while they're stuck here working at the parts shop with kids and rig pig husbands. Except that I can't leave. There's no revenge. We'll be the same when we graduate, stuck in this buttfuck town, working crummy jobs, except that I'll be alone and I won't wanna be here. A toilet flushes, another. They slam the stall doors open, turn on the taps for two seconds, then leave, the sound of air rushing in and the spring in the door. I count to fifty before I go.

The bell rings. People trickle then pour out of classrooms. Won't be long till they all know. I find Nancy walking down the hall, probably going to the library. I follow her.

"Hey," I say.

"Hey." Not even a glance in my direction.

Ms. Jamieson, the librarian, perks up as we walk in. No talking allowed. Nancy goes towards the carrels.

"Wait," I say. She turns around. I could make a scene. She knows it'll make her look bad. She comes back out to the hall.

"What's this about?" I say.

"I just want to read." Her eyes on the lockers on the other side of her as a couple of people pass us, whispering.

"You'd rather read than hang out with me."

"Let's hang out in a couple of weeks," she says, her voice low. "Or we'll talk on the phone. Just —"

"You don't wanna be seen with me." She looks like she's about to say sorry. Or not. "What kind of friend are you?" I say. More people pass, stare, give her the eyebrows.

She lowers her voice. "Sorry."

"Fuck you."

"Chris, don't be like that."

"I don't need you," I say, and storm away. Around the corner, I hear people laughing. A crowd. Mike Brown's in the middle of it screaming, "Treeeee-naaaaa!" Everyone laughs till they see me. Then they watch, smiling, to see what I'll do. A few of them don't look at me. They act noble like they weren't just laughing or like they feel sorry for me. Fuck 'em. I won't need anyone else when she's here.

The nearest exit: the front doors. Another thirty feet of shame before I reach them. I crash through, then walk past the church, where Ty Rodriguez is leaning against some girl, her arms draped down his back, his hands invisible. It's cold out. I go down side streets, past the drugstore window advertising Christmas, paper Jesus on a crucifix, a nativity scene. I'm still looking for Trina, still looking for her car, past the clinic and the SAAN store. I slip in through the back. It's 12:05. I go upstairs and lock the door, read then fall asleep. Thank god it's Friday.

I WAKE TO A smell and come out squinting. Spareribs for dinner. My dad made them especially for me. My mom hates meat. My dad can't take the sugar in the sauce. He puts a piece in my bowl, on my rice. It's garlicky and coated with hoisin sauce, one of my favourite foods before today. *Pigs have personalities and are as smart as three-year-old children.* I retch, then eat all the rice the rib didn't touch, and throw out the rest. I hide the rib, refill my bowl. When I sit back down my dad asks if I'm on a diet.

"Yeah, I guess," I say.

"A little bit won't hurt," he says. I shrug but he puts another rib in my bowl.

The purpose of a rib is to protect vital organs. This one was taken from a pig that loved its mom and kids. It liked eating. What else? Was it silly, sad, affectionate? I think of those guys on Sunday, just living their lives and looking for plants to eat, then boom, a car. I don't even know what kinds of animals they were. How is an animal food? Silently, I thank the pig and apologize to it, to the other animals.

I go back to my room, unsatisfied, my stomach half-empty. Nothing fills you quite like meat. The house smells like barbecue pork, the plate on the table is still full. My dad is hurt, confused, worried about me. He comes from a peasant background. Meat is precious — the most expensive and best kind of food. It doesn't make sense to him for me to not eat it. I'm wasting it if I don't, and insulting his cooking. It's the main thing he does these days, and he's fucking good at it. Maybe he's thinking, *Am I losing my touch?* Maybe he's thinking, *We moved to Canada and we work hard — just so you can eat this.*

When I come back out, my parents are in the living room watching the Miss Hong Kong pageant. Schmaltzy music. Thin, short women in ugly shoes. My dad points at a horsey-looking one and says, "Kuey emdem leng." *She seems pretty.*

My mom looks up, she's surprised to see me. I ask if she can talk a sec. She gets up and we go to the other side of the house, by the washing machine. I wrap my arms around her as tightly as I can without hurting her. It feels good. I wish we could stay like this. Would she mind? I wish I could climb back into her, all small and cozy and safe. I could come out when Trina came back. But while I'm waiting I wouldn't know my mom at all, wouldn't see her with her socks half on, scowling like a kid when she didn't wanna eat something or my dad happy and excited about animal shows or this special food he made just for us. I wouldn't see a sunset in Easter colours or hear Joy Division without it sounding like I'm under water. No.

"I love you," I say, arms still around her.

"I love you," she says back, by rote, without thinking.

"Have you ever thought Trina might come back?"

Her baby scent, her bones. The hug quakes. She's shrugging, not a thing that comes naturally to her.

I let go. "Well, where else would she go?"

"The city," she says, enunciating the *T*.

"Why do you think that?"

"She like shopping."

Pause. "I had a bad day at school," I say. Her face. It's like I'm not even talking. My mom never knows what to say. "Some kids were making fun of me."

"Why?" she says in a concerned mom voice.

There's no one else to tell. "I thought I saw Trina today."

She's alert.

"Out by the woods near school," I say. "But it wasn't her, and now everyone thinks I'm crazy." I tell her about Mike Brown, the crowd of kids around him, Carrie and Meaghan in the bathroom, Nancy, how it'll get worse once the whole school knows. "Maybe I should quit school, or do it from home or something."

"You almost graduate. Just a few more month. Can you be tough?"

Can I be tough? No. "I don't know," I say.

"You have to be more normal." She says it like it's my fault.

"This doesn't have to do with me being normal," I say, even though it does.

THE WEEKEND IS A kind of reprieve: two days without the mob at school, two days for it to blow over, for me to figure out my next move. But Monday morning comes, an unwelcome guest. I wake up and know I'm gonna get it. I skip first period English so I won't have to talk to anyone. Second period, Band class, I'm late as usual. Sloppy Scott Joplin as I walk in. The music farts.

"Class, look alive," Mr. Buckner drones. "A late arrival is not a licence to stop playing." Half the class's eyes are on me as I grab sheet music and my baritone from the front of the room. I go to the back, sit next to Luke. His eyes on his music, he finds the notes with his right hand while waving hello with his left. When he gets to the end of the page, I reach over and turn it for him. He gives me a thumbs-up.

Band's not bad. There's safety in the moment, this jaunty carefree brass moment from a hundred years ago. People with fancy clothes in ballrooms did the quickstep to this song. I think of people cheering on around-the-world car races, the first passenger flights, long voyages on massive boats — women with dresses, hats, handkerchiefs, and black lipstick waving goodbye.

As we play, though, I feel it in the air like it's about to rain: nerds poised to make themselves feel better about themselves at my expense. Right now, there's not much they can do. They're busy and Buckner is watching. But when the bell rings, the teasing starts. I pack up my baritone and something pings off my head. A ball of paper. I know I shouldn't open it, but I do. On it is the word CRAZY and a drawing of a penis spurting semen. People leave in groups, whispering, tittering, giving me a wide berth.

The rest of the day I feel the eyes, hear whispers and conversations and assume they're talking about me. So when I go into Home Ec and Mike Brown sees me and yells "Treeeenaaaa!", I've had it.

"You miss my sister, eh? Not getting any or what? In case you're wondering, she's not into limp dick losers."

That shuts him up. No one talks to me for the rest of the day.

ON THE WAY HOME, I check the post office. There's another letter from Trina. She and Billy tried going to Dawson City after hearing about the arts festivals and the Top of the World Highway, which is all hills in different, zany colours. Partway there, though, some guy at a gas station said the Top of the World was closed till summer. *Who ever heard of a road closed in the winter!* Trina wrote. Too bad. So they went to Alaska instead. There're festivals in Anchorage, too, a fur auction, a running of the reindeer, a big dogsled race. They've been trying to take their time getting there, going down whatever side roads they've seen, going on little trips. They got to Prince William Sound, one of the prettiest places she's ever seen, that way. She said things were going well with Billy, only a few disagreements, but at a town called Mentasta Lake, Trina went off road, down a hill because she could, and got stuck in the mud. It's gorgeous like you wouldn't believe. So many mountains, all that water. She bought a CD in Valdez, this Alaskan punk rock band. She said she made friends with the people who helped her out of the mud and that this was a great country, where someone could help you if you needed it, even if you didn't necessarily deserve it.

I'm mulling over the letter, how I feel about it, when the phone rings. Do I pick it up?

"Jack's Western Wear," I say.

"Treeee-naaaa!" someone yells on the other end.

What will I do tomorrow? Can I home-school?

Gene spent two years in his room because he was sick, because he was sad and scared, because people can't keep their fucking mouths shut. If Trina were here, she'd understand. *Fuck 'em,* she'd say. But that gives me no relief, and anyway, she's the source of my problems.

17

GENE HAD A REAL connection with Stef. It was a special one. Throughout his life, he had this tough-guy front — he'd never hug you or say anything nice, and he made fun of you if he saw you being nice to someone else — but he was softer with her, even though she did things he'd call out in anyone else. Like watching soaps. Her favourite was *Days of Our Lives*, so he watched it while she was at work. He'd take notes, then go downstairs when it was done to tell her what had happened that episode.

We used to jibe him for it, but Stef loved knowing that stuff. It seemed worth it somehow. "Oh, my god! I wish I could've been there!" she'd say, pricing jeans or dressing a mannequin, while Gene told her that Hope recognized Bo despite her amnesia or that Patch got caught in a boat explosion planned by Lawrence Alamain.

Gene had a dark side, but somehow Stef got through. They used to stand on opposite ends of the store, tap dancing certain beats, back and forth like call and response, and I remember a few occasions when he came from out of nowhere and jumped on her back, expecting a piggyback ride. He had to have been, like, seventy pounds heavier than her, but she loved it. We took a photo of it happening one time. It's probably one of my all-time favourite pictures, they both just look so happy, but it's lost now, gone to wherever my mom puts the pictures of her kids who are no longer with her. Stef taught Gene how to use the cash register, she taught him how to drive, and before he went out she used to say to him, "Don't do drugs," "Don't crash the car," and "Wear a condom." He took it.

Another thing Stef did was defend Gene from my dad. About a week before she died, Gene crashed the car, and that same day, we had to keep our dad busy while she snuck off to get the dents pulled.

Gene pretty much gave up on life after Stef died. We tried to step in, but *you* try replacing someone's favourite person. It can't be done. Gene turned up his music, took up smoking, and it all went downhill from there.

One day my mom got a call from school saying he had stopped doing the work. She couldn't keep her mouth shut that night at dinner — Gene still came out to eat sometimes — and my dad figured it out and flipped. For the next few weeks, he got mad every time he saw Gene, and sometimes even when he didn't. He'd be in the middle of some unrelated task like cutting onions and he'd put down the knife or whatever, walk down the hall, and yell a new thing at Gene's closed door as if he'd just remembered he was mad. We all caught shit in those weeks. My dad yelled at Trina, saying her outfit made her look like a beggar, and he yelled at me for not helping with meals, even if I had already helped plenty.

My mom nagged and nagged and my dad yelled and yelled, and we never saw Gene at dinner again. Thing about my parents? They've never quite understood certain basic things about parenting. One? You attract more flies with honey. Two? Some kids are rebellious and don't want to be controlled. Three? Parents are not the kings and queens of their homes, they are not cobblers with faulty machines that miraculously work when they hit them, or shopkeepers that might succeed if only they worked and ran hard enough. Life doesn't work like that. It's something we kids came by the hard way. My parents? Probably never learned.

Still, they were worried sick. We all were. We started leaving plates on the shelf outside Gene's room. In the morning, sometimes the food was gone. We never knew if he was home — his door was always closed — so it took a bit of work to figure out if he was there.

Trina and I came up with the idea that she should get his assignments from school, same as how Stef used to for his episodes. She went to the office to figure out who his teachers were, then went to talk to them. One by one, they all said the same thing: he hadn't been to class for weeks.

Sometime later, after all of this was over, Trina found out what he'd been doing. She went into his room and looked through his drawers, saw his pictures of disfigured humanoid shapes and drowning robots. It sounds cheesy but that was his style, he was good at it. She also found notebooks filled with a lot of dark shit. Some of it we couldn't read, and sometimes he used words wrong. Whose fault was it that he felt so bad and didn't have anyone to turn to? It might have been his. Maybe it was my parents'. God, I hope it wasn't ours.

JOSH MCMURTRY COULD HAVE been tried for manslaughter, but it was a flimsy case. His friends would've stood up for him in court, and there were no other witnesses and no evidence she was thrown in. The Crown would not press charges, so I tried to get my family to. No one bit, and I don't blame them, we were all so sad and tired. But I was angry, too, got to picturing all the ways he could die: forest fire, flash flood, cancer, snake bite. One time he came into the store and Trina, my mom, and I hid in the back despite there being customers. He came back a few weeks later and we did the same thing. My mom got a kick out of it, as much as you can get a kick out of something like that.

I thought we were all on the same page about Josh, but at some point, a few weeks after he came by the second time, Trina and Kirk went down to Red Mart. Fifteen and they were already dating. Josh wasn't there but his mom was, and gave Trina a hug when she learned who she was. She said he was at home, and he'd wanna talk, so they walked over to McMurtry's place in the new subdivision and rang the door. No one answered. They rang a few more times and looked in the windows, then gave up and went to cut across the back, a shortcut to the river, past the house, past plants staked into the ground, branches heavy with tomatoes. Kirk wanted some, but Trina didn't feel right stealing.

"Come on," Kirk said. "You've never had a tomato till you've had a garden one."

They heard coughing then, a smoker's cough, and a raspy voice saying, "Hey." They looked up and saw someone on the back porch. It was Josh. He was wearing pyjamas, and even from where they were, they could see his complexion was pasty. He invited them to sit, so they did, Trina on the porch swing, Kirk on a reclining wooden chair.

"Nice day," Trina said.

Josh nodded. He was staring at the end of the deck.

Kirk said, "So you've got tomatoes."

"Yeah," Josh replied.

"They're pretty awesome."

"Yeah." Josh nodded and went quiet again.

Eventually Trina said, "My sister Chrysler wants you in jail."

Josh said he could see my point.

Trina said, "Did you know that for the last few months we've been getting letters for Stef from the university? Letters saying, 'Please enroll in courses and pay, or we're cancelling your registration?'"

"No, I didn't know," Josh said. "She was gonna go to U of A."

"Yeah. Reg is buried in Edmonton. You probably know. We had this plan we'd all live there together. But she applied everywhere. Berkeley, Santa Monica, Seattle, New Mexico ..."

It went on like that, Trina making digs at Josh, Josh taking it, obviously hurting. For a while, she didn't care — he deserved it — but eventually she softened up, started telling stories about Stef. He drank them in. Josh must have had his own stories about Stef, but he didn't share them, just asked questions when Trina stopped talking. The sun went down, and they kept at it. When Josh's mom came home and offered dinner, Trina knew it'd mean something if they stayed, so they did.

Trina didn't tell me all of what they said that day, but it must have been something good, because when Trina came home, she said she'd made her peace. It took a few months more, but I made mine, too. There's no explaining it. I was mad every day, then one day found I was less mad. Josh is an okay guy. He cared about her, like, a lot. He didn't mean for it to happen. And you can't hate someone forever. Or maybe you can. Gene's door stayed closed, his music always turned on from the afternoon till the middle of the night. I knocked on his door a lot those first few months. So did Trina and my mom. But he almost never answered.

ONE NIGHT IN OCTOBER, more than a year after Stef got thrown in the river, I woke to something on my bed, a little mouse on my shoulder. I twitched. It was Trina, saying she'd just seen

Gene in the kitchen. He was thin, his clothes baggy, and she could smell him from ten feet away. *What can I do?* I thought, but I went with her because I wanted to know how he was.

Gene was making a sandwich.

Trina's voice was low and even. "Gene. Hey."

Long fluorescent lights in the kitchen, same as in the store. Roast beef, white bread, processed cheese, Miracle Whip. An empty glass by his plate. His dull eyes, hand on the butterknife. He said, "Hey," but didn't look up.

I felt like an ass standing there. Trina did most of the talking. "What's up?" she said.

"Not much."

"It was busy at the store today," she said. It was. Midnight Madness is a sale we have the Friday before Halloween. Every year, on just that night, the store opens till eleven and we all dress up in costumes. Trina picked meat off the leftovers plate. "You should've seen the way we dressed Mom."

"Yeah. She was a punk rocker," I said. Our mom didn't normally dress up for Halloween, but somehow that year we'd convinced her. "She wore my Union Jack shirt, one of Triny's leather jackets, and cherry Docs. I swear, she never looked so cool."

"Yeah, and Dad was a cowboy," Trina said. He went every year as a cowboy. He held court. People would come by and remark on his costume and he would smile that photogenic smile.

Gene smiled a bit, too, held his sandwich in both hands and took a bite. Didn't even cut it first.

We all stood around for a while till Trina said, "Gene, what're you doing to yourself?"

He opened the fridge and filled his glass with milk. "Sorry," he said, then picked up the food and walked away.

"Gene," she said, but he didn't turn around.

TRINA AND I STARTED hearing rumours about him at school.

Mike Brown said, "Your brother's a fuckin' weirdo."

I said, "Yeah? What else is new?"

He said, "He's on the prowl. I saw him talkin' to some cougar outside the Bottom last night."

Gene was good-looking till around the last year of his life. He was cute as a kid and it shows in all the photos my parents took — way, way more than they took of any of the rest of us. Girls liked him, too. He used to have trouble juggling them. Still, he'd been pretty chaste for most of his life. Who knows why — older siblings, upbringing, plain decency? The funny thing about Gene is that the time in his life when he was at his ugliest was also when he was having the most sex.

Mike Brown was right. Gene *did* find older women outside bars. He also found teenaged girls in the school parking lot, at the Dairy Burger, outside their houses when they went to take out the trash. We didn't know how he was able to attract girls in his state, but we had our theories. "Some older women just like a younger guy," Trina said. The ones closer to his own age, I thought, he was able to get based on his past glory. If there was a lesson to be learned in that twelve-step program he worked out for Reggie, it was that confidence and charm were more important in seduction than looks. Plus, people tend to look better in low-light situations, which is maybe part of the reason why he always went out at night.

He started sneaking girls home. One time in the middle of the night, after half an hour of moaning and screaming coming from his side of the wall, I went out to the hall. What was going on? Was he killing her? What would our parents think? I stood at the door for a while, gathering the courage to knock, but I didn't have to. The screaming stopped. The door eventually opened partway, warm air rushed out from his room, and my school friend Maddy Hawkes scrambled out, naked except for Gene's towel, her skin pink and flushed.

"Your brother's a maniac," she said, stepping past on her way to the bathroom.

"You could've fooled me," I said, and went back to my room.

18

✳

FIRST THING I WANNA say, you never wanted to go to the Yukon. I did. Not you. Do you remember? I said, *It's not that far, but there's lots of animals there you can't see here.* I said, *I wonder where the trees stop.* You yawned, remember? Wondered how we could possibly ever be related when I'm always asking questions like that, even though we have the same fucking chin. Do you remember? Now you and Billy are hatching plans together. You wanna do it right. You're going to Anchorage. Fuck you, Trina. You and your girl-friend can both go fuck yourselves.

Oh, and thanks for waiting half a year to write. *I'm sorry it took so long*, you said. It was no big deal, actually, I only spent every waking moment of the first five months wondering whether or not you were dead and how you died and where you were and why the fuck you just up and left without a single fucking word.

Stop telling me you miss me. Stop saying you think about me every day when you obviously fucking don't. All that we've been through, the both of us, and two years of trying to keep you home, then you shack up with the first head case you see walk into a diner? You find this girl and talk to her and let her make you feel less lonely? Earth to Trina: *I'm* lonely. Here. I'm lonely. God, you better not be telling her anything about me.

Also? What the fuck kind of name is Billy for a girl?

EVERY LUNCH HOUR FOR a week, Mike Brown has done a comedy routine at my expense. Trina's name has become the non-sequitur answer to all the questions at school. Tuesday, in Chem, Mr. Birch asked how many water molecules would be produced in a reaction where two molecules of sulfuric acid were combined with three of ammonia, and Derek Mason put up his hand and said, "Trina?" People laughed. Mr. Birch shrugged and said with a tone of forbearance, "No. Would anyone else like to try? Chrysler, what about you?"

It'd be funny if it weren't me. If Trina were here and not the source of so much of what's wrong with my life, I'd tell her all about it. She'd laugh. But she's not here and I don't want to tell her shit, don't want to remember or speculate on anything about her. But it's not like I have a choice in that. Thoughts come, memories, whether or not I want them to, and I'm confused about how I feel. I want to think about her. I don't want to think about her.

The first few days after I thought I saw her, no one talked to me but Kay and Luke. But they don't know what it was like to be with her, or how it was when my whole family was together. Neither of them has lost anyone. I'm lonely, but sometimes talking to the wrong people makes you feel even lonelier, so.

My parents aren't any better. After all these years, I'm gonna, what, talk to them about feelings? Reveal to my dad what all went down at school over Trina? Would I show him the letters? He doesn't talk about anyone after they've gone, it's not like he'd want me to bring them up. No wonder Trina was his favourite. He wants ignorance, she fosters it.

Friday after school, I'm at cash, making change for Mrs. Emery's shoelaces — she wants quarters for bingo — and when I look up, Conrad's there.

"Hi," he says. "Is it all right if I come in?"

Yes, it's fine. Come talk to me. No, please go away. But we have a connection, don't we? What does the heart want? To hide or to be recognized? You can't have both at once.

"I'll come outside," I say. I get my jacket and tell my mom, who's at the back, that I'm leaving. It's cold outside, wispy clouds. There's a little girl in a snowsuit riding a bike yelling bye.

"So how are things?" he says.

I look at him, shrug.

"That good?"

I look down at the old sidewalk. It's worn down. Grooves where the cracks are, filled with snow. "Yeah, it's pretty bad right now."

"I'm sorry."

"Yeah, school is shit, people are assholes. If this doesn't all blow over, it'll be months of this before I graduate. But like, I'm not going to university anyway, so why should I feel the need to finish high school?"

"I guess to keep your options open?"

"How about you? What's happening? What brings you here?"

"Ah, same old. Basketball games. Doing the helicopter with little kids. I put my back out once doing that. Did I tell you? I'm, like, eighteen and my body's already falling apart."

"Just, you know, pump some iron. You got a weak back? Back extensions could be your best friend."

"Thanks for the tip." He's laughing. Am I funny?

"Where's your bee costume?"

"Left it with Dean Willis. He's had a tough time, too — got rejected by some universities this week."

"You're a good man," I say.

Hands in his pockets. More than half a foot taller than me, but he talks and acts like he's on your level. "Got plans right now?" I say.

He shrugs. "Thought I'd try on a bonnet, go churn some butter at the museum."

"We could, umm, grab that pizza if you want?" It's hard to look at him.

Something in his eyes, like we've been through lots of shit together already. I look away then back like it's a scary movie I wanna watch. "I'm vegetarian now. Did you know that?"

He nods like an old farmer chewing straw. "It's the better way," he says.

We walk up the street together, side by side.

GETTING TO KNOW SOMEONE is a kind of journey. At first we're as wary as guard dogs, but gradually trust grows. Things are fun, things get easier.

One day, Conrad brings this set of fake fucked up plastic teeth he bought from a vending machine in Edmonton. He puts them in before ordering at the Dairy Burger, and gets no reaction at all from Sara Stephenson. I laugh and laugh. He wears them the rest of the day. We go for a walk and he keeps saying hi to people we see on the street. It's awesome.

Another day, he gives me sea glass. One piece is flat and round and blue. The other is green and has an arc to it. They're frosty, smooth, and hard. I don't know what they are at first. "Don't worry," he says. "I have more."

But I do worry. Conrad lays off on the *I like you* stuff, but I know he feels something because of how he looks at me sometimes. It makes me shy. But he's been there for me.

Most of our hangouts are spent walking and talking outside. It's freezing cold, but Stef once said I should only do what feels comfortable, and that seems like good advice for a time like this.

AROUND THEN, CHRISTMAS HAPPENS. My parents and I are in a low mood. I try to make them happy. I find Christmas cartoons on TV for my dad, then give him an expensive frying pan and say, "Your wok is too big. If you use a frying pan, you'll make smaller meals." I give my mom a ceramic cottage, a special order from the gift store, for her collection. It makes her cry. Christmas is a hard time for us. She wipes snot and tears from her face with a used paper napkin, then gives me clothes from the store. She says they're from my dad, too.

Later in the day, she says, "Nei yaht yaht huey bin?" *Where do you go every day?*

"It's not every day. It's only, like, once a week." And I go to my room.

The worst my mom can do is worry and nag. My dad is the one who can do real damage. To be honest, though, I'm not that worried because he's not the observant type.

NEEDLESS TO SAY, I don't visit Conrad in Eckville. He's cool with that, says he's glad to come in because it gives him a reason not to spend time with his dad.

"You really don't like him," I say when he calls me at the end of February.

"Yeah," he says curtly and doesn't elaborate. I shouldn't've brought it up.

"But, like, he's your dad."

"Yeah, to like or not to like as I see fit. It's not as if he's not in my life. I do live with him five days out of seven."

"Okay," I say, guard up. He's gonna get mad, even madder than he already is. He's gonna get mad and he's not gonna want to spend time with me.

A spoon clinks in a cup on his side of the line. "Like, most kids with divorced parents want them back together," he says.

"Me? No. I'm glad they're apart, even though Bob's like —"

"Why are you glad?"

He pauses. "Because my mom, she's nice — really nice — but she's fragile, too. My dad was mean. Called her fat, even though he knew it really hurt her. She took up jogging, every day in the morning — she's not a morning person — and she lost, like, thirty pounds, and he still didn't love her. Man, she used to ask me what I thought was wrong with her. How do I fuckin' know? I'm a kid. She'd come home from work and make a nice meal, and before my dad got home, she'd come into my room with two dresses and ask me which one I thought he'd like better. But the problem wasn't her. Obviously. He's a fucking coward. If you don't wanna be with someone, you should end it. You know? Or you should try and see if there's something in them you can love. Don't have a fucking affair. You know?"

I don't know. My parents fight and sometimes the fights get bad, but at least they stay together. My dad knows what my mom likes and tries to give it to her. Sometimes he's mean or annoying, but she tolerates it, and maybe she gives more than he does, but they'll stay together. I wouldn't call it love. Or maybe it is, just not the kind I want. When I was younger, I tried to get her to leave him, but she didn't and she won't and I guess that's a good thing.

"Anyway, yeah. D'you wanna come over?"

"It's a sheet of ice outside. Didn't you hear about that twelve-car pileup?"

"Yeah, that's on the highway, though. I'll come get you if you want. My mom wants to meet you."

Why would she want that? "Sure," I say.

His mom *is* nice. We make pizza, and his mom talks to me: "Jack's Western Wear. That's you?" "So you go to Palliser." "You know I see him more often, now that he's met you." — as I cut vegetables for a salad, looking over at Conrad from time to time, the muscles in his arms as he presses out the dough, then throws it like that guy I saw one time at Papa John's during a field trip. "Look at you!" I say to him. "Show-off!" When he starts to explain why you throw it, I say, "Centrifugal force," and he smiles.

Before we eat, Conrad's mom and stepdad pray. I try not to watch, but honestly, I'm curious, envious. God's a simple explanation, somewhere to direct your hopes and dreams. The pizza is amazing. I've never had pizza like that. Basil, home-made sauce, the crust shatters in my mouth.

After dinner I help his mom with the dishes, and as she's telling me they have Monopoly and that four is a good number for it, Conrad grabs me by the arm and starts pulling me to the door. He says to his mom, "We're going now. I'm taking the car, okay?"

I give her an apologetic shrug on my way out. "Maybe next time," I say. "It was nice meeting you."

Outside it's cold, and the air makes a sound like cracking ice. We get in the car and he calls me a suck. "Better than you," I say. "'I'm taking the car, okay?' You don't even wait for her to answer. Your mom's nice. Plus, it's rude not to help. She fed me, right?"

"I fed you, too." We drive down the highway, turn off at the Voyageur Motel, then cruise past Spring Hills Elementary. We move slow and safe like sleep. "I got an idea."

"Yeah?"

"You ever walk along the edge of town?"

"No."

"Would it be fun for you to do?"

Trina listening to Athapascan punk rock on an ice floe, making friends on the fly. How would it be to live like that? "Maybe?"

The car slows down at a stop sign. Conrad's got his hand by his mouth like he's an undercover bad guy in a cartoon and whispers, "I think we have ourselves an afternoon plan."

WE'RE PARKED AT PUDGEE'S. The sky is white, and there's ice on the ground, tamped down snow that's thawed and frozen again.

"Ready?" he says.

I look at him. He gets out of the car. *Come on, Chrysler.* I get out, too. "Where we going?" I say.

"You trust me, right?"

"Maybe. It looks slippery."

He runs ahead on the sidewalk, holding his arms out beside him, and slides two feet before falling on his ass.

"Oh, my god! Are you okay?" I say, catching up.

"You didn't see that," he says.

I help him up. Though there isn't an obvious place to go, he guides me off the sidewalk and to a downward slope — the riverbank. It's worn smooth from the bottoms of sleds, and slick.

"I'm not going down there," I say.

"It's not that steep. And it's nice down there. You ever walk on the river before?"

"No," I say, like *duh*.

"It's pretty great. Or we could walk down to the bottom of the bank and just have a look." He holds out his arm. I take it, look down the hill, and don't move. "Or we could stand like this all afternoon," he says.

"How strong are you?"

"Strong enough."

We find a place by the trees where sleds haven't been. He lets me set the pace. I take a step, and another, and another. It still feels dangerous, but something about the adversity, my fear, makes it fun. Step. Step. Step. Slow. I watch my feet the whole way. A few times I tentatively ask if we can stop. It scares me to ask because he could say no, or maybe something worse would happen, I don't know what. But each time I ask, we stop. He does that for me. Imagine asking for something and actually getting it — without a tease, without refusal or guilt or punishment or conditions.

This valley like I've never seen it before. The trees are covered in frosty gloves of white, the graffiti on the bridges is quaint and not just in an ugly way, the river's solid, dark grey, and unmoving. And his arm is strong, I can feel it, wiry under his jacket, and when I slip, I grip it harder, his muscles tense, he supports me, and I don't fall.

"I can't believe you're not scared," I say.

"What's the worst that could happen?"

"You fall, break your neck."

"Okay, but what's the most likely bad thing that would happen?"

I look at him. He looks back, smiles.

"Thank you," I say, like I know I'm a burden.

"You're doing well."

He's right. I'm doing it. I really am. And I know it would be easy for someone else, but it doesn't matter. It's hard for me, and I'm doing it. When we get to the bottom, I feel so good I say, "Fuck it. Yeah," and rush ahead onto the frozen river. I can do this. It's only deep in a few parts, and I won't go on those parts. I turn to him.

"You did it," he says.

"I did it!"

He catches up to me, and we walk. I keep holding on to him. He gets his flask out and asks if I want a drink. I say okay, take a little swig and it burns my mouth and throat.

"This tastes like shit!" I say.

"Point taken," he says. "Wait here?" He starts walking away.

"Where you goin'?" I say, but he's already gone, sliding down the river and running up the bank.

He's mad at me. He's abandoned me. Or it's revenge for me hurting him before. I think of things that could happen. Thieves in pursuit and me a slow runner and bad slider. The river cracking and swallowing me whole, even though it's three inches deep where I'm standing. Why did I come here? Why did I do this? I hold the ends of a tree and walk back in the direction we came from, one foot ahead of the other like a toddler learning to walk. It's the slowest I've ever done anything.

When I've made it off the river and have started to climb the bank, I see him at the top. He starts walking down, fast, he's almost running, and in about eight seconds he's beside me, asking where I'm going.

"*Me*? Where'd *you* go?"

"I went to Pudgee's. I bought you something." He pulls a ginger ale from his pocket. Another can, orange pop, comes out of his sleeve like a magic trick. He lets me pick the one I want.

"You sure?"

"Yeah, I'll just take the other one."

I look at him, trying to figure out which one he wants. I pick orange. We start walking again, under the bridges, between trees and tall, dry grass on either side of the river. A whole new vantage point. I hold on to his sleeve. He carefully pulls out his flask again, tips some into his open pop. "Would the lady like a drink?" he says. I nod and he pours some in, and it doesn't taste as bad this time.

We walk and drink and slide. We pee in the bushes. *Don't look. I won't.* And when we get too cold we go back, stumble up the hill in the dark. The sun sets at four-thirty in winter here. I'm uncoordinated, but it's faster going up than going down, and

I'm not afraid. Not really. I look down and notice I'm holding his hand. I let go. We get in his car. It's quiet, cold, and still.

"You can't drive like that," I say, taking another swig.

"I won't drive like this." His smile. Whoa.

"Yeah, so that was fun."

"Yeah, it was," he says with an even bigger smile and his eyes on the dashboard, and then fast, before I have time to react or even think, he leans over and kisses me.

What? Umm. Oh my god. No. Yes. No. No. Yes. No. Yes. So much fear, but I kiss him back, it must be instinct. I kiss him again, and again, blind fear and desire mixed together. Is it desire? Kiss. Yes. I yawn open, you could yawn open like the sun, till you're all mouth, and we kiss, and we kiss, and we kiss, his fingers on my neck, light, breathing, it's mine, why am I breathing like that, and then he unzips my coat, and I gasp.

"What's wrong?" he says and kisses me on the neck, under my ear.

I close my eyes and tilt my head to give him room.

"Does that feel good?"

"Yeah."

"You're so amazing," he says. "You're so pretty and smart and —"

"What?" I pull away.

"What?" Confusion on his face like a distress call.

"No."

"What do you — What?" Hurt colouring his face like ink in water.

"No. Just —" I shake my head. "No."

"What?" He makes a face. "What?" he says louder, more emphatically. "Why?"

"I just — I'm sorry. I don't know. Can you take me home?"

"Just tell me what you're feeling."

My hand in my hair, closed eyes, crumpled up. "Sad."

He puts his hand on my shoulder. "Why?"

"You're just — so nice to me."

"You deserve it," he says.

"I have to go."

"Okay." He starts the car. He's drunk.

"I have to walk."

He turns the key and the car dies. "I could walk with you."

"I think I want to be alone."

So I get out of the car, sadness filling me up. He'll be mad or frustrated, and that makes it even worse, but this is what I have to do. I start walking up the hill, head down. He's sad, too. Who am I to make him feel that way? I walk slow, not noticing the cold or the snow or anything but the black black black of night. Up Fiftieth, down Main, up the sidewalk stairs, then the yellow light of home, steamed fish for my parents and rice for me.

I go to the bathroom before I eat. My face. Will they be able to see? Conrad and me in the car, me like the sun. I dump a can of beans on my rice, my lips tingle as I eat. I look for signs on my parents' faces — of anger, worry, recognition of what I've done — but no, at least I don't think so. My dad asks if I want vegetables. Otherwise, the TV talks for us. After dinner, I go to my room, lie down, and there's no one to talk to and nothing to say. I'm like King Midas, infecting everything I touch, and any good thing that's ever happened to me is not something I deserve at all.

19

※

MONDAY MORNING, I'M LYING in bed thinking of Conrad and me in the car, thinking of him. His eyes, his smile, his strong arm and patience as we went down the hill and slid across the river. I like how weird he is. He's easy to talk to. We've got shit in common. What's wrong with me?

At school, I ask everyone I can about love — and by everyone, I mean Kay and Maddy Hawkes. Luke is out for being a boy, Nancy and I haven't talked in weeks, and I'm not close to anyone else. I'm not even that close to Maddy, she just happened to be there and I figured she could help. She and Kay claim they've been in love a few times and that it's great. But how do you know when it's love?

"Oh, my god. You slut!" Maddy says to me.

"What?"

"Ty Rodriguez?"

"No."

"Then Luke? I always wondered if you guys —"

"We're friends. No."

Kay watching us like we're playing Ping-Pong. Smiling.

"So who is it?"

"No one."

"No one I know, no one you wanna say, or no one no one?"

"Bye, Maddy," I say, signalling to Kay to start walking.

"See ya." Maddy's throaty giggle. "Don't do anything I wouldn't do," she says, loud enough for half the school to hear.

Breathe, I say to myself. *Nothing confirms a rumour like a strong reaction. Just breathe.*

Kay and I have a spare, and we wind up downtown at Marlene's. She gets a bowl of broccoli cheddar. I get one, too, pay for both of them. Us with our bowls of liquid comfort.

It feels weird sitting here, asking her for advice. We're not that kind of friends. Still, there's no one else to ask. She won't betray me. Can she help me? Her eyes are down, she's blowing on a spoonful of soup. We've been friends for years, I've been to her house. I start us off. "It's kind of weird talking about this."

"I dunno. If something's on your mind, I'm happy to help." What is that in her voice? Is she being falsely chipper?

"Were you ever scared to be involved with someone?"

She looks at me, head cocked to one side. She shrugs, her hands on the table between us. Looks like she has tyrannosaurus arms. "I dunno. Maybe scared I'd screw it up?"

"Were you ever scared you'd hurt the other person?"

"Yeah, I guess," she says lightly, maybe without thinking. Then she sees my face and starts laughing. "What?" It's not something she'd be afraid of at all and she knows it.

We go back and forth. It gets less awkward. I ask her things — what is love? How should it feel? Do I really want it or do I only think I do?

She makes the point that most of the people I've loved have died. "You're wondering if it's worth the risk," she says.

I don't answer. And I sure as hell don't tell her about Conrad, or the kiss. When it's time to go back to school, I'm as confused as ever. If it were Stef or Trina here with me, I'd know how I feel. We'd have worked it out. It's kind of amazing, actually, how good Trina's advice was, considering she's only a year older. But she's experienced a lot in her life, or maybe just a lot more than me, and she's understanding when she wants to be. Stef was five years older and a really good listener. Half the time with her, if you talked long enough, you'd reveal your own feelings to yourself.

Kay and I come back to school through the north door. She goes left, to the washroom, while I go right, by the chicken-wire office windows, see Mrs. Blackburn at the copy machine, and walk in like an object coming down a conveyor belt. She says hi to me.

"Hey, Mrs. B.," I say. Then it occurs to me. "Can I talk to you?"

"Sure. Now good?"

I have class, but I tell her I have a spare. We go into her office. She sits across from me, an expectant look on her face.

"I don't even know where to start, to be honest," I say.

"Why don't you start by telling me what happened?"

Will she judge? "Okay, so, uhh, I've been hanging out with this guy for a while, and yesterday we kissed."

"I can give you condoms, information on —"

"No. I won't need that."

"What's the problem, then?"

"I'm scared."

She tilts her head.

"He seems to really like me," I say.

"Okay."

"He's really nice. I've never been in a relationship. I've spent my life liking guys who didn't like me back."

"Okay, so you're scared because you don't know how you should act?"

"Maybe?"

"It's normal to be scared. It's scary if you like him because the kiss means more, and it's scary when you kiss your friend because everything could potentially change. If it doesn't work out, you might not be able to go back to being friends. You might be better as friends. You have to keep asking yourself how it feels. And know that if it doesn't feel good, you can always stop it."

"If I do that, he won't like me."

"Chris, being liked isn't the most important thing." It's easy for her to say. "Most important is feeling good. Also, liking him now doesn't mean you'll have to like him forever. You're smart enough to know if something isn't working out."

Am I? During the next period and at home I think about it some more, weigh the things I like about him against the way he was in the car, those things he said to me, his eyes closed and he's groping at me like a blind baby animal for milk. My conclusion? I have to let him down. I practise breakup faces in the mirror, sad wheezing in the middle of saying variations of *it was a mistake*. Can you even break up with someone you're not technically dating? He might never want to talk to me again.

A few days later, he calls. I tell it to him straight, I have to. I say I think I like him but that I'm scared and that I'm sorry about how shit went down in the car. He says that it was weird what I did, but that he understands, and that we can go slow, that we don't even have to do anything if I don't want to.

On Sunday we hang out. His mom and stepdad are out of town for some Christian conference. He surprises me with takeout from Edmonton: Korean, Japanese, Indian, vegetarian Chinese, this thin spongy pancake with stuff on top that he says is Ethiopian. Lemon cream pie from his favourite place. It smells funny but nice, all those different foods together. He did that for me, broke the bank, says he got so much because he didn't know what I'd like. I like it all. I didn't know you could eat this way and still be vegetarian. I eat and eat till I'm sick. I think of him going all that way for food — a five-hour round trip — and knowing what to order in every place.

After lunch, he puts in this movie, *Harold and Maude*, about this weird guy who falls in love with an eccentric old lady. A good movie, sweet and sad. After that, we watch a New Order video, live concert footage from 1984, four years after we were born. Epic synths, bass, drums, and guitars. I've never seen it. Conrad says the tape is rare. He had to order it from Europe. I sing along — can't stop myself — and he doesn't mind.

We move the couch closer to the TV. I look over from time to time to see his reaction to stuff in the video, and some of those times, he's looking back. Whoa. We get closer on the couch, closer, it's innocent at first, like when you're sharing a chair with your friend and your legs are touching. Then he reaches up, touches my arm — my whole brain in those inches of skin — and I tell myself not to freak out. He puts his arm around me. Nerves. I seize up and he tells me it's okay. I stand up and so does he. I feel drunk. We hold hands and go to his room while the video's still playing, "Confusion." We kiss and kiss some more. It feels better than it did last time, and after, we just lie there talking. I keep looking away, but something always brings me back. Those eyes, they're huge. His face, I like to look at it.

ANOTHER LETTER FROM TRINA comes and I barely care. She says the Anchorage festivals were fun and there's more to do there than she originally thought, but she's running out of money so she's going to have to stay a while. She's still with Billy. They want to take a ferry somewhere. She's amazed by the amount of choice there is — how can she choose? Each route so breathtaking and remote, yadda yadda.

Glad to know you're still alive, Trina, good to know that the North is your oyster and that you're still having fun, etc. etc., Trina. Whatever.

CONRAD COMES TO THE store, even though I told him not to. I'm serving a customer — telling this guy with a flat ass that the jeans he's trying on look good on him — when I notice him in the gloves. I finish with the customer, then go off and do some freight. *Don't think of him. Don't think of him. Don't look at him don't think of him.* I fold jeans, check things off on the invoice, count out tags, calculate retail price on the adding machine.

A breath in my ear. "Hey."

He's right behind me, the heat of his body, his hand sweeping down my back — my whole body tingling, I close my eyes, oh — under the band of my underwear then out and he's gone.

Dinner is scrambled eggs. I eat slow, hoping my parents didn't see. I've never fought with my dad over a guy before. It isn't that hard to imagine — the tone of his voice and the volume, the things he'd say, how it'd make me feel.

My dad asks me why I'm not eating. Aren't I hungry? I wolf down my food after that, and my dad makes some worried remark about how not eating meat has given me an irregular appetite. I'll have to eat more eggs now that I don't eat meat, he says. Yes, Ba. Is it religion? No, Ba. He hates religion, except for ancestor worship, which, for some reason, doesn't count. Sometimes he says, "Of course you're hungry, you don't eat any meat," or, "You make it really hard for me to cook for you," as if he still did.

After dinner, I help with dishes, the whole time picturing a series of complex looks on my mom's face — rare for her — expressing surprise, shame, nosiness, embarrassment, criticism, disappointment, and false authority. Too playfully, too eagerly, and also reluctantly, she would say that she saw me with Conrad. *Don't have sex, okay?* she would say with a bit of embarrassed laughter. She wouldn't want to know anything about him. She'd assume he was bad news. She's not the kind for a birds-and-bees talk — maybe only had sex five times in her life — and believe me, I don't want one. Don't even really want to have sex, but that wouldn't stop her from talking. She puts dirty dishes into the rinse water. Normally, I'd give them back to her so she could do them again. This time, no. I think, *please, please, please, please, please*. She says nothing.

After dishes, I do homework, take breaks to show my parents I'm still around, then sneak out. It's dark and the town is almost beautiful. I walk up the street and meet Conrad by the old IGA.

"So you're coming by the store now," I say.

"I just wanted to see you, you know, at work. Like, 'How does she look when I'm not there?'"

"You know I could have gotten in shit, though, right? I spent the last hour and a half waiting for my dad to start throwing things at me."

"Okay."

"You know what could happen to me if they knew?"

"No," he says, accepting blame. "I don't know."

"See, it's easy if you don't know."

"Sorry," he says. "I just wanted to see you."

We end up at Ridgemore School Park. He keeps trying to apologize. At first, I let him. Later on, it hurts. I don't want him to apologize so much, not like this, not for something I liked. So when he asks if he can give me a piggyback ride, I say okay. We go around the playground like two kids in one big guy's trenchcoat. He carries me like it takes no effort. I'm gripping hard so I don't fall off. It's nice being so close to him.

I bend down and kiss him on the cheek. He says, "You keep

that up I'm gonna lose balance." I kiss him some more. He wanted to see me. I get off. He backs me up against the school and it's spring, things are melting. Our jackets make shush shush sounds. His soft stomach, his hip bone, the hollow. I put my hand in and push it into his pants. He starts whispering. I don't know what he says. Nonsense, prayer, a command. Cars go by, shoes on gravel. Someone's coming. Conrad doesn't want to stop. I don't want to, either. We stand there listening, but whoever was there is gone.

We go to his house, the basement spare room. His mom and Bob bumping around upstairs, talking with the TV on. A solid relationship. We have books on the bed in case someone walks in. We kiss each other wherever we can. Mostly on the mouth, but he kisses my nose, my neck. He touches me on the back and it makes me jerk like a fish on land. It's embarrassing. "I like that," he says, and keeps doing it. We start rocking and rub- bing against each other — instinct rearing its ugly head. You'll make a baby if you're not careful, if you only listen to instinct. It feels good, a little weird. He wants to take my pants off but I don't let him, then I worry he won't like me if I don't do it. I don't normally have this effect on guys.

Just past ten-thirty, I think of my parents at home, about to sleep and unaware I'm lying in bed with a white boy. I imagine Conrad and me ten years from now. I'm still at the store. What does he do? Work the rig? No. Does he live somewhere else? Yes, and he can only visit on weekends, which isn't enough.

I tell him I have to go. I can never be seen in public with him. Maybe he should find someone else. Love is wanting what's best for the other person, after all.

He says, "They find out about us, what's the worst they can do?"

"Disown me, yell at me, hit me."

"You know there's laws against that."

I look at him like, *You think I don't know?*

"Well, you're gonna make your folks mad at some point," he says.

A FEW WEEKS LATER, we're on his living room floor, a Trivial Pursuit board open between us.

"So one thing I've been meaning to ask you," I say.

"Arts and Literature? Sports and Leisure? History?"

"You could be with anyone."

"You're great. Do you need me to list off reasons?"

I shrug.

He says: "You care. You're sensitive. You're, like, this totally unique person. You say random shit sometimes, and I'm a sucker for random shit, and what you say is funny and cool. You're smart — like really smart. You're like a walking encyclopedia." He points at our little game pieces. I'm two pie slices up on him.

"Total fluke," I say. "There's tons of things I don't know."

He rolls his eyes. "Yeah, also you're strong. You don't think so, but you are." He looks at me, shy, above his thoughts. "And you're pretty."

I'm not the pretty one in the family. I'm not the pretty girl at school.

"No one's said it to me before."

"You're pretty," he says, leaning across the board, disrupting the pieces to kiss me and I accept it. "I can't believe no one's ever said that. You're so pretty." He wraps me in a squeeze. "Your hair is nice, I like the way you dress, you've got really pretty eyes and nice hands and I like your smile. Holy shit, do I like your smile."

I close my eyes then, my hand over my grinning mouth like

it's a secret.

Later he says, "I got some responses." From universities, he means. U of A, U of T, UBC, Hunter College, a few others. Some scholarship offers, too.

"Which one are you going to take?"

"Thought I'd wait and see. We could go together. You should apply."

"I don't know."

"Well, you are going to university, aren't you?"

"I don't think so," I say. He laughs. I don't.

Something drops in his face. "Are you serious?"

I shrug.

"I'm just, what, some guy you make out with sometimes?"

"Yeah, it's why I'm spending all my time with you. I don't know what we'll do. We don't have to think about this now," I say.

He says we do.

"My family, everything I know, is here."

"But if you stay, will you be happy? Don't you ever think how things could be? About how you might change if you left? Think of the books you'd read or classes you'd take or people you could meet. We'll go to school together, start an adventure tour operation when we're done, make money, grow old. I can see it. You got a walker, I've got a cane. You're old and smart and beautiful."

"That's romantic. I've known you six months, and you're already picturing me old. I turn eighteen next month, you know."

"I know," he says, "and I planned you something good."

No one outside my family has ever planned my birthday. "You know what happens when I turn eighteen."

"You can drink legally and vote. I know what you think's gonna happen."

"What if it does? Say I die. You'll be stuck in, like, Buttfuck, Ontario or something." Like Peggy McInnes. Her mom came in the store recently, said Peggy was still in Michigan.

"Just apply to some places," he says. "You got calendars for fun. Why not apply for fun? See who accepts you."

"I don't even know what I'd take."

"So make a list."

He gets a pen and paper. I start writing, he looks over my shoulder. Sociology, English, Anthropology, Astronomy, Botany, Ornithology, Mammology.

"Someone likes Biology," he says.

"I love it. But I wanna study other stuff, too, maybe do a double major. Do most schools offer these subjects?"

"Most decent-sized schools."

"So why don't you decide?"

"We can go by city."

The next day I bring over application forms. He guides me through it as I fill them out, and follows me to the mailbox to make sure I drop them in. I never thought about it before, but mail is a lot like hope, isn't it, like little prayers you send out into the world, announcements of your existence. It takes a lot of effort to send a piece of mail. It takes thought, intention, physicality, your words like a thread sewing you to the piece of paper. Out through your hand, in through your eyes, again and again and again. Backtracking if you said it wrong, or wrote it wrong, it's a painstaking venture, and sometimes it actually hurts to hope that hard. You request an audience, acknowledgment, a response — a favourable one. You go down to the corner, pull out the wide screeching handle of the box, and put your letters in, you say one last prayer before the door bangs shut and your letters fall back to a place where you can't reach them. Then the real anxiety starts, moments where you think, Did I write the right address? Did I say the right thing? Should I have sent it at all? It's a stupid old saying, but it's true sometimes: be careful what you wish for. Someone in Vancouver, Toronto, or New York might open the envelope, take the letter out, read it, then what? Throw it away? You want someone to want you. What if no one does? What if someone does? What then? Do you really want what you say you want? Are you ready to get it, to embrace that kind of change? At what point are you unable to turn back, stop the flow of change, withdraw your neck from risk?

Conrad pats me on the head.

"All done," I say. It's a hazy day. The sun is shining, sick and yellow.

"It'll be great," he says. "You'll see."

I walk him back to his house, then I go back to mine.

20

※

LATE AT NIGHT ON October 16, 1995, we got a call.

Trina answered the phone. It was just past one and she was falling asleep after a late night out with Kirk and their friends. She didn't want to answer it at first. Who calls at one a.m.? She thought that if she ignored it, the person would give up. But the phone kept ringing.

It was someone from the hospital with news about Gene. He'd shot himself in the head in a barn. It belonged to Jim Mendel, a farmer who came into the store sometimes to buy dubbin and leather laces. Could be Gene knew where Jim's guns were from that blabbermouth Mendel kid. They weren't even friends, just in the same grade.

Trina woke us all in hysterics and we drove the two hours down to Foothills Hospital in Calgary still wearing our pyjamas. I sat in the back, head between my knees, as my dad asked my mom about the details. He asked why Gene would do something like that. When my mom said nothing, he said, "I told you this would happen."

When we showed up, Gene was in surgery, and they didn't let us see him till he was out. He was unconscious, then — on life support. Most of his head and face was bandaged up, and what wasn't was badly bruised. I hoped it wasn't him, I know it was a dumb thing to think. The doctor came by and said his brain was bleeding and the pressure in his head was high by the time they got to him. He could heal on his own — that happens sometimes — but there was a chance that he wouldn't, and we had to prepare ourselves for that.

We waited hours. They carted him away a few times for tests and procedures to relieve the pressure, but in the end he took a turn for the worse. The doctor came back and said brain function tests came back negative and that machines were keeping him alive. She gave us a choice, but it wasn't a choice.

"I was holding his hand," I said, "and I could feel him holding me back."

She said that was a muscular reflex. Trina asked if there was any chance Gene could come back. The doctor said it was highly unlikely. Once she left, Trina and I explained it all to our parents to make sure they understood, and then we sat in silence. A few minutes later, Trina got up.

"Are you sure he can't come back?" I asked as she left Gene's bedside.

I left, too, and saw Trina in the hall with the doctor. She asked about the chances. She wanted numbers. I wanted to know and also didn't, but I stayed to hear the doctor say there wasn't any chance at all.

We weren't halfway back to Gene's bed when my dad asked, "What if we keep him alive?" My mom looked up at us. She wondered, too.

"He's not really alive," Trina said. "He can't think or talk. He'll never wake up."

"No chance?"

"I don't think so, Ba."

We couldn't stay there forever. I thought of Gene connected to machines in Calgary while we went back to Spring Hills.

Lonely. People talk about a light at the end. Do we all see that, or is that just if you're in between? Maybe Gene saw that light now. He couldn't pull back and he couldn't go towards it, so long as we didn't let him. It seemed wrong, somehow, to keep him alive. He tried killing himself, after all.

"I wouldn't want to be kept alive by machines," I said. "Like, if there was a chance I'd come back, then fine. But don't say no just because you're not ready."

My dad didn't understand, but my mom did. Gene was her baby, her favourite.

"I understand if you need time, but this is a choice we have to make."

"Why?" my dad said, angry.

"Because he's not coming back," I said. I was angry, too.

No one said anything after that. All together in that big blue room under artificial light, each of us was nonetheless alone. I looked at the floor, at my knees. I thought of Gene. What does a person need to feel in order to choose that? Could we have done something else, something more?

Trina said to our mom and dad, "I don't want to tell the doctor to unplug him, either. It's gonna hurt. A lot. It's gonna hurt if you tell her in an hour and it's gonna hurt if you tell her in a month or a year. You might need time to say goodbye, but you'll have to say it. He's not coming back."

Gene was lying right there. Could he sense our depleting hope?

"It's gonna be okay," I said to him, but I didn't believe it. I was horrified by what he'd done. I couldn't understand it at all. It was disgusting. Still, if he was in there, I wanted to comfort him, tell him I loved him and wanted the best for him. "Whatever needs to happen's gonna happen."

I stroked his arm, and tried to think of something else. I remembered a time at the dinner table. Gene's spot was across from my dad's. One night, their eyes locked. My dad has this way of not turning away sometimes, even when you look back. Was it curiosity or a challenge? In the wild, the lesser animal is the first to look away. They stared at each other for three seconds — then the soup came, shot like fountain water from Gene's mouth. It was a weird way to ease tension but it worked. Soup in the fish and chips, my dad rat tat tat swearing in Chinese, though he wasn't really mad. It was funny, and I'll always remember it.

"Remember his drawings?" Trina asked. "Garfield?"

Garfield was his favourite when he was young. "Yeah," I said.

We went on like that. My mom cried, talked about how much he liked corn when he was young. I thought about his fifty-dollar allowance — I only got ten — and about how my mom, all through August, would say, "Happy birthmonth," to Gene, even though he was born August 29.

Finally, my dad said, "If there no chance for him come back, I think we should unplug. I feel so sad see him lie there."

We all stopped talking then. Trina watched her own feet kick forward over and over. Then she nodded and looked at me. What could I do? I nodded, too. My mom needed more time, but eventually, she agreed. Trina told the doctor what we'd decided, and our parents signed some papers. We went back to Gene with the doctor. It was morning. I thought of people waking up, padding through their morning routines. I tried to feel like we hadn't just betrayed him.

"We need time," Trina said to her.

When she left, I put my arms around Gene, careful not to disturb the tubes in his nose and arms. I put my ear to his chest, heard a sound like hydraulic brakes in reverse, a slow ascending *kshhh*, and after each forced inhale, a passive exhale, air rushing out on its own. He smelled like B.O., farm, chemicals. I whispered in his ear, "Gene. Wake up." Then, more urgently: "Come on, man. Get up. We're gonna unplug you." But I wasn't dumb. I knew how things worked. I just said it to say it.

Everyone had a moment with him. Trina lifted the sheets, looked at his hands: swollen, bigger. He would've liked that. His long, skinny, flat feet. No one else has feet like that.

"Goodbye, Son," my dad said. His last son. He put his hand on Gene's head to shove it around, and almost dislodged some tubes.

"Ba, careful!" Trina said, rushing in to rearrange them.

My mom held Gene's hand in both of hers. "Wah, jong nuen," she said, hopeful, to my dad. *He's still warm.* We had to tell her that's just what bodies do, and it didn't mean what she thought it did. It hurt to say. She started crying again. "I'll miss you," she said to Gene.

Trina and I gripped each other and wondered what was wrong with our family that we kept dying like this. We watched the monitors, the numbers — heart rate, blood pressure — that peaking green line.

A nurse came in. There was nothing else to do. She asked if we were ready. All the hinges and metal on the bed, which was not like a bed at all. Your body is a fortress of life. Most of what it does — breathe, eat, fight disease, remove wastes — is to protect against death. In the room where Gene died, each unplugged machine pulled away a barrier. We crowded around him, watched as numbers on the monitors slowly dropped. Every time they went up, we cheered, out loud but quietly. We thought he was rallying. We'd seen enough reprieves in movies and on TV to think it might be possible. We didn't touch him or interfere in any way.

A rustle of curtains. The nurse showed up, muted the monitors before he flatlined, and then she left the room. Trina started singing, didn't care who heard. The song was "Babe" by Styx.

It was cheesy but appropriate. Plus, who am I to shit on someone else's way of grieving? My dad stood stone-faced. My mom, by Gene's head, bawled. I went over and held her. Trina held my dad's arm. Every time I felt the tears subside, I looked at Gene. Though he was paler and skinnier than before, he was still handsome. The nurse came back in and said she'd never seen such a strong family. I couldn't see it.

GENE HAD WRITTEN IN his journal about how he felt bad, both for making us go through his shutting us out, and for the times we had to take care of him. He wrote of how bad things got sometimes. Imagine not having control of your body during what should be the prime of your life, always wondering how bad your next bout would be and when it would come, and on top of that, losing your family confidante, the only one who really got you. He wrote of how it didn't seem worth the effort for us to knock on his door and for him to open it. That was something he felt sad about. He wrote of feeling like he was at the bottom of a well. Above him, people were going about their lives. He could sometimes see their shadows move, and he sometimes wanted to call out to them, but he knew there'd never be enough rope, and he doubted two young girls and two old people would have the strength to pull him out. And why should he rely on us anyway? There was nothing that could be done, he knew that death was on its way. It was he who came up with the idea that we would all die at eighteen and out of town. If that was true, time was ticking. He felt sorry for us not knowing, and at the same time envious that we could live our lives unfettered. He hadn't known what to do with the rest of the time he had, though. He wasn't sure he was living the right way. How do you choose to live when you know your time is running out?

21

SCHOOL FINISHES FOR THE year. I study like crazy because department-
mentals count for half my final grade. I write a few, do okay.
Mike Brown still pipes up with his old Trina chestnut but no
one laughs. In the middle of it all, envelopes with university
logos on them find their way into the mail.

I'm carrying the first few upstairs when my mom sees me,
her eyes bugging out with curiosity. I tell her what they are, and
I love myself a little bit for making her smile so wide. I open the
letters with her, give her the play by play. One single-page reply,
the rest acceptances. I can't believe that they want me. Toronto,
Edmonton, Calgary, Vancouver, Hunter College. U of A wants
to give me a scholarship. My mom tells me how great this is.

I try to picture myself somewhere else. New York. Brown-
stones and fire escapes, corner stores, that accent. Lots of crime,
but the sun's on me as I walk down the street. Toronto is good
but not as good as New York. Vancouver would be okay,
except it rains. Edmonton or Calgary to be close to my parents.
Edmonton, so I could visit their graves. I imagine my parents
alone after I've moved out, working till they can't, then selling
the store or trying to give it to me. No pressure. It's only everything they've worked for their whole lives. I imagine them
upstairs, watching TV all day long, my dad making two sandwiches

and a can of soup for lunch, them never leaving town, no one phoning them but me.

Maybe no one, period.

"Mom, what should I do?"

Her pink cheeks. Limp bangs on her forehead, and the rest of her hair looks crooked. "Go." Her eyes are filling.

"If it's gonna make you sad, I won't go."

"I'm not sad. I'm proud."

"You're not sad?"

"No."

I go to my room, call Conrad. We both want to go to New York, but it's expensive, so we settle on Toronto, though it's not really settling. Toronto.

"We'll need to go this summer," he says. "Look around, find an apartment."

"I've gotta tell my parents first." Knocking on the door. My mom. "Hey, I gotta go. Call you later?"

"Sure."

She takes me to the bank to set up a joint account. She saved money for five kids to go to school and now only one of us might be going. In the teller line, I say, "What would you think about me going to Toronto?"

Her eyes open extra wide. "So far?"

"It's the best school in Canada, the biggest."

She knows. Her first deposit's ten thousand dollars.

It's lunch when we get home. My dad's complaining again about how much work it is to cook an extra set of meals for me. Then he asks what I want on Thursday.

"First you complain, then you ask me what to cook? I don't know." I want to tell him about schools, about how I've been accepted and wonder if I should go, and all he can think about is food.

"Well, it's your birdday," he grumbles, defensive. "You choose."

My birthday. I guess it will be. Thursday is four days from now.

Later on, I bike down the hill towards Pudgee's. I'm thinking of Toronto and I'm sailing, the road like a parabola with individual houses on one side, gone before you even realized they were there, and it's sunny, bumpy, fun. Almost the edge of town: on the left hand side are fields and the railroad tracks. Gravel. I skid once by accident, the most fun on three wheels, but still I slow it down. Skidding's not a safe thing to do. The turn at the bottom of the hill comes faster than I expect. I push back on my brakes and my front end starts to slide. I realize what's happening three seconds too late to do anything other than panic. I fly through the air, hit the ground so hard my sinuses clear. I'm Wile E. Coyote, punished by a giant anvil for hubris, for hatching a complex plan. Straw poking through my clothes, at my face. I'm on my side. Stay down.

A voice. It hurts. Bruises, worse. A truck on the side of the road.

"You all right?" he says again.

I don't know. I wanna stay down.

"You were biking pretty crazy. I didn't know whether to stop or go. Are you hurt?"

Yes.

"Did I hit you?"

I don't know.

"You need a ride?"

My mom runs out when she sees me. Toronto — what the fuck was I thinking? I go upstairs and lie down. Blood on the sheets when I get up. I wash my stinging leg in the tub, my head full up with cotton and worry.

GHOSTS AND REBIRTH AND heaven, oh my. What happens to us when we die? What I want is for the spirits of the people we love to remain on earth, not in a haunting, horrible way, but in a way that they can see what you're up to sometimes and still exist and not be nothing. Maybe they could give you signs of their presence — flicker lights or play significant songs on the radio. Maybe but probably not. What if the only way we live on is in the memory of others?

SO HOW DO YOU prepare for what might be your last birthday?

That night I go through all my stuff, the shoeboxes under my bed. Trina's letters, pictures, old stories and poems, clothes that belonged to my siblings. I make lists: favourite colours, songs, moments in life. I write eighteen poems, one for each year, even the ones I don't remember. My parents down the hall, watching TV, are oblivious. I clean, go downstairs and get boxes to pack away the rest of my stuff, everything but essentials, just in case. I call Conrad three nights in a row and tell him everything he might not already know about me, starting from the top.

Wednesday night, Conrad drives into town, asks me to come over. His mom opens the door. Suitcases sit in the living room overflowing with stuff. She and Bob are going off to Tanzania to be missionaries. She says they're leaving tomorrow. "Conrad didn't tell you?"

"No." He must have forgotten to say. "How long are you gone?"

"Just under three months. Don't worry, we'll be back to see you off for university."

I ask about the trip while she fumbles around, holding up shirts and asking me which ones are nicer. She's excited, lists off the shots they had to get: tetanus, diphtheria, the hepatitises, some others. Imagine going somewhere so dangerous you need shots. She mentions cholera. My dad's mom died of that when he was young. I didn't think people got it anymore.

"All these shots and pills," she says. "I tell you, people better appreciate what we're doing for them."

"Shouldn't the grace of God be enough?" Conrad says as he comes into the room.

"Here he is," she says. "You invite your girlfriend over and leave her waiting?"

The word, like a halter, I accept without argument. *Girlfriend.*

"There's pizza in the deep freeze and little quiche things," she says. To me: "You can come over anytime."

"Oh, Mummy." He takes her in his arms. "Can I throw a party?"

"No parties," she says. She's already uncomfortable leaving him behind. He's only allowed to be in Spring Hills a couple of nights a week for his summer job at the Double Scoop. His dad agreed.

"It's Chrysler's birthday tomorrow."

"Why didn't you tell me sooner? I would have got her something." She hugs me, soft and fragrant. "I hope you get a car, a Chrysler. Wouldn't that be perfect?"

She thinks she's being smart. I don't mind.

"Don't be dumb," Conrad says.

"A car is a great gift," she says. "I wish my parents had got me one."

"You don't need a car in Toronto," he says. "There's bikes and transit and —"

"Biking in Toronto. Good grief. Can you believe this, Chris? Promise me you'll take care of him."

"I'll do my best," I say.

Later, in Conrad's room, he turns down the light, and we kiss.

"Sorry about my mom," he says.

"I don't mind. I like her." There's music, slow and sad. We hold each other awhile, then I pull away, put on a brave smile. "It's my last day of seventeen."

"Yep." His eyes are a little sad, too.

"So I probably can't stay long. Sorry you came all this way."

"You apologize for the dumbest things, I swear."

"Yeah? Fuck you," I say.

"Fuck you, too."

He lifts me onto his desk. I wrap my arms and legs around him. I'm wearing jeans, he's in khaki shorts. So much fabric between us. I breathe him in, vanilla, eggs, sugar, musk.

"Wanna do it?" I say.

"Play Parcheesi?"

"Backgammon. It might be your last chance."

"That's some pickup line," he says.

"I cut my nails today. They say your nails keep growing after you die."

"Morbidity. I like that in a girl."

"You should date Jess Henry. She's the goth in my school. She'll probably be at my funeral, if you wanna meet her."

"Is she cute?"

"In a Victorian kind of way."

"I'll think about it," he says, and starts kissing me. Random places on my face. "I love you," he says. "Please don't worry." To distract me, he asks about my brothers and sisters, wants to know what I like about my mom, what I'd build a house with given the choice of sticks or cardboard boxes.

I ask him again if he wants to do it. He doesn't say outright that he doesn't, but we don't, not even when I put my hand on it. The first time I do, he sings a funky seventies song and thrusts into my hand as a joke. The second time, we're talking about whether or not I'll ever want kids, and I stroke till he pulls my hand away.

I leave his house around nine. He asks if he can come, but I tell him I should be alone. "I'll see you tomorrow," he says. He's made a plan for after dinner, but who knows if I can make it.

"We should have done something tonight."

"I'll see you tomorrow," he says again.

WARM AIR HITS ME out the front door, carries me uphill past lit windows and trailer parks. The sky is a wide and blue rainbow. It's quiet. Town shuts down around now. I try to take it all in: the sudden smell of lilacs at that one particular place, familiar cracks in the pavement, the order of businesses and houses. I pass the hospital, think of the times I've been there, the hot chocolate from their machine. I pass the old IGA. It's a furniture store now. The real IGA is on the highway, but I used to get free cookies here. I'll always remember how it looked inside, even though I'll never see it again.

The familiar slide-click of the side door lock as it opens. The lino pattern, the dirty stairs. My parents watching TV. Thick rice noodles in a bucket of water on the kitchen floor, softening for tomorrow.

"What time are you guys going to bed?" I ask, even though I already know.

"Long about ten-thirty," my dad says. I've got time.

I go to my room, count the money in my little toy safe. I've got a lot of stuff. A computer, a printer, a bike. I decide to write a will. Will it be legally binding? There's so much the average person doesn't know how to do. I write the date, print my name and also sign it, use *hereby* and *therefore* and *bequeath*. First dibs on my books and music go to Conrad, so long as my parents don't mind. He can share the computer with my mom, so long as he leaves my files intact and shows her how to use it. I'm giving money to Mac's school clubs. The rest of my stuff I want to give away so it'll get used, but my mom would be sad about that, so I leave it all to her. I imagine her riding my trike. She never would. She probably wouldn't even look at my stuff once, but she'd be glad to have it. My will. Seventeen and I have a will.

I leave it in an envelope on the desk and go back out to my parents. They're in the same positions I left them in before — my mom slumped in her chair, her flaking feet stretched out on the ottoman, my dad half-asleep on the couch, hands on his stomach and half the blue blanket on the floor.

I pull up a chair and put it between them. Together, we're a little wall of Wongs. The show is boring, a family drama with lots of courtroom scenes. I lean over and kiss my mom on the cheek, half a dozen times fast, so it seems comical. "Mummy, I love you," I say, and tonight she's so glad to hear it she kicks her feet in tired glee. I picture her in bed half an hour from now, a stack of books on the bedside table. I should read, she thinks, before falling asleep, sinking into the crevasse on her side of the bed. My dad has his own, just inches to her right. My god, if I ever live to share a bed, please let there be no crevasses. I want lumps because we sleep in a different way every night or a trench because we fall asleep hugging.

My dad wakes in a daze, looking weak and old. "*Fun*," he says. *Sleep*. I move out of the way as he hobbles by, placing his hand on my shoulder. I follow them to the bathroom and watch him brush his dentures, wash his feet in the sink. My mom fills her denture mug with the tub faucet, her eyes half-closed.

"Nei yao mo hau see?" she asks, gummy-mouthed. *Did you study today?*

I have one exam left, Biology. I'm not sure when it is. "Yep," I say. It's a lie.

When my parents go to bed, they turn off all the lights and the house feels lonely. I go to my room, slip into bed, and call Conrad. He picks up after one ring, his voice hushing through my ear in the dark. "Your birthday's gonna be awesome," he says.

"We should have done something tonight."

22

BY THE TIME I was fifteen, Trina sixteen, we were old hands at funerals. There was a wake this time — Gene liked to party — and a slide show: pictures of him playing basketball and of him being a kid with Stef. There was a picture of them in tracksuits in a dark room, lit from the front and with looks of glory on their faces like they'd just won at the Olympics. There was a ten-year-old picture of us in Banff National Park. Our parents are in it, too, and we're all looking down a hole.

Trina and I each gave a eulogy. Rod Miller, who owns the pet store, came up to me afterwards and said how good mine was and I shrugged. No one expects a kid to write anything good, so it's easy to make an impression.

We buried him in the same part of the cemetery as Stef and Reg, by the river. A few stones between them. My dad wondered aloud if he should buy the four next to Gene, my mom chewed him out, but I said, "May as well."

At the end of the service, I went for a walk and ended up on the edge of a steep, snowy valley. Evergreen trees. I tried to see the bottom and imagined going back later to throw myself down. I was musing. It felt like an act without consequence. How would it feel or sound to fall that far? Like flying at first, like a very large stone thrown in to fresh snow, that crinkle.

Birds. They weren't singing, but you don't always need a voice for someone to know where you are.

"It's nice out here."

I opened my eyes and turned around. Trina.

"Stef picked a good spot," she said, shaking out a cigarette. Little hands on a lighter, flame to the filter end first.

"What are you doing?" I said it hard. I meant the cigarettes. I didn't know she smoked.

"Burning the cancer away," she said.

"Most of the carcinogens are in the filter," I said. I did the research when Gene started smoking. "You shouldn't do that. You'll disrupt them."

Trina took a drag, then started to cough. It could have been she just started that day. She was smoking Gene's brand, DuMaurier. Our mom would have gone crazy if she knew. She was always asking me if Gene and Trina were doing drugs or smoking. "Yeah," I'd say, grouchy. "Every night. Why don't you ask them yourself?" Watching Trina, I imagined a future career with an anti-smoking group. Part of my job would be to travel to high schools and put on a cancer slide show — pictures of felty lungs, yellow fingers, and raw holes in lips and throats like second mouths.

"Are you dumb?" I said. "You wanna die, too?"

"Whatever. It's fun."

"Fun? Those things'll kill you."

"I'm gonna die anyway. I may as well go down laughing."

I stormed away, found the car, and lay down in the back alone. I closed my eyes. It was quiet. I didn't want to be a part of the world. When I woke up, we were in Spring Hills. In the weeks that followed, I read Gene's journals, that thing about the curse. I didn't leave town much after that.

Trina, though, went out even more. Parties, joyrides, road

trips. I tried to make her stay — "We don't have much time," I said, "together, I mean" — but all she wanted was to leave.

We had two years of that, two years of me staying in doing homework, watching TV with my parents, and dreaming up ways to keep her home safe. Two years of tension and fights between her and my dad — he took it out on my mom, they fought at least once a week back then. Two years of her coming home late and acting weird — high or sad or drunk and smelling like beer or marijuana or someone else, telling stories about her night, how she'd high-centred on a snowdrift out in the country or drove on the running track at school, or how she and her friends had to get away from these older guys.

I wrote stories for her. If they were good enough, she'd stay home an extra few minutes, sometimes longer, and listen to me read them. I thought about things she'd wanna talk about, read the TV guide to see what she'd want to watch later in the week, thought of ways to rephrase the fact that she was gonna die soon and that she ought to spend more time with us. Sometimes she did and we'd have a heavy talk. We'd wonder aloud, speculate, reminisce. A couple of times she suggested a movie, and we'd get one from the megastore, pop some corn, and watch it in Gene's old room. At some point, we'd started joking around again, talked more about guys and music. It was a return to closeness. We used to be close, guess we always were in a way, but this was nice.

But I should've known that my conversation skills or my dad's cooking or whatever else we had to offer wouldn't have been enough to make her want to stay in the end. Still, somehow I didn't expect her to go, didn't think it was even possible. It's kind of like travelling back in time and showing the people you meet some piece of technology, say a Thermos or a car, and the cave people scratch their heads when the water comes out three hours later just as hot, or your car beats the shit out of their fastest runner in a foot race. They don't understand what's going on. They don't even want to believe it.

23

✺

I OPEN MY EYES and there's light under the door. Eight-thirty-two a.m. June 11, 1998.

Eighteen and I'm still here. I didn't die in my sleep, no one killed me in a botched robbery last night, and it's spring, almost summer. I've got a family and a boyfriend.

Something sizzling in a pan. I come out to Birthday Meal #1: pancakes. No one makes them like my dad. My mom is singing atonally, walking in front of Chinavision news, twitching her hands like she's screwing and unscrewing light bulbs. Moss green fleece and jeans, looking me in the eye, smiling. How do you explain love? How do you describe it?

"Good morning," I say.

"Good morning, Chrysler," my mom replies, comedically emphatic. "You got exam today?"

I check the schedule in my room. She's right. Biology, nine a.m. I come back out, grab three pancakes, some butter and sugar, take them back to my room, eat while I cram, then get dressed and run to school.

By the time I get there, my side aching, heads are bowed over desks, an imperfect pattern. Ms. Germaine wobbles up to me, a spinster in high heels, sheets in hand, stern and chipper, if that's possible.

"I'm sorry I'm late — I slept in," I say in a low voice, smiling hopefully. It's pathetic. Will I charm her? "It's my birthday."

A cloud of salt and pepper hair, a schoolmarm dress, gold wire-rim glasses. She scowls then cackles, brushing her hand through the air like *pshaw!* "Everyone is allowed some exceptions on their birthday," she says.

There is one empty desk, near the back — in front of Mike Brown. He says something as I sit down, and I imagine whaling on him in the middle of the exam. I look at the booklets. I'm still half-asleep. Two hours and forty-five minutes to go. I wish I'd studied. Some of it I know by heart. I could fudge answers, but I shouldn't have to. This could be my last test ever, and it could've been an easy ninety.

At halftime, ten-thirty, Luke Carcadian gets up. He's done, and when he leaves, the lab door slams shut behind him. Twenty minutes later — SLAM, SLAM, SLAM, SLAM — everyone is leaving. Shuffling behind me. Mike Brown gets up, kicks my desk. I hear him scream "TREEEENAAAAAAA!!!!!!" in the hallway. A ripple in the room. I have to focus.

By eleven-thirty almost everyone is gone, and at ten to, when John Stevenson leaves, I'm the last one left. I start the last essay question — something about tracing lineage through mitochondrial DNA — and fire everything I have at it. Some of it doesn't even make sense.

At twelve, Ms. Germaine tells me to finish up. I've written so much my hand is cramping. At 12:03, she looms over my desk, and I start abbreviating.

"Chrysler," Ms. Germaine says at 12:07. If I don't stop, she can't take it away.

"I just have a couple more points to make," I say, without looking up.

At 12:08, she takes the booklet away while I'm still writing.

A line down the page from my pen. "Shoulda come earlier, Chris," she says.

But I was only fifteen minutes late. The thing I should've done was study.

The lab door pounds shut behind me, and there's no one in the hall. My last exam. I won't be back again. Twenty feet away, a door leading outside. I go the other way. It's quiet and I'm at peace, a swimmer at the end of a race, bobbing in the end of a pool, wiped out and innocent from all of that exertion. Funny how different it feels when it's all over and no one's there. Mr. Anderson's room, Ms. Patrick's. Mac's with our *Lord of the Flies* dioramas, his globe and Shakespeare posters, his books.

I walk slow and tentative like I don't know how to, like I just got out of jail and don't know what to do yet with my freedom. Free. The last Wong to walk these halls. The floor is baby blue and light grey. Lockers blue and dented. The crazy days of high school. Photos above the lockers. I stop at one. The class of '95. I look for Gene. The pictures are small, but I find him. I find Stef and Reggie, too — '93 and '92. Then I'm running, and there's Trina, looking merely pretty and not like the heart-breaker she was. I stare at her picture a while, imagine her standing on a rocky coast looking at out at the water, or at hills and little towns. I don't know where she is now.

Outside, it's too bright and too hot. My birthday. I close my eyes, start walking across the field. Cars shoosh on the streets. Once when I was young, I wore a pillowcase on my head and walked around the house. I wanted to know what it was like to be blind. My body knows the way. Ten blocks. My finger on the doorbell. Is it okay to come by unannounced? My heart on my sleeve, a crack in the door.

"This is a random check," I say. "Do you have anything to declare?"

"You'll have to come in and see," Conrad says, then steps back, pulling the door open wider.

I fall forward and he catches me.

"Chris? Chris? Are you okay?" He picks me up, runs me off to his room, sets me on the bed, rubs my sternum with his knuckles, which hurts, and then he shakes me, gives me fake CPR for a while, his hands on my chest. "Oh my god, oh my god, oh my god." My head rolls to the side. "Noooo!" he shrieks. "Noooo!"

He starts crying. I keep playing dead. He gets in beside me and buries his face in my neck, whimpering as he holds me. I cuddle into him, start drifting off, and then he's talking.

"They're gone," he says. "This summer's gonna be good." He tells me the vegetables he wants to plant in the garden: beans, peas, tomatoes, basil, broccoli, chard, lettuce, spinach, and carrots. He wants to dig up the lawn to make a bigger garden, he wants to move his telescope to the roof, and he's planning a trip to Toronto to find us an apartment.

Me, I dream of leaf shadows. I dream I'm riding a bike, my whole family on there, and Conrad, too — a whole pyramid of us packed on like Shriners and we're going down a trail like the bike path, only it isn't, sun and shadow, sun and shadow. We're going fast and it's easy, then suddenly a feeling creeps up. It starts really small, a bit of uneasiness, but then gets bigger and bigger. What's the problem? Trina's holding her hat to keep it on. My mom is scared. There's something wrong. Are we actually skeletons — or skeletons and people at the same time? And will my dad be mad at me, like really mad, World War III mad? There is no "will." He already is. Only thing that's keeping him off me is our riding the bike with a few people between us. It'd be dangerous for him to lose control now, but as soon as we get off I'm gonna get it, that much I know. We can't ride forever, the path ahead is running out two kilometres from here. And what if we crash before then? I know we're going to crash, but where? What's the best place? Can I jump off? How about those trees? We veer, correct ourselves, then veer again, into the trees. White blinding light.

I wake up with a start, check the clock. One-forty-one. I forgot about lunch. How long have they been waiting? I get up. Conrad's still in bed.

"I don't know about Toronto." I'm not sure why I say it.

"What do you mean?" He looks concerned.

"I mean, what if it's not safe?"

"But you said."

"I didn't say I'd go, just that I was thinking about it."

"Cities are safer," he says.

"I don't know."

"There's nothing to dispute. They have statistics on these things."

One-forty-two. It's a twenty-minute walk.

"I have to go," I say. "I forgot about lunch. My dad's gonna shit."

Conrad follows me out. He's not done talking, goes on about emergency response times and how much safer giant highways are compared to little ones, about how much better the hospitals are and how much more exercise I'd get in a city like Toronto just from walking around.

I practically run down Fifty-Eighth and up Fifty-First, past the cinder block apartments to the top of the alley. I stop to try and shake him. "Gotta go now, Con," I say. It's hard. I hate interrupting, hate shutting people down, but this is what I need to do. "You really have to go. I'm gonna get in trouble."

His eyes go wide before I finish talking. He's looking over my shoulder. I turn around.

My dad's at the back door, holding a bag of trash. He

immediately starts yelling, doesn't care who hears as he goes
back into the store. "Goddamn son of a —"

Conrad walks away. "Sorry," he says.

UPSTAIRS, THERE'S A PLATE of fried noodles drying at the edges
on the dinner table. My special meal. I eat, then put the rest of
the food away, clean the kitchen. I want to hide, but in my room
it feels like I'm waiting, so I go downstairs. It's quiet. I find
things to do. I serve customers, receive stock, tidy jeans. It's a
form of apology.

I'm sweeping the floor near the counter — tags and bits of
plastic, pins, dust, and lint — when a sound like chickens starts
to come from the back. It takes a minute to realize it's my dad
yelling at my mom. There's nothing to do but own up. I wait
for him to come. When he does, he's running at me. My mom
is there, too, trying to calm him down by nagging.

"Why? Why?" he keeps saying. "Why?"

"Sorry I was late."

He's stuttering. I keep apologizing because I can't understand him, until I realize he's talking about me in third person.
He's saying in Chinese how I'm always telling him to make
special food. "Why can't she eat normal? So trouble."

The store is quiet except for him yelling. Customers are
watching.

"Mo gong la," my mom says. *Don't talk.*

"We were waiting," he says.

"Sorry. I lost track of time."

"With that white boy? Ew neiga ma." *Fuck your mother.*

My legs wobble.

"He's my friend," I say.

"Friends," he says. "How much per pound? You don't know.
I know how it is."

"What do you know? What do you know?" I scream.

He screams something, too, about religion.

"What do you know?" I say. "You don't know him. He's better to me than you are. You act like nothing happened. The worst things have happened to our family and you act like they were nothing. You don't help. You just yell and yell and —"

"Fahn leen hee!" he says. *I hate you.* "All your trouble and you mouthy. You just open the mouth and talk talk talk. You think you so smart."

"And you think I'm dumb, which shows how smart you are. I'm going to university. I'm going to go as far away from you as I can."

My mom screams at us not to fight.

"Who will pay?" he says.

"I got scholarships. They're paying me to go to their school." I say that, even though U of A only offered a small one.

"Go! I have no kids. Fuck you. All my kids are dead."

I'm gone. I shove the front door so hard it bounces off the building. I cross Main fast, then jog down Fifty-First. I turn and look, but no one's following me.

AN HOUR LATER I'M at Anders Park, five blocks from my house. I'm on the swings, going fast and high. If I pump hard enough, I'll fall off and break my neck. He'd be sorry — or would he?

We fought last year on my birthday, too. Our last big fight. Trina came and got me. I complained about him, his temper, the way he's never there for us. Now I wish we talked about something else, like, I don't know, the fact she was planning to walk out on us later that night? Now there's no one left to look and no one to talk me down.

The nearest payphone is up the street. You can see it from our living room window. When I'm tired of the swings and just full of sadness and yearning, I take the long way there, put a quarter in, dial the number. It starts to ring, I can almost hear it from the street. But my dad picks up, not my mom, so I put the phone back on the cradle.

It's dinnertime. I could use something to eat. It would have been good tonight, something with tofu, maybe vegetable dumplings. I could use a jacket, too. Hungry, cold, sad, locked out. Happy birthday.

I call Conrad.

"Hey," I say. "I know we weren't supposed to hang out till later, but —"

"What's wrong?"

"We had a fight. I just need a place to be now, please."

"Of course," he says. "Yeah. Come over."

24

BY THE TIME I get there, he's set up candles. Bowls on the kitchen counter, a roasting pan, some vegetables. He's got an apron on, Snoopy on a weigh scale, Woodstock and his yellow bird friends stacked on his head. *Good grief. I need to lose some weight.* He asks me if I'm hungry, and I hug him long and hard, tell him I'm starved. He says he's making dinner. A block of tofu on a plate, another plate on top of it. "To get the water out," he says. "It's gonna be simple. I wasn't expecting you till after dinner, but this is good, too."

He peels and I chop the vegetables. They go in the roasting pan. Conrad adds spices, puts stuff in a bowl for a marinade. The house is cozy and dim. He asks if I want music. I put something on by the Velvet Underground — a bad name for a band, but I like the picture on the cover: a black and white shot of these guys, one shy in a stripy sweater and cool tall boots, looking away like he doesn't know a picture's being taken. I find a blanket and lie on the couch. The music is perfect and sad.

I wake to a good smell, two plates on the table in front of me. A weird mishmash of food. Roasted veggies, tofu in some kind of sauce, rice, and peas from a can. Conrad is sitting on his haunches, feet on the floor, his old mauve recliner tipping forward. He's watching cartoons, Bugs Bunny on mute.

My dad likes Bugs Bunny, too. He used to watch it and the Flintstones with me while making breakfast or lunch, back when I wasn't old enough or headstrong enough to be a disappointment.

Light flickers over Conrad's face. Elmer Fudd in a Viking hat, stabbing a spear into a hole. *Kill the wabbit, kill the wabbit, kill the wabbit.*

"You never see this one," I say. "Turn it up. It's no good if you can't hear it."

So he puts the sound on and we watch it all unfold — the disguises, the chase, the magic and lightning. Bugs Bunny dresses up as a woman and Elmer Fudd falls in love with him, a great courtship, they sing a romantic duet dripping with longing, till Bugs's helmet and wig fall off and the chase resumes. Bugs Bunny is comforting, predictable, he always wins, except for one time, this time. The magic gets him, his limp body on a rock — can you believe it? He actually dies, and Elmer Fudd carries him away, sorry for what he's done.

"That's encouraging," I say.

Conrad stands up. "Kill the wabbit, kill the wabbit, kill the wabbit," he sings, wagging his head. "Ready to eat?"

I make space for him on the couch and he sits next to me. We watch cartoons over dinner. The food tastes better than it looks. From time to time, Conrad disappears, each time coming back with something else for us to eat. A small second helping, cake, popcorn. We lean against each other on the couch.

He asks about the fight. Was it about him? I say yes, partly, but that he wasn't the only reason. Conrad defends me, says my dad can't handle having a smart, independent daughter and that's his loss. He says people make mistakes and should be forgiven. I don't want to talk about it, though.

"It's just a difference of opinion," I say. "He told me to leave, told me I was dead to him. So I went. I should probably call my mom."

I find a phone in the next room. My mom picks up. She's worried and asks me where I am. I ask if my dad's still mad. "A little," she says. The TV on on her end. "Dim gai nei gum stubborn?" *Why are you so stubborn?*

"How come it's my fault? I should let him yell at me? I said I was sorry. But it's none of his business who I'm friends with."

"Respect your olders."

"My elders aren't always right."

"Still, you must respect them."

A worn blanket around me. Patchwork, fraying. I pull it tighter. My dad's voice in the background, asking about the show they're watching.

"Come home," she says.

"No," I say. "Sorry, but not tonight. I love you, but I can't be there right now." I give her Conrad's number. I tell her it's for emergencies only even though my mom's not one to call a stranger's house.

I can hear the TV on her side: footfalls and a scuffle. Someone, maybe the hero, says something self-righteous. Someone yells back. The fight resumes with punching sounds you could make with your mouth.

"Hello? Mom?"

"Yah?" she says. She's crying.

"I'll call you tomorrow, okay?"

"Do you still have exam?"

"No, it's all done. I'll call you tomorrow, okay?"

A fake Hong Kong gun sound.

"Okay?"

A woman screaming.

"Okay?"

Dramatic music.

"Are you there? I'm gonna go if you have nothing else to say." But nothing.

"Okay, I love you. Bye." I put the receiver down, go back and watch TV. Nothing funny, nothing overly dramatic. Cartoons, music videos, *Star Trek* reruns, infomercials. I'm not a TV person, but we watch all night.

IF YOU ASK A bunch of kids what they'd eat if they didn't have parents, some would say things like candy, burgers, and chocolate shakes, but lots of them, I bet, would pick proper meals — chicken pot pie and Caesar salad — ordinary foods their parents never make. That's why, on our first morning together, I decide to make French toast. Because my dad makes oatmeal, he makes pancakes, he makes a mean bacon, egg, and cheese sandwich, but he's never made French toast. Not even once.

I slip out of bed early, with the sun, hours earlier than I would at home. Conrad's sleeping on his side, drool on his pillow in the shape of Mongolia. I find eggs, bread, a frying pan. This could be my new life. I stir the eggs, dip a slice of bread. Sizzling when I lay it in the pan.

Less than three miles away, my dad will be wearing an old plaid shirt and nylon vest, cutting their morning fruit. He'll feel a fart coming on and let it rip. Oatmeal slow bubbling on the stove while my mom watches TV.

"Hey," a voice behind me says. His breath on the back of my neck. Sunny day out the window, a bird. I turn to kiss him on the cheek then pull away with a shy smile that says I want to be loved.

"Hey yourself," I say.

His ratty white T-shirt, his small loose-fitting shorts, his cowlick. Arm across his belly, his other hand scratching his head.

Small feet, his eyes like an old man's. No boner in his shorts or anything. This one is the one I want.

He looks past me into the frying pan and says somewhere between a period and exclamation point, "Food."

We eat, then drift in and out of sleep on full stomachs. We talk and read, watch the sun on our arms as we lie in bed. Soon it's noon. My mom will be trying to keep up with the lunch rush. My dad will be making something in a frying pan. Conrad leaves, comes back two hours later with quiche. Says he made the crust and everything. Quiche.

"I didn't know we were showboating," I say. What should I make for dinner? Mushroom burgers. Tacos. Lasagna.

"We weren't," he says. "It was good, wasn't it?"

We go out to Mac's to get slushes. I kick rocks down the street. The sun is hot on my head and the back of my neck, the street quiet like a ghost town. We wander down the bike path then go into the trailer park. Somehow, we wind up downtown. By the time we round the corner at the Mountview Hotel, Conrad knows where I'm going. He follows me down the block.

"You have to stay outside," I say.

"I have to get some gloves."

A big black metal truck, rusted out, chugs up Main.

"Gardening gloves," he says.

I wish he'd leave.

"It's June. I gotta plant the beans."

I stare him down, and he crosses the street. I don't see where he goes.

It's around four o'clock, but the store is quiet because it's summer. No one will see me if I'm careful. I peer around the outside wall. My mom slouches behind the counter, her hands clasped without authority. She looks defeated, but she always looks that way. I go up to the glass door and motion for her to come outside.

"Chrysler," she starts in before the door's even closed behind her, "where were you?"

At my first sleepover. "Where's Dad?" I say.

"At the back, fixing shoes."

"Is he mad?"

"No. He's not mad."

I look in the store. I don't believe her.

"Mom, what should I do?"

"Come home."

"I don't know."

My mom's worried look, her stinky breath. "You always cause problems."

A tall forty-something blonde in denim watches us as she walks by. She turns her head as she passes so she can keep looking, her meaty paw holding the hand of a little boy in denim overall shorts. *Don't touch my son, you ugly chinks.*

"You don't think he's to blame at all?" I say.

"You know he's stubborn. Come home."

I see him through the glass door. Pot-belly, spindly legs. Short for a man. He's near the back walking mostly with his knees. His thighs have no say in the matter. My dad.

Say it quick. "Mom, I need money."

She looks around — no one here but us chickens — then awkwardly pulls a roll of bills from her pocket. Green, red, brown. Why so much? I put it deep inside my pocket, like she taught me. And even though she sees me do this, she still says, "Put it deep inside your pocket."

"Thanks, Mom," I say. My mom. "I gotta go."

"Come home," she says.

I shake my head. "It doesn't feel right."

He's probably already wondering where she is.

"I gotta go. I'll call you."

She just stands there, staring at me. I take her hand — warm, thin, bony — and I pull her past the door, past the windows, out of view of the store. Then I put my arms around her, breathe her in.

"What if Trina did the right thing?" I ask. She doesn't reply. "Dad's always mad. I don't want to be here." Then I get a crazy idea. I know what she'll say, but I still say it. "Maybe you could come with me."

"I have to stay," she says without thinking. "To work."

It's not about the money. What then? Duty, keeping herself busy so she doesn't have to think. Plus, she likes it, she'll keep selling boots at age eighty if she can. Will I be there to help, to take on the store when she goes, or will it all turn to shit? She holds out her hand. I take it, and she pulls away. Something in my hand. A bank card. Our joint account.

"I'll support you," she says.

"Thanks, Mom."

"Oh," she says, remembering something. "Tong mai gnoa yao bao shun bei nei." She goes back inside, comes out with an envelope: S&B Contests International. The writing contest. I open it and read the letter. I got second place, the prize is travel vouchers. It's like that stupid O. Henry story where the couple gives each other useless gifts. But when I tell my mom — about the contest, the prize, everything — she says, "Good to win."

"Thanks," I say, then walk away.

FIFTEEN MINUTES LATER, I'M in the IGA. It's weird being here alone, amidst daytime-shopping moms and their screaming kids.

I'd like to think you can tell something from the things a person has in their cart. Sugary cereal means kids or white trash;

flats of cans at a case lot sale means a big house, thriftiness, or both; and canned ham, well, it depends, but generally, it means the person's poor, or has been through some kind of famine. When I see an old person with a can of ham in her cart, I wonder what she's seen. Maybe someday my dad will buy it, too.

Standing in line at checkout, I realize I grabbed too much. I put half my food away then pay. I pick up the bags, thinking I'm pretty badass. I can do this. I carry freight at work. I help my dad with groceries and parcels all the time. We have a hand cart, though. The first time I put the bags down to rest my arms, I'm still in the parking lot, sweat trickling down my neck and forehead.

Sometime around the forty-minute point, despair kicks in, but then I turn a corner and see his house. I walk the entire block without putting down the bags. I turn onto the walkway with authority, like someone who actually lives here, and ring the bell. I wait then ring again. No one answers, so I plop down on the step. Across the way a mom is getting bags from her trunk. I look down. There are ants. When I was young, I liked kicking in their hills. I liked watching them go all crazy trying to figure out what to do. Now it's good enough to watch them crawl around carrying stuff, bits of food, maybe nothing, in their crooked triple file.

Neighbourhood moms and dads are starting to come home from jobs and errands. Rush hour in a small town is not a lively affair — just one car at a time, several minutes before the next. Maybe Conrad's staying away for a reason. It might have been something I said or did. Maybe he doesn't want me here. The sun is in my eyes.

A little while later, a speck on the horizon that might be him. *How do you know?* I have a feeling. The clothes are shaped like his and maybe the speck is wearing a hat. How long do you maintain eye contact? I squint at the sun. I bought all this food, carried it all over, for what?

"You again," he says, as I'm looking down at my knees. "Can't get rid of you."

I shrug. He doesn't want me. I shouldn't be here. But I can't go home. *Don't say it. If you say it, it makes it truer.*

"You don't want me here," I say.

"I want you here. But I want you here because you want to be here, not because you have nowhere else to go. You know how I feel about you."

I don't say anything. He touches me on the back of the neck then sits beside me.

"Food," he says, looking at the bags.

"Yeah, dinner."

"Really big dinner."

We see an ant. It's carrying a dead something. Another ant.

"You get your gloves?" I ask.

"Yeah. Stopped by your store after you left. If you were there, I would've walked right past."

"You see my parents?"

"They looked how I thought they would. Your dad is small and wiry — perfectly capable of kicking my ass. He didn't see me, though. But your mom sold me two pairs of gloves."

I smile. Typical Mom.

"She convinced me I needed two kinds, a heavy duty one for weeds and another for bumming around."

"How did she seem? Nice?"

"She seemed sad." A fly comes to hum around our heads, one of the slow, stupid ones you feel sorry for killing. "She was nice, shy, eager to help."

"She's also distant and responsible."

He shrugs. "I wouldn't know." The fly goes away.

"I hate you having to sneak around like that."

There's something weird about that, the existence of two sets of people you care about and who care about you who will never actually meet. It's sad, but there's no other way.

We go inside. I make lasagna — fry stuff, season it, grate cheese and boil noodles, put it all together. I can do this. It's delicious. Conrad thinks so, too. I cut us an extra serving because it's novel — something I made — and because I'm feeling something, I don't know what, but I hope eating more will make the feeling go away.

25

THE FIRST FEW DAYS with Conrad are easy in some ways and hard in others. Things begin to slide. We get less ambitious with meals, we're not as nice, we start farting in front of each other like we're my parents or like we're friends trying to gross each other out.

One time he says to me, "I'm running out of frozen piz-zas," like I hadn't bought us groceries already. He still hasn't thanked me for that. Still, it gets tiring eating crackers, frozen food, canned food, so I buy groceries again, a bag of spaghetti, jar sauce, a head of lettuce, a carton of juice, and two packs of veggie ground round with a mantra — *he doesn't appreciate you, you need him, he doesn't appreciate you, you need him* — playing through my head the whole time.

We do some fun things, though — go for walks and bike rides in the sun, plant the garden, sit around reading in the yard. Times when he's asleep and I'm awake, I imagine him as a sensitive, curious, lonely little boy who loves his dog and wants to protect his mom. But he isn't that person anymore, is he?

He buys me gifts, mostly books, some highbrow stuff, includ-ing love poems by this guy Pablo Neruda. "We could read them together," he says.

"I could pretend you wrote them."

"Unlikely," he says. "They're Neruda. Only Neruda writes like Neruda."

IN THE SLOW SNOW-GLOBE tumble of our life together, something else happens: we have sex for the first time. What I mean is, I do.

We're sitting on the couch watching *Jeopardy!*, and out of the blue, he starts kissing my cheek, like full-on making out with it. My first kiss from him in two days. Alex Trebek says, "This physicist was instrumental in developing atomic models and the 'exciting' field of quantum theory. He won the Nobel in 1922."

Who is Niels Bohr? "What's this about?" I say, edging away.

Matt, the guy on the left, rings in and says, "Who is Niels Bohr."

"Correct," Alex says.

"I want you," Conrad says. "Did you know that? We fart in front of each other and I still want you."

"That's romantic," I say. But does he love me?

"Great Danes (and Swedes) for 600," Matt on TV says.

"This Danish filmmaker, best known for *Breaking the Waves*, is closely associated with the Dogme 95 collective."

"Lars von Trier," Conrad says into my neck. He's right.

"Mind if I change the channel?" I say.

"Come on. Aren't you even a little bit, umm … interested?"

"In what?"

"Sex."

Oh, that's what's happening. "Fine. Yeah. Sure," I say.

"You can be on top, if you want."

I shrug, get up. He's sitting down. I don't know what to do, so I straddle him.

"Well, you'll have to take your pants off," he says.

Taking your pants off doesn't mean you'll have sex for sure. I do it nervously — my pants and underwear. He does it, too.

"Dogs for 200."

I get back on him.

Alex says, "Famous one in a movie named after a composer."

"Who is Beethoven?"

I can do this. Remember he was weird when he was young — into science, talked a little too much, too smart, and like an adult, spent recesses alone. He may have never thought he could get a girl to be with him. I'm doing him a favour. Plus, he's handsome. His eyes, you like his eyes. And it's nice of him to let me stay at his house. And look how weird he's acting. He's nervous, too. Isn't that sweet?

"Do only as much as you want," he says.

I nod. What I want mostly is to kiss him. I kiss his mouth, it's soft. He's a good person. I think of how rich the lips are with neurons, it starts feeling good. We kiss some more, he puts his hands on me under my shirt, it feels good, I can't stand it. There's a noise. Where'd the noise come from? The answer on *Jeopardy!* is, is, is … Rottweiler. I didn't know. The sound must have come from me. I can make a sound like that? I kiss him on the neck, really burrow in there, he's making little movements like he likes it, then he bucks up, it goes in a bit, and I'm split with pain, the first time I've ever felt anything there. He sees it in my face and goes soft, it's sweet, I keep kissing his neck, move up to his ears, his hands on me and it feels good.

"You're lovely," he says.

It makes me want him, but I'm shy, I'll always be shy. Still, instinct knows the way. We're all hands and mouths and other parts, and I'm thinking, *Stop thinking*, and then I think about how I feel, whether or not I love him, and it makes me queasy. He goes back inside me and I'm split with pain again, but this time he doesn't see or I hide it well. I don't want him to leave me, and he will if I don't satisfy. Somehow, I'm not sure how, he winds up on top, thrusting hard and fast, making sounds I've never heard him make before, he's making faces like we're in a tribe and it's his job to scare away the monsters. Fast and hard and fast and hard, then he takes it out of me, it spurts on me, my shirt.

He kisses me on the cheek then stays there, lying on top of me, constricting my breathing. What's he thinking? Maybe that I'm satisfied, too, or that sex makes up for the things I lack as a girlfriend, or that he's glad we finally did it. I look down. He's not thinking anything. He's asleep. Did he think I'd like that?

I wonder if I love him. I thought it'd be different. I think I'll probably regret it.

The room is cold. A blanket on the floor. I try to reach it. My one arm squished into the L of the couch, my other arm free. Something wet. My chest. He's drooling. I get out from under him, stand and take a bite from a half-finished piece of toast on the coffee table. No pants on, I feel exposed. I was not his first. Carla Kilpatrick was. Does he love me? My underwear stuffed in the couch cushions.

I put on my jeans and bra and go for a walk. The whole time I can feel him there, like when you ride your bike for hours, your shitty, heavy one-speed, through rutted grassy fields and up and down hills, down alleyways and the bike trail past Mac's house, everywhere you can in town without actually leaving, and for days after your crotch and ass hurt like you pushed down on your seat with all the fury and fear you had, and your seat pushed back.

There's nowhere to go, nowhere that interests me, nowhere I haven't been.

The idea of sex makes me sick. I walk around town, stop in

at the store, then go to the IGA. I go to the industrial part of town, the library. Everywhere I go, I think I see my dad. I wind up on the highway, at the town limit sign by Joe Play's. I look out at the suburbs. Car dealerships, hotels, Boston Pizza, the church. All that neon. Town is growing. Maybe someday someone will come and move the sign. Maybe there'll be an oil boom and Spring Hills will quadruple in size overnight and there'll be more space to stretch out.

I want pizza, a simple one with mushrooms. Pizza's in the sauce. That's why Perry's is the best place in town. Sometimes my dad will taunt me, same as he did when we were kids.

Hey. You want to have peesa for lunch?

Yeah!! we used to say.

Naw. And he would chuckle.

We've only had pizza as a family once since Trina left. My dad has diabetes and can't stand the starch. And my mom — are you joking?

Perry's is two hundred feet past the town limit sign like some kind of beacon or holy carrot. The wind picking up around me, I walk slow on the highway shoulder towards it, slow like I'm on a tightrope. It could happen anytime. *Fuck it*, I think, then start to run. The wind messes up my hair. There's a feeling you get on the side of the highway, nice when no one's there. There's no other feeling like it. Today it's different, all these cars, how I feel, it's like the whole world's rushing with me. I slip on gravel, and when I recover, a car in the other lane zooms towards me. I stand my ground, keep running. Another car passes me in my lane. I'm fine. Then another. Whoosh whoosh. After that, it's a sparse parade, cars from out of nowhere. Maybe it's a normal amount. I'm usually in school this time of day. Cars sound mean, scary, when you're not in them. I tell myself to be bold. Mostly, I succeed till a Mack truck splits the air with its horn, roars by, makes me jump to the side, it's more of a fall, the guy pulls his horn again. I'm in the ditch, watching truck exhaust spread into the sky. Cars slow down, one after another. I hunker down and hope that no one stops.

Once things settle on the highway, I get up, dust myself off, and limp back into town. Nowhere to go so I get a table for one at Giorgio's, order spaghetti and salad, a glass of milk. I eat slow, count my bites. After that I cross the highway — playing chicken with imaginary cars — to Petro-Can, where I drink three cups of coffee, the first three cups of coffee of my life.

Somehow I end up on Main, across the street from my house. Lights on, the ceiling fan, they're watching TV. Which show? The one with Fei Fei.

There's a cluster of middle-aged drunks outside the Mountview Hotel. It's dark. Are they looking at me? I hear the words *little girl*. I keep walking, fast, get off Main, go a couple of blocks, turn around. No one there. I turn again, jaywalk across the empty street, look in the windows on Forty-Seventh, keep turning to make sure I'm not being followed. Ugly old dresses on pawnshop mannequins, transparent yellow shades drawn. Bars on the window at the Music Den. Bryan Adams uses Ernie Ball. I slouch on the bench outside the library, stare at the railroad tracks. There are stars. Which ones are planets? Every passing car is Trina. There are no passing cars.

Someone comes and sits beside me in the dark. It's Rick Jones, town drunk. Hit on my sisters for years, came into the store just to find them. I smell like coffee, garlic, ditch, sex. He smells like beer, sidles up like he wants something. I get up and speed-walk to the end of the block, then turn the corner and run like hell. The streets all blur together. Am I going the right way? Homing pigeons, magnets. I don't have magnets in my head. White house, red house, the one with the fences, then Conrad's.

The door's unlocked. I lock the deadbolt, knob, slider behind me and turn on all the main floor lights, grab the biggest knife I can find in the kitchen drawer and sit in the corner of the living room, clutching it. I listen hard, keep looking around. The ghost of someone there, a half image, yellow. What if I've locked myself in with it? The heat clicks on, and I jump. The heat turns off, I jump again. The house moans, creaks, grips its foundation as the wind shoves it. There's nothing to do with fear but have it.

Then Conrad shows up, hair standing in the back, just another yellow ghost until he says, "Where the hell have you been?"

I clench the knife, stare. I imagine him attacking me. I can fight if I have to.

"Chris."

The woman who pries a car open to save her family. The kid who climbs a tree to escape a bear.

"Chrysler, it's me." He approaches me slow, talks slow.

My hands are sore from clasping the knife. I look down. They're shaking.

"Chrysler. Put down the knife."

Why should I?

"I stayed up waiting," he says. "I watched the door. There's no one else here."

Then why'd it take so long for you to come? Where were you when I got here? Felt like two fucking hours sitting here. I was scared and alone — really alone.

"I didn't know where you were, if you went back to your parents or what. I didn't think that you'd come back. I fell asleep."

My head slumps down into my arms. My sleeves are wet and warm — have I been crying? — my legs curled under me, an ampersand. And. And what? Sore down there. Conrad, naked, above me. I'm tired. But I'm still clutching the knife.

"Chris, talk to me. Did something happen? I swear, I'll fucking kill anyone who even tries to hurt you."

My first words in hours, I say them. "I didn't want to have sex."

"What are you talking about? Who are you talking about? I'll fucking kill him."

"You," I say, raspy. "What you did. The way you did it. The way you looked."

"You should have said something."

"I went to the highway, almost got hit by a truck."

Air comes out of him, slow like an old balloon, his eyes like open sores. I go into my pocket. I wish I had tissue. I never do. He wipes his eyes on his sleeve. "I'm sorry," he says. "I got carried away."

He asks me if I want a hug. I don't know if I do. I let him hold me, but don't hug back.

"I'm sorry," he says. "It'll never happen again." I let my eyes close. "I'm sorry." I let go of the knife. "I'm sorry I'm sorry I'm sorry," he says.

I make him check all the rooms in the house — in the closets and under the beds. We sleep with the lamp on and his room door locked. His bed is big enough we don't have to touch. Before he falls asleep, he says, "Remember all the good stuff."

I think of him as the bee, doing the helicopter with a kid, the kid squealing with delight. I think of him making pizza, his hands and arms, how he went to buy gloves so he could see my parents. I picture him standing up to his mom and Bob, telling them he doesn't believe in God, even though he loves his mom — a lot. I think of him alone in a clearing, drawing plants, happy and in awe, all alone. I think of him in a jungle somewhere, after a long flight, looking up at all the trees, all the different kinds of plants and animals and bugs in every shape and colour. What would it be like to see those birds in person — say, a splendid astrapia, whose feathers are red, yellow, green, and an impossible shade of electric teal, or a toucan with a beak like a lobster claw — when all you've ever seen are sparrows and magpies?

I wake up on the edge of the bed. Windows dark. I can feel him there. You could fit two people between us. Without moving, I go back to sleep.

We wake up after noon when the phone rings. Conrad picks up, talks, and hands it to me.

"Hello?" I say.

It's my mom. My dad's gone missing.

26
※

SHE SAYS SHE LAST saw him last night. They fell asleep together. She didn't say goodnight, just turned the light off after TV, washing up, and reading. When she woke up, he was gone.

"Why'd you wait so long to tell me?" I say. They wake at five. It's 1:30 now. More than eight hours.

"I wanted to make sure."

"Sure of what? Are you crazy?" My dad needs so many things. Food, insulin, medicine. "You didn't look for him?"

"I did," she says, exasperated. "I did look for him. Dan hai kuey ja truck, a maa."

"The truck is gone?" *For fuck sakes, Mom!* I almost say. He hasn't driven in more than two years, and he's been in half a dozen bad wrecks. "Did he say anything about where he would have gone?" I say it loud and slow like she's stupid. Eight hours! She fucking is.

She says he didn't tell her anything.

I meet her at the Radio Shack to grab some walkie-talkies. She insists on paying, holds hers in two hands like it's heavy. We separate, my mom to walk the streets, and me to search the highway. I walk to IGA, the Co-op, the industrial part of town, my eyes peeled for him and for his truck. In my head, *shit, shit, shit, shit*. Out loud to everyone, "Have you seen my dad?" All the cars are his, all the red vehicles. I picture the truck smashed up, parked, puttering along. I stand on the highway shoulder and stare.

Another one gone and I didn't fucking say goodbye.

I go to the railroad tracks, check the hospital, call every hospital within fifty miles. But no one knows anything. I picture the truck in the ditch, the driver's side smashed in. I look for him in every store in town. Some places I check twice. Back at the Co-op, I imagine myself buying a roast beef and roasting it with all the windows and doors open to lure him home. That's when I see the in-store pharmacy. Of course. The pharmacy. I really should have checked there first. He'd be dead without his insulin.

Neil Carson behind the counter. I've never seen Neil without a cowlick. Maybe he gets it permed that way. I go up and ask him when my dad last got his meds and he says that information's private.

"Even to family members?"

"Yes."

"I really have to know."

"Sorry, no can do. Why not send him over, have him check himself?"

I end up having to spell it out for him and, finally, Neil sees it in my face. He checks his files and says my dad topped up his medicine yesterday. Then he comes out from behind the counter, checks a shelf of travel medicine bags — pink, yellow, turquoise swirls like eighties windbreakers — and says one is missing and that my dad maybe has it.

Outside, it's sunny and hot. I cross the highway and imagine the bag riding shotgun in the truck, stuffed with ice and insulin. The ice is melting, water seeps into the seat. Where is he? Did he go back to somewhere important? Houseboat fishing in the Shuswaps? His paper father's grave in Saskatchewan? Maybe he wants a new life. Daughters fucked off, other kids dead, boring wife. Maybe. But he's seventy-two, has fucking vision problems. Why wouldn't he stay somewhere safe? There has to be a reason.

As I run home, an idea pops into my head. I get to the store, come in through the front door like a customer.

"Mom!"

She's at the counter, ringing in boots. She says to the man buying them, "Do you need extra laces?"

"Just the boots," he says.

"Polish, waterproof, insoles?"

He wants her to get on with it. Her fingers slow and sure on the till keys.

"Mom!" I say again.

"That's one hundred sixty-three thirty-five," she says. He pays by credit card. "Do you need written receipt?" she says.

"I think your daughter wants to tell you something," he says.

"Yes," she says to the air before turning to the credit card machine. She doesn't look at me. It spits out a receipt, he signs it and leaves. She makes sure the register's all closed and everything's put away before she gives me her attention.

"Mom!" I say as she finishes. Third time. Angry.

"What!" she says, defensive. The ghost of a British accent.

"What happened yesterday?"

She looks at me.

"What'd he do yesterday?"

"Nei sheung wa mut?" *What are you trying to say?*

"Well," I say, "he cooked?"

"Yes."

"Kuey yao mo bo hai." *Did he fix shoes?*

"Yao." *Yes.*

"Kuey yao mo mai sic mut?" *Did he buy food?*

"Yao."

"Did he serve customers?"

"No."

You served them all by yourself? You've been serving them alone for a week?

"What else did he do?" I say.

"Have nap."

"What else?"

"Loa shun." *He got the mail.*

No. No. No. No. No. "Did he tell you anything? Did he say if you got any letters?"

"He give me bill."

"Anything else?"

She thinks, then shrugs.

"Mom, I have to tell you something."

She looks at me.

"Promise not to get mad?"

Mild expressions on her face: a little sad, a little curious.

"I've been getting letters from Trina," I say. She sags before it's all the way out of my mouth. "He must have seen one. That's why he left. To find her."

She looks at me, but it's like she's looking through me.

"I'm sorry I hid them from you, but now we have to go."

Silence.

"Mom," I say, annoyed, "let's go!"

There are still people in the store. She can't go. She has to wait until they leave and sell them stuff before they leave. A young family — man, woman, and baby — comes in.

"We need to close the store and go," I say.

Kyle Bigchild comes to the counter with a frilly pink shirt. He wants to know if it comes in extra-small. My mom rushes out to help, but I hold her back, my hands on her shoulders as she struggles and tries to pull away. My wrist pops. Throbbing pain. She's stronger than she looks.

"I'm sorry, Kyle," I say, "but we have to close the store right now. It's a family emergency."

"Let go!" my mom says. Anger is rare for her. My wrist hurts, but I don't let go.

"I'm sorry," I repeat. I mean to say it to her. He drops the shirt on the counter and beelines for the door, probably thinking *how fucking rude.*

I stand on the stool at the front counter and announce to the store that we're closed. As far as I know, this is the first time in the history of Jack's Western Wear that we've had to close early. People think it's a joke. "Please leave," I shout, pausing between my words for effect. "There is urgent family business to attend to. We need to go."

My mom, trembling and agitated like seaweed in changing currents. "Why you do that? You don't have to do that. They'll come back." A customer comes up to the register and she starts ringing him out.

I'm still trying to get everyone to leave. Some are quick to go, others dawdle. I speak to the stragglers individually. Luke's mom, Ruth Carcadian, asks me why. Her daughter Laura's getting married tomorrow and her youngest son Les has nothing to wear.

"It's my dad," I say. A blank look on her face like she's acting dumb on purpose. "He's gone. He went away. We need to find him."

"We need five more minutes, okay, Chrysler? He's in the fitting room. And he's got a couple of pairs in there with him."

"Mrs. C., it's an emergency."

"Just give us one or two minutes."

Ruth Carcadian is the biggest gossip in town. I picture her

making small talk at the IGA over what that Wong brat said to her as she kicked her out of the store. She'll say, *Those Wongs are rich enough to turn away business. I'll bet they jack up their prices.* She's got me and she knows it. She starts acting like I'm not there, like the case is settled and her chubby son can go on trying pants till close, or later if he wants. She pulls a pair off the shelf by the waist, *fwaps* them open to see the fit. Pair after pair she does this to. Leaves a mess. Someone'll have to fold them back up. Me or my mom. My fifty-eight-year-old mom, taking all kinds of shit from people just to make a couple of bucks. After combing through the aisle, Mrs. C. turns to me, a pair of pants flopping in her mauve-taloned hand like a dying fish. "Could you see if you have this in a thirty-eight?"

"No, I can't. Your one or two minutes are up now, Ruth."

I head to the back of the store and turn off most of the lights. Back at the front, I hold the door open. Hundreds of dollars of sales walk out, my mom watching as I spit in the face of everything she's worked for, eleven hour days six days a week, tens of thousands of work hours, more than twenty years in business. A bony hand on her chest, she's leaning forward. She could have a heart attack now, and it'd be my fault. Both parents gone because of me.

Mrs. C. guides Les out the door. "No wonder he left," she said. "Crazy family like you."

Trina would've ran her out, would've screamed at her and her tires as they screeched up Main, would have screamed at the dust clouds and the settling dust bowl. My dad maybe would have, too.

My mom's eyes on me. I shrug. If she had better English, she'd say, *I hope you're happy.* If she were the swearing kind, she'd call me a stupid fuck. Instead, being who she is, she tries cashing out the till, setting up for a regular start tomorrow.

I lock the front doors, scribble out a sign and stick it in the window: *CLOSED UNTIL FURTHER NOTICE.* Then I pull her away from the till towards the back of the store, careful not to hurt her, though she struggles. Bills in her hands, she yells at me for fifteen feet to let her go. When I'm convinced she won't go back to the till, I do, I follow her to her office, where she sorts the bills in her hand and puts elastic bands around each of the piles.

"Ready?" I say when she's done.

She's not ready. She needs her licence. We go upstairs. I look for Trina's last letter, if there really was one, and come up empty. There's no telling where he is, how long we'll be gone. I pack bags for my mom and me: coats, clothes, and toiletries, put some books in mine, a Walkman and some tapes. A musty smell from my mom's closet as I try to pick her some clothes. Which one of thirty plain long-sleeve T-shirts will she want? Which one of thirty pairs of loose-fitting blue jeans? This is the plight of someone who spends eleven hours a day in a clothing store. Sometimes there's nothing to do but look for a new shirt.

While I'm in her room, I go into the top drawer of her dresser to make sure she got her licence. Two dust outlines, one for each of their wallets. Right now, my dad's — brown, greasy, over-stuffed with cards — is in the truck glove box, rattling down Highway 11. Or maybe 22. I picture him thumbing through it in some faraway small town pharmacy. *Oh. You need ID? I got some right here.* His cute accent.

IT TAKES SOME STERN talking, some pleading, but I get my mom inside the car. This is a job for two, after all: one to drive, one to keep a lookout. But she looks small and powerless and just plain wrong behind the wheel. It's the first time I've ever seen her there.

She's barely in the car before she gets back out again. What's she doing? Wiping the mirrors with tissue. Side windows, too. I get out and help. Napkins from the glove box. I do ninety per cent of the work, run back in like I'm in a car chase scene. *Where's Mom?* I roll down her window, stick my head out. She's picking shreds of toilet paper off the car.

"Mom!"

She gets in, shuts the door twice, and adjusts the mirrors. I help her pull her seat forward. She adjusts the mirrors again, brings down the wheel height, and pulls out the seatbelt. I help her buckle up. I do mine up, too, even though it'd be easier to look out all sides without it, because it's safer and because I don't want to give her any reason not to leave.

"Okay," I say. "You remember how to do this?" As far as I know she's driven a handful of times in her life. Plus the test.

She's quiet.

"Well, do you?"

"Yeah!" she says, annoyed, like she's the kid and I'm the mom.

I open the garage door. She puts the key in the ignition, looks down at the centre of the wheel with mild interest, as if the answers to the universe's big questions were there if only she wanted them.

"Mom," I say, softer this time. "Ready?"

She turns the key like it hurts, puts the car in reverse. It creeps out slow as shit, straight out, she almost nicks the mirror on the wall. She backs out an extra ten feet over Current Electric's gravel pad across the way before turning down the alley. Her foot barely on the gas, it feels like gravity pulling us down the hill, not combustion. My mom is even worse than me when it comes to being scared. She probably thinks of cars as death machines, especially after Reggie. She hasn't been in one since Gene died.

I'm proud of her. I wanna say so. Instead, I suggest we tool around before we leave, to ease her into driving. She likes the idea, so we go for snacks, run over the curb on the way through the Dairy Burger drive-through. My mom is a healthy eater so I love watching her enjoy junk food. Next stop: Red Mart. I fill the tank and buy a bag of ripple chips, a tub of garlic dip like old times. Add a couple of sandwiches, and a big bottle of water for good measure. I pay for it all on the debit card my mom gave me.

Josh McMurtry asks if I'm going camping. His nice blue eyes.

"No," I say. "Road trip."

Back in the car, my mom wants to tool around some more. Every minute, my dad gains a few kilometres, but what can I say? I'm not the one who's driving.

We pull out of Red Mart and cruise down the highway at forty. It's fine till a truck comes up fast in the rearview. He rides our ass, a young annoyed guy in a red ball cap, he horns us, swerves, barely misses an oncoming car before he swerves back in.

My mom tries to be attentive but is so consumed by fear and is thinking so much about safety that she doesn't see all the cars. She's nervous like a little bird, one I'd keep in a cage to protect, but I don't want to die, and for once, there is something more important than her or my or someone else's feelings.

"Mom," I say, trying to be gentle.

She turns off the highway and we chug down dirt roads, end up in the industrial part of town. We head for the new subdivision, cross into older neighbourhoods, spend entire minutes trying to three-point-turn out of crescents. We sail past Conrad's house, past Mr. Berkson's house, famous for its Christmas display, dormant now and gaudy as hell when it's turned on. There's the trailer park, the junior high school, the town's second elementary school. Churches. That hill Gene broke his leg on being front man on a toboggan. The park where

I got drunk with a French exchange student. Cops came. We hid our bottles under the table behind our poker hands. Everything, all I know, all my stories, set here. We cover it all twice in just over half an hour, even pass a couple of spots more than that. The beauty of being young in a small town is that you can only go as fast as you can walk.

I keep half-expecting to see my dad's truck, his hunting cap crooked on his head, age spots on his face like a constellation, let's call it the Old Traveller. But that would've been too easy. I tell my mom it's time to leave town.

"Which way?" she asks.

If my dad is looking for Trina, he'll be driving either west on Highway 11 or north first on Highway 22. Twenty-two is the more efficient way, faster, but 11 is a bigger road with wider shoulders and fewer animals.

"Highway 11," I say. "West."

He'll be stopping in towns along the way to stay the night. His eyes get worse at dusk. He knows this. He'll do what's safe, won't he? But what if he doesn't? I imagine him losing control on a curvy mountain road or slamming into an elk or bighorn sheep. Maybe he gets out to take a look at something, stretch his legs, go for a walk. Maybe he encounters a bear or someone who sees he's by himself. Sees the bulge in his front pocket.

My mom takes the long route to the highway like she's hoping to get lost on the way. This town she's lived in for thirty years. We pass the Presbyterian Church, the Catholic Church, the Lutheran, on that strip Stef nicknamed Saviour's Way.

"You know where you're going, right?"

She knows. We drive in a jagged arc towards Highway 11. She turns and turns then turns again. Why is she doing this? It's fine. At least I know we're leaving now. I put my feet up on the dashboard. She glances sideways. I slouch down further. My feet stay where they are. I check the map, though I already know a route by heart.

We'll take the 11 to the 93, then drive north through the mountains to Jasper before taking the 16 west. Highway 16 was the road Trina took, and once we're on it, we'll go pretty much the way she went, except we won't stop in Prince Rupert. We'll take the 16 to the 37, the road that runs parallel to the islands, then we'll take the 37 up to Upper Liard, where the 1 to Whitehorse starts. I've been tracing this route for weeks now, months. We'll stop and look for his truck in all the bigger towns. Stop in Jasper, Prince George, Whitehorse, plus anywhere my mom wants to rest. We'll go to places he likes to go. McDonald's. Arby's. Tim Hortons. Tony Roma's if there is one.

Right now, it's four o'clock. Can we make it to Jasper by the time we have to stop? Look up at the highway businesses. This may be your last chance to see them. 7-Eleven, Fountain Tire, strip mall, Red Mart, Treasury Branch, IGA, then nothing for a while, and then the high school, the water tower in behind. It's the side of the highway I like less. The other side, the way to Red Deer, is more familiar. But we are, of course, here by necessity. Community centre on the left, then eventually we run out of businesses, hit the 80K speed limit sign going sixty, pass kilometres' worth of houses — suburban Spring Hills — then the pond, a town limit sign, on the right. This is it. We're finally leaving.

Without warning, we lurch to a stop. I'm thrown forward and the seat belt locks me in. Vehicles horn, almost rear-end us, shake the car with their wind as they pass. We're not even on the shoulder. There are no stoplights or stop signs here. What's wrong? Is it something with the car?

"What's going on?"

Silence.

"Mom?"

Her hands are on the wheel and she's staring straight ahead, out the windshield, like she's still driving. I lean over. The engine's still running. No warning lights on. The car is fine.

"Mom. Is everything okay?"

My dad on a quest to find his favourite living daughter, leaving his wife and the daughter he likes less behind. If that was the only way to think of it, I'd say fuck it and leave him to it. But it's not. There's family togetherness. Life and possibility. And danger. His failing eyesight, poor driving, the mountain passes, the bad roads. If we find him in time, we can save him, keep a lookout. If they're both in Anchorage, we can meet them, bring them home.

The air splits open, roaring. The car shakes. A semi.

"You're gonna get us killed. Mom. Go."

She acts like she doesn't hear me. I'm in a TV nightmare. Waking up invisible to the ones you love the most.

"What is it? Are you scared? So am I. But I need you, Dad needs you, to keep going."

But she can't do it. Or she doesn't want to. Reg died in a car. Stef in the water. Gene with a bullet in his head. No wonder. But I have to try.

"Is it any safer here?" I say. "This last year alone, I've been hurt at least half a dozen times. Who's to say that you're not gonna be working some day when some guy comes in and tries to rob you? Someone with a gun, trying to get your money."

Silence.

"People burn down buildings here, they get into fights. Remember that guy who died last month? Larry Kneebone? Got hit by the train. It's not safer than the outside here. You tell me how it's safer and I'll be fine with you not leaving."

Her bitter face, like I'm my dad forcing her to eat when she'd rather starve.

"Larry slept on the track," she says. "He was drunk. So stupid. He deserved to die."

"Mom, I swear. Are we going or not?"

She turns off the ignition.

You know sometimes when you do something and don't realize till after you've done it? Some actions are beyond logic, beyond thought, beyond feeling. Either that or they're pure feeling. A hand pulls a lever, a leg pushes a car door open, feet hit the pavement. I grab the bag I packed, put the sandwiches, water, and my wallet in, sling it over my shoulder. Leave the rest.

My mom turns to me, opens the window, but has nothing to say. We stare at each other. I'm waiting — for last words, for wisdom or something. But words have always failed her. Nothing to say, even when it counts. But all it takes to talk is an open mouth. It's mechanical — larynx, pharynx, palate, tongue — it's something we're made to do. But words have always failed her.

I look down the highway, then back at her. My mom's small hands on the wheel. Big knuckles. Her eyes, soft and blank, on me. Only her eyes will ever look at me that way.

"Bye, Mom. I'll call you," I say. She has no friends. She'll be lonely. Working all by herself at the store. Eleven-hour days. But this is an emergency. This is how it has to be. And maybe sometime down the road, I can visit. Maybe we can all come back.

I turn, take one step down the highway, bracing myself, expecting to fall down or die, expecting a herd of wild bulls to come charging. I take another step — tell myself to breathe — then another. And another. So far so good. I turn around to see if she'll follow. She doesn't. So I walk faster. So I run. It feels good, moving like this. Soft, flat shoulder. I wobble because of the bag, I'm not in shape, and I keep looking back — she's still there, crying? — I'll miss her, already miss her. But she'll take care of herself.

Slower, I say, *be careful for your heart, it's okay if you walk instead.* But I don't, I keep running, round the bend on Five K Corner, the loop on a track and field course that leads you home. Only this time it won't. I've only ever gone over Five K Corner in a car, with my family. My mom and dad singing along to Chinese opera, my mom with her socks half off, the pull of the turn, my mom's head swimming with private thoughts or maybe there weren't that many. A side of the highway feeling, freedom. Where to eat, sleep, go, what to do — all scary thoughts for me to put out of my mind.

Will I call Conrad? If I don't, what will he do? When will he start to wonder where I am? What will he be like in ten years?

Something in that field. A broken down vehicle. Gene broke all my dad's cars, his audacity the thing I loved best about him. Stef, her forthrightness, attentiveness, and wilderness knowledge. She could've taught me how to do this. I'm sorry I didn't know Reggie that well. Five K Corner — this is where he died.

I imagine my mom driving home, parking the car on the gravel patch because it's too hard to get in the garage. Alone, she can eat whatever she wants. Shrimp or fish twice a day plus oatmeal in the mornings. Stir fried veggies. Tofu. Soy milk. Fresh fruit. It's not that she dislikes eating, more that she's picky and hates being forced. Mom. Take care of yourself.

Trina. Where is she now? In Anchorage, maybe somewhere else, maybe no longer with us. My dad. Is he gone forever? How will I find him? What if he doesn't make it to Alaska?

I've already half-decided I'm going to Sifton. I've never spent any time there. It's a buttfuck town even worse than Spring Hills, but the bus stops there. Still, it's, like, 20K away.

Lots can happen in 20K. I don't have a light. Maybe a car will hit me when it gets dark. But if I hurry and get there in one piece, I can make the seven o'clock bus. Trees approach, slow. I can't believe I'm doing this. Yellow fields on either side, huge blue sky above. Clouds. A picture postcard scene and I'm running through it, trying to get it over with. A new scene, after all, means distance travelled.

ACKNOWLEDGEMENTS

The good folks at Cormorant Books, past and present, including Marc, Barry, Alessandra, and especially Bryan for patience, understanding, and acuity during a difficult birthing. Thank you all for having faith in this book and me. And thanks to Gale Zoe Garnett for the introduction.

Instructors and writers involved in the early days of the Guelph MFA. Thanks for admission, commiseration, early feedback, and telling me I was a writer. It seriously changed the course of this girl's life. Specific thanks to my instructors Michael Winter, Catherine Bush, David Young, and the late Connie Rooke, and colleagues Kathrin Hüsler and Todd WheeltonLukaniuk.

Other folks who have been supportive during the writing of this book: Pam Pua, Dana Mills, Cosmina Ionescu Vaccarino, and other confidant(e)s. You know who you are.

Nathan Moore, my own Mac in my wee hometown. (A shout-out to inspirational teachers everywhere!)

Everyone who informed characters in this book. Writing inspired by real life is sometimes an attempt to fix the ephemeral. I hope you don't mind.

My sweetest one, Terry Vaios Gitersos, for late, vital, manifold contributions.

My family — for the past, present, and future. For love. In loving memory of Philip Mah, black sheep of the Mah clan, without whom this book would not be possible.